The floor creaked and an older female cleared her throat.

Rosalind worked her jaw. "Did you just 'hush' me *again*? In all my life, I've never been hushed once and you've managed to hu—"

He clamped one hand to her mouth, the other to the back of her head. "Someone is coming," he rushed out in a whisper.

Rosalind's eyes widened in revelation. Nicholas nodded gravely.

Swinging a startled Rosalind into his arms, he threw her roughly on the bed. She landed with a bounce and a squeak, but quick-thinking lass that she was, Rosalind lifted the covers up, inviting him inside. Without a moment's hesitation, he dove under them.

He couldn't see a thing, thank the good Lord. He did not forget—indeed, how could he?—that Rosalind wore next to nothing and her face was above the covers. If there was a smidgen of light, he could feast his eyes upon her without her ever knowing.

He swallowed, his mouth watering.

By Olivia Parker

GUARDING A NOTORIOUS LADY
TO WED A WICKED EARL
AT THE BRIDE HUNT BALL

OLIVIA PARKER

GUARDING A NOTORIOUS LADY

AVON
An Imprint of HarperCollinsPublishers

AVON BOOKS
An Imprint of HarperCollins*Publishers*
10 East 53rd Street
New York, New York 10022-5299

Copyright © 2011 by Tracy Ann Parker
ISBN 978-0-06-198840-0
www.avonromance.com

First Avon Books mass market printing: June 2011

Printed in the U.S.A.

10 9 8 7 6 5 4 3 2 1

For my brother, Frankie.
Thank you for carrying me in from the rain,
defending me from my bullies, and for sharing
your secret stash of watermelon candy.
I love you, too.

And for Mom.
Thank you. But I'll never believe
that you actually like doing laundry.

Acknowledgments

A special thank you to Esi Sogah

Chapter 1

Lackington's Bookshop
London

There were three activities in which Lady Rosalind Devine considered herself quite the expert.

One: She had a keen eye for fashion and eagerly shared her talent with any young lady in need, often turning veritably invisible wallflowers into quiet beauties with crowded dance cards.

Two: She possessed undeniable skill at matchmaking, her efforts often undetected by the blissful couple.

And three: She could eavesdrop with the practiced ease of a master spy.

That is, if there wasn't a giant buffoon standing in her way.

Before today, Rosalind had never given much thought to throttling another person, but the idea was becoming more appealing each passing second.

The object of her frustration happened to be the *gentleman*—and Rosalind highly suspected he was nothing of the sort—on the other side of the bookcase who kept blocking her view with his impossibly broad shoulders.

However was she to spy on the couple behind him if he kept moving about?

She was already standing on the fourth rung of the bookshelf ladder, teetering precariously in her slippery soled half boots in order to see past the man. *Just how tall was he?*

If she climbed any higher, she would certainly lose her balance. Heights made her dizzy and frightened, and she needn't be terribly high up at all for it to affect her. She had only ever been compelled to climb a tree once in her life . . . and it had nearly ended horribly.

Closing her eyes briefly, she took a deep, measured breath to steady her nerves—not to mention her temper. The stale, but strangely appealing, smell of paper and ink pervaded her senses.

Surely the man on the other side of the bookcase didn't intend to be deliberately disobliging, she assured herself. And besides, Rosalind wasn't one of those females who indulged in exaggerations. Well . . . not very often. Usually. Sometimes? All right, quite frequently, actually.

She nodded, convinced now that his shadowing movements were purely coincidental. It was absurd to believe otherwise, she assured herself. He stood there nonetheless, vexing her.

With a viselike grip on the sides of the ladder, she stretched as far as she dared in order to peer over the tops of a row of books on the next shelf over . . . and blast it if the infernal man didn't move and obstruct her view again!

Was he doing it intentionally? How could he know she was spying?

He *wouldn't* possibly know. Besides, for all he knew she could be merely perusing any of the books stacked next to bursting.

But then why was it that every single time she moved her head, he inched over to obstruct her view? Perhaps he *was* doing it on purpose. And perhaps she ought to put her suspicions to a test. Right now.

Cautiously, she stepped down from the ladder, minding the hem of her pale green day dress. The ladder creaked and snapped with her movements, sounding overly loud in the quiet bookshop.

Reaching solid ground, she looked casually up and down the aisle, satisfied no one was watching her.

After scooting the ladder down about five feet, Rosalind carefully ascended the rungs once again, stopping at the fourth—she dared not go much higher.

For the whole of five seconds she had an unobstructed view of Lord Beecham and Miss Honeywell . . . until a tall, dark shadow came to block her range of vision once again.

An angry puff of air blew past her lips, momentarily suspending an errant lock of coal-black hair that dangled above her right eye. Perhaps she ought to give in to her primal urge, dive her hands through the stacks of books and grab him by his loosely tied cravat. After all, he wouldn't have any time to react.

She held on to the sordid fantasy for only a moment longer, then shook her head. No, no, books would get knocked down in the process and would undoubtedly create quite a clamor. And the likelihood that she was strong enough to do the job was slim. His neck appeared rather sturdy. And truthfully, she really didn't fancy spending the rest of her life rotting away in Bedlam for a brief moment of madness. Ah, but the idea was ever so tempting—

"Bloated toads they all are!"

Jolting in surprise, Rosalind nearly toppled to the floor. Hugging the sides of the ladder now, she gulped down a scream, a mere squeak escaping her lips instead. The bothersome man on the other side of the towering shelf seemed to jerk in reaction as well. Their gazes met and held between the books for a second—long enough for her to discern that his eyes were an impossible shade of sparkling gray.

She'd only ever known one other person with such a uniquely colored gaze, but it couldn't be . . .

Breaking the shared glance, she forced herself to ease her grip on the ladder. Surely she'd find bruises blossoming on the insides of her arms later.

Shaking slightly, she forced herself to look down. The flaxen-haired Miss Lucy Merlwether stood directly below, fists on slim hips, looking quite put out.

"What is it?" Rosalind asked.

Lucy stared at her mutely, light-blue eyes narrowed, lips pursed. "The wager," she whispered. "To think of such a thing!"

Rosalind blinked down at Lucy, wondering if

the dear girl had lost her mind. For she certainly felt as if *she* had. It had happened so fast, but Rosalind couldn't seem to shake the memory of those devastating eyes staring back at her. Perhaps he was still glaring at her even now?

Little by little, she turned her head to verify, toying with the idea that she just might reach through and poke him in the eye if he was still there.

But he was gone. Her shoulders instantly relaxed. Was the tension thrumming through her body from the exasperating man, or was it from being nearly jolted off the ladder by Lucy's sudden exclamation? It must be the latter. Rosalind fancied herself like a stone when it came to most men. All but one failed to move her to feel anything other than polite regard. And he would never come to London.

Lucy gave a sigh of frustration. "How can you be so calm? Those insufferable nabobs have made a wager with you as the prize. It's created quite a stir already."

"Oh, pish," Rosalind muttered, finally able to focus on what her friend was talking about. "I find it slightly comical and completely absurd."

Indeed. Upon news of her brother's approaching

wedding trip, madness had swept over the gambling men of London. Apparently with the daunting duke away, the bachelors of the ton decided to play, placing secret wagers projecting themselves the future brother-in-law to the duke.

"It will amount to nothing, I assure you," Rosalind replied. "Last year they wagered daily on my color of dress. As soon as I found out about it, I made sure to come and go several times a day, changing my clothes each time. After half of one day, they lost track, fought over the validity of the reported hues, and had no choice but to relinquish their game. Utter foolishness."

"Well, seeing as your family is hosting a ball this evening, perhaps we ought to lament on the sorry state of the available bachelors attending," Lucy said impatiently. "Or at least I'll discuss it. You seem to be busy flirting with the man in the next aisle."

Rosalind straightened. "Indeed, I was not."

"You were," Lucy accused jovially. "I think you must fancy him."

"I do not," Rosalind whispered. "I don't even know who was there."

Lucy giggled. "Anyway I'm only teasing. Lord knows no one is good enough for you."

"That is not true," Rosalind said in her own defense. "I'm only waiting."

"For . . . ?" Lucy prompted.

"Well, for my match, obviously."

"And how do you suppose to find him? You've occupied yourself each and every season since your debut doling out fashion advice to newcomers in need and finding them love matches. What if your match is standing right before you but you fail to notice?"

"Then I shall be alone."

Lucy gave a delicate snort. "A daughter of a duke. Wealthy, respectable, and *unmarried*? They'll think you're mad."

"Perhaps they'll think I'm romantic and melancholy," Rosalind said, forcing a grin, her tone deceptively light.

Lucy raised a golden brow at her remark and began searching in her reticule for something. "Ah, here it is." She unfolded a wrinkled sheet of paper and grimaced. "It is a list I made of the available bachelors this season. Very thin, I'm afraid." She clucked her tongue. "What am I going to do? My grandmother said I'm old goods, and Father said I've already started to wrinkle around the eyes. Lara claims her husband has a cousin named Eustace, but I'm not sure I like that name. I've known two Eustaces and they were both rather . . . well, unclean. Mama said that Lord Kenton will be looking for a bride after his mourning period is over, but that'll be a year hence, and by then I'll be even more old and wrinkled and—"

As it was an ongoing, rather tedious subject, Rosalind quelled the urge to groan. Lucy was two and twenty—not ancient by any means, but the women in her family had all married by their nineteenth birthday. It wasn't that Lucy hadn't any proposals; she simply refused them all. According to the Meriwethers, the finicky Lucy might as well don a lace cap and start leading apes. A hasty prediction, Rosalind believed, but perhaps not inaccurate. None of the numerous bachelors Rosalind had suggested had met Lucy's approval, so Rosalind had learned to simply listen to all of Lucy's worries with a patient ear and plenty of reassurances.

Before long, Lucy started to scan her list again, murmuring to herself. Rosalind glanced to the bookshelf. With the irksome man gone, she would now have an unobstructed view of Lord Beecham and the young lady. She trailed her fingertips over various leather spines, pretending to peruse the titles.

How wonderful it would be to witness the fruits of her labor, to see these two besotted people finally embrace their fascination with one another.

"However am I to find a proper husband amongst them?" Lucy complained quietly from below.

"The *'bloated toads,'* you mean?" Rosalind asked out of the side of her mouth, her eager eyes fastening on Lord Beecham as he reached up to take down a book for Miss Honeywell.

"I even danced with Old Lord Utley twice at the Montagues' little garden party yesterday," Lucy nearly groaned. "I fear I'm growing so desperate, if he'd managed to get down on his one good knee and ask me to marry him, I just might have accepted."

"The new Lady Utley would not approve," Rosalind muttered, unable to help herself.

"Oh, Lord. I had no idea. *He remarried?*"

"Two days ago. Surely you read the announcement in the paper?"

Shaking her head, Lucy threw up her arms in disgust. "Leave it to me to waste an entire evening dancing with a married old man."

"Shh," Rosalind implored, trying not to laugh.

"Go ahead and giggle at my expense," Lucy continued, whispering. "I only wish my brother were a duke. Then I could afford to be picky and enjoy all the attention that comes with it."

"Don't be absurd. I cannot abide all their misplaced servility and false adoration. 'Tis not a sincere man amongst them . . ." Her voice trailed off as a man passed in front of the couple. For a second she thought the tall, broad-shouldered man had returned to further vex her, but this particular man kept walking and wasn't nearly as tall.

"*Oh . . . my*. Who is that?"

"Who?" Rosalind asked, turning to look down at Lucy. "Who? Where?" Something about her friend's nearly worshipful tone had Rosalind following Lucy's gaze down the narrow aisle they were standing in.

At the end, near the enormous circular desk where patrons paid for their books, stood the rude man from before. Rosalind would know the broad expanse of that particular back anywhere. Well, really, she ought to, as she had been trying to see over and around it for the last half hour.

Light spilled from the tall, gleaming shop windows, streaking gold through his tousled deep mahogany locks. His expertly cut black frock coat stretched across his back, pulling tight slightly as he bent to speak to a rosy-cheeked shopgirl.

11

Whatever he said made the girl giggle, her entire face sparkling with glowing admiration. He dipped his head and turned, his new direction allowing Rosalind to view him from the front for the first time.

Her mouth dropped open.

A rare, lingering grin curved one side of his mouth upward. His jaw was strong; defined, yet strangely elegant. Under dark, straight eyebrows, his eyes were deeply set, and they seemed to smolder with a brooding quality that made it seem as though he regularly stunned the women in his life into awed silence with just one glance.

Tall, broad-shouldered, and tan, he stood out easily amongst the other men shuffling about the bookshop—an eagle amid a covey of partridges.

Rosalind knew this man. He was their closest neighbor at the ducal seat in Yorkshire and her eldest brother's closest friend. And she had loved every stubborn inch of this man with every breath in her body ever since the day before her nineteenth birthday.

And he was here, right here. She couldn't quite believe her eyes.

Seven London seasons—seven *long* years of dutifully traipsing down to the marriage mart all the while leaving the man she loved behind in high country. And now he was here. Why?

Her gaze swept downward. His cravat was slightly crooked, quite like he had slipped his fingers in the top of the knot to ease its hold on his neck. She supposed he wasn't accustomed to dressing thusly.

Nicholas Kincaid was a reclusive country gentleman. His usual dress was composed of loose white shirts rolled up to his elbows and snug breeches tucked into tall, scuffed boots. But even in those simple clothes he exuded coiled strength and nearly overwhelming virility. Of course, on the occasions he had come to dine with her family at the castle, he had dressed in a more formal manner, but nothing like this.

His new direction put Rosalind (and Lucy, too, but by this time she had quite forgotten other people existed) in his view for a brief moment. Those dazzling eyes of his connected with hers.

A hot sting jabbed low in her belly. Her heartbeat faltered and her limbs felt weak. Dry. Her lips felt dry. She ran her tongue over them, belatedly realizing that her mouth must have been agape for quite some time.

Smile, you idiot. You know him and he knows you.

13

Wiggle your fingers or give a small nod of acknowledgement.

But before her fogged mind cleared enough for her to react, Nicholas's gaze turned a cold, gunmetal gray. Rounding a support column, he strode out of view.

Her shoulders sagged.

If he barely spoke to you in the country, why would seeing you in the city be any different?

His indifferent manner toward her (coupled with an almost permanent scowl—which in Rosalind's opinion looked more like he was always thinking about something rather than a true frown) had never deterred her from liking him.

Over the years she'd learned that Nicholas was gentle and protective, intelligent and strong, curiously secretive and handsome as sin. His only flaw was that he habitually kept his distance from her; sometimes she likened him to an impenetrable wall.

Certainly it would be easy enough to believe that he simply wasn't fond of her, but Rosalind was a perceptive young lady, and she did not miss the spark in his eyes when he spoke to her or the way his touch lingered when he handed her a book she had (purposely) dropped at his feet.

His behavior confused her, and because she was uncertain of his true feelings, pride kept her from blurting her admission of love.

From below, Lucy gave the skirt of Rosalind's dress a twitch. "Rosalind? Are you all right?"

Rosalind blinked and stuttered, "Yes, yes, I'm fine."

Lucy nodded knowingly. "Flustered you, did he?"

"No, no. Not at all," Rosalind rushed out. "It's just that I didn't expect to see him . . . here. In London."

Her friend's expression turned hopeful. "You know him, then?"

"Vaguely," Rosalind lied.

A memory sparked in her mind. Once, in her youthful vanity, she had asked Gabriel if she could have Nicholas for a husband—as if he'd been a particularly fetching bonnet she'd seen on a fashion page. Her brother had laughed and tugged her braid, telling her "he would never do that to his friend."

She almost groaned aloud at the embarrassing memory. Brothers could be so cheeky.

"So you *don't* know him very well?" Lucy persisted, redirecting her thoughts.

Rosalind exhaled and wobbled her head in a

funny, not quite a nod, not quite a shake, manner.

"Right," Lucy answered slowly, drawing out the word. "Well, when you're done finding Miss Honeywell a match, I'd like you to make me one. With him." She sighed, staring blankly at the spot where he had last stood. "All that's left to do is find out who he is. Lud, I hope he's hunting for a bride."

"You wouldn't want him," Rosalind said, discomfited at the note of defensiveness in her own tone.

"Well, I can't imagine any woman not wanting such a fine specimen for a husband. That's it, isn't it?" Lucy gasped. "He's married?"

"No," Rosalind muttered, feeling a bit adrift. "He's not married. He's a . . . he's a farmer." Her insides burned with shame for misleading Lucy.

"A farmer?" Lucy muttered in disbelief. "Here, in London for the season? Business perhaps?"

Rosalind nodded, her own curiosity wrecking havoc on her concentration.

"A farmer, as in a *yeoman farmer*?" Lucy whispered her question. "Or farmer as in a landowner? A *gentleman* farmer?"

Rosalind gave a small nod. "Gentry." With a twinge of guilt she withheld the rumor that he had a distant aristocratic relation. She had overheard

Gabriel mentioning that fact late one night while at the billiard table at Wolverest. The men hadn't known she'd been in the hall, her ear pressed against the closed door.

"Is he a man of substantial funds, then?" Lucy asked, giving a frustrated sigh when Rosalind failed to answer her.

Just what was Nicholas Kincaid doing here?

Gabriel would know. A surge of anticipation quickened Rosalind's pulse. She wouldn't have to wait long to ask her brother. Gabriel had requested her presence in his study for a brief discussion before their guests started to arrive this evening. She suspected she was due another lecture about her meddling—er, *matchmaking*.

Although it ought to be praise. Lonely Mr. Thwaites and the spinster Miss Crofton were now the happy Mr. and Mrs. Thwaites as of just last season. And by the looks of things, Miss Honeywell here would find herself a viscountess very soon. Rosalind itched to take another peek in their direction.

"My Lady. Miss Meriwether," a gentleman intoned from behind them.

Rosalind turned to see Lord Stokes stepping past the other end of the aisle. A veteran of the marriage mart, the redheaded viscount was rather reserved, but friendly. An acquaintance of Gabriel's, he often attended all the Devines' parties.

He tipped his hat, smiling at them in turn. His gaze lingered a touch longer on Lucy, which hardly went unnoticed by Rosalind.

"Well," Rosalind whispered in her most beseeching tone. "Whatever are you doing here talking to me, dear Lucy, when there is a highly available bachelor right here in this very establishment? I daresay, he is completely smitten with you."

"You think so? I rather thought he only had eyes for you."

"Don't be silly," Rosalind replied lightly.

"Well . . . perhaps," Lucy answered, sounding unsure.

"Why don't you go and speak with him, then?"

Lucy blinked in surprise. "I shouldn't know what to say."

"We are at a bookshop, for heaven's sake. Ask him a question about a book."

"What book?"

"Any book. It doesn't matter."

Hesitating, Lucy tapped her finger against her teeth.

"Go on," Rosalind urged, jerking her chin in the

direction Stokes had gone. "If I were you, I should think I'd sidle up next to him and start fretting about not being able to reach a book. It's bound to work."

Lucy gasped, her eyes wide and her smile alight with enthusiasm. "A test of his gallantry," she replied in a loud whisper. "Brilliant!"

Rosalind nodded in encouragement. "Why don't you give it a try?"

"Yes. Yes, I'll do just that. Superior idea!"

As Lucy sped off down the aisle—busy with thoughts of snagging Lord Stokes—Rosalind turned her attention back to peeking through the bookshelf in order to gauge Miss Honeywell's progress.

"Oh, dear," Rosalind whispered, her shoulders falling in disappointment. It appeared they had gone separate ways.

Rosalind carefully slid a particularly meaty tome two inches further down the shelf in order to get a better view. Lord Beecham had rounded the corner and was clearly exiting in a rush. What had happened? Completely enthralled with just what exactly had occurred between the couple, she forgot her position on the ladder. She arched her feet and now stood on the tips of her toes.

Her head now in the shelf along with a dusty book, Rosalind nudged the thick tome further out of her way with the side of her forehead. Had they argued? And Miss Honeywell . . . where had she gone? She gazed up and down the aisle as far as she could see. Was she upset as well? Oh, dear, what had happened?

If Rosalind had been paying any attention at all to just how far she was leaning to the side, she would have surely caught herself by grabbing hold of the sides of the ladder. Instead, her toes slid on the rung.

She didn't have time to scream. With nothing underneath for purchase, she toppled backwards, her knees bending. Gloved fingers grasped for the ladder but failed. Her entire body hardened, preparing for a jarring impact with the hard floor.

Her backside never found it.

Two strong hands caught her swiftly underneath the arms, her back slamming into the unforgiving wall of a man's solid chest. While the air in her lungs seemed to be locked on a frozen scream, his warm, even breath feathered the top of her head. It felt as if time had been suspended.

The backs of her calves rested on the fourth rung, and her feet had pushed a row of books through to the other side. He held her thus, in this ridiculous position, before she realized he was waiting for her to pull her legs out and stand on the floor.

A scorching blush inflamed her entire body. How ungainly, how graceless.

Trembling, she pulled her legs through one by one, while he held her steady. With both of her feet firmly on the floor, he hesitated, his hands firm and reassuring against her back. She exhaled shakily before he finally let go.

Pressing her lips together, Rosalind wavered, reluctant to turn around and thank him for saving her from numerous broken bones. Perhaps he would just walk away and she could pretend this had never happened?

No. That would never do. Good manners decreed she thank him. Straightening, she turned and found herself staring at the middle of his chest. She cleared her throat. "Dear man, I must extend my sincerest . . ." She tilted her head back and met disapproving gray eyes.

"Nicholas," she barely choked out.

"My lady," he murmured with a slight dip of his head.

"I . . . I—"

"—should watch what the devil you're doing?" he reproved, one brow arched. "I certainly hope this isn't a habit of yours—to behave so recklessly."

"Er, not usually," she managed to mumble.

Oh, what a witty girl, she thought, nearly rolling her eyes at herself.

He opened his mouth as if to say something, then paused, his eyes narrowing on her as he apparently weighed the words on the tip of his tongue.

"What is it?" she whispered.

He bent his head even closer, apparently so that no one else could overhear. Warmth spread from her head to her boots, and she felt her body tremble slightly. He was looking so intensely into her eyes that she blindly gripped the nearest shelf to brace herself for whatever it was he was about to say.

I love you, Rosalind. I worship you, Rosalind. I followed you all the way to London just to tell you that you are my sun, my stars, my moonlit . . .

"Apple tree."

Rosalind blinked. "What?"

"Do you remember that day in the apple tree? I shall never forget it." His voice was low, his slight Scot's burr seeming to thrum through her. Having his silvery stare centered on her so unexpectedly and after so long fairly turned Rosalind's mind to mush.

"It was the first time I saw you." He shook his head slowly, his intense look never softening. "I spotted you sitting in one of your brother's apple trees in the walled orchard. I had no idea what you were doing up there. It took me a half a moment to realize you were spying on a man and woman enjoying a picnic luncheon on the lawn."

Oh, yes. Rosalind remembered that day. And she had arranged that picnic, too. In fact, she'd picked the menu herself and packed the basket as well. She had been helping a footman woo a scullery maid for weeks. The girl had finally relented, agreeing to an outing. Within the weeks that had followed, the happy couple had married.

But contrary to what Nicholas believed, she had *not* been spying on the lovers. She had been spying on Nicholas. He had just finished helping their groundskeeper burn a diseased tree on the border of their properties. Believing he'd been alone, Nicholas had slipped off his shirt and washed up over a tub of rainwater near the wall of the orchard. Fascinated, her eyes had lingered upon the flat plane of his stomach and muscled chest, the light trail of hair that circled his navel and disappeared in the band of his breeches. His skin had looked like the color of tea with two drops of cream—and just as warm and inviting. When he'd straightened, shaking the water out of his hair, she had thought he'd caught her eye. She had lurched back . . .

"You tipped backwards and would have come crashing down, but by some miracle you hung on to the tree limb by the backs of your knees." He shifted his weight. Lord, he smelled wonderful and warm. Light cologne and utterly masculine. "And there you swayed back and forth. The only thing that ended up falling to the ground was your bonnet."

Her skirts had flipped over her head, too. A flush of heat fanned through her upon realizing that Nicholas must have seen her unmentionables that day. She was just glad he didn't reveal that particular fact.

His eyes sparkled mischievously, but only briefly. It still managed to trip up her heart. Perhaps he was remembering that flipped skirt after all.

She inhaled slowly, shakily, and rallied her composure.

"So this is"—he looked off in the distance briefly, then swung those eyes back to her—"at least the second time you've fallen off or out of something."

The corners of his mouth turned downward in a teasing manner that made her feel like she was a debutante again. "One would think you would have learned your lesson."

"To not climb trees," she answered cheekily.

He sighed, giving a nod to the next row. "Perhaps if you weren't so preoccupied spying on people," he said, a muscle twitching in his jaw, "and paid attention to yourself, you wouldn't have fallen off the ladder."

All of a sudden, her mind seemed to awaken out of a blanket of fog. Her eyes narrowed on him. "You *were* deliberately blocking my view," she accused in a sharp whisper, taking a step closer to him.

"And *you* are ever the wee snoop, I see," he whispered back, his warm breath dusting her cheek as he, too, took a step closer to her.

Her mouth opened on a silent gasp. "How dare you make such assumptions," she whispered as loudly as one could and have it still be considered a whisper.

A wicked gleam lit his gray eyes. "Is it quite beneath you, then? Women of society don't meddle in people's lives?"

Her mind, refined and knowledgeable in the art of giving someone a fantastic retort, went startlingly blank. Not only was he accusing her of spying, which of course was exactly what she'd been doing, but they were also standing so close to each other now that a deep thrumming began to vibrate through her. Did he feel it, too?

Giving herself a mental shake, she reminded herself that he was chiding her as if she was some vexing creature—a little sister, perhaps. Frustration simmered inside at the thought.

She might be someone's little sister, but she wasn't his. And she certainly didn't want him to view her that way—not when she was undoubtedly a woman full grown, not when her feelings for him were so strong, so lasting. Her love was not a transient thing, an infatuation.

It occurred to her then that he was waiting for her to say something. Refusing to take a step back, she held her ground and blurted out the first thing that came to mind. "If you must know, I was trying to get a book down." She lifted a shoulder daintily, her face a mask of nonchalance.

"That's all?"

"And I couldn't quite reach it."

One brow raised in apparent disbelief. "Indeed?"

"Indeed."

"All right then, which one?"

"What?" she hedged.

"Which book?"

Her eyes flew to the shelf.

One long, blunt-tipped finger gently tapped her chin. "No peeking."

A shaky sigh escaped her—as did the title of the book she wanted. Of course, as the book was imaginary, that was to be expected.

"Now, lass, tell me which book it was that you couldn't reach," his eyes dipped to her mouth briefly, "and I'll get it for you. Easy enough."

She swallowed, and then without looking, she reached upward and pointed in the general direction of the shelf she had been poking her head through. "It was on the top shelf."

With his serious gaze still upon her, he reached high above her head. His chest so close, the stiff lapels of his coat almost brushed her cheek. His scent surrounded her, warm and clean, and making her want nothing more than to bury her face in the soft folds of his cravat.

"There's only one book up there," he said, his eyes lifting away to look past her.

"Then, that's the one," she chirped, banishing her absurd face-in-the-cravat fantasy.

"If that be your wish, lass."

"It be," she said, then cleared her throat. "I mean, yes. Yes, it is."

Voices whispered nearby. He took a step away from her, seeming to finally acknowledge that they might be creating gossip fodder.

He pulled back further still, and suddenly the thick book she had nudged with her forehead earlier was thrust in her face. "*This* book?" he asked suspiciously.

"Indeed." She took it with two hands, nearly losing the thing when her wrist twisted from its weight. He caught it before it slipped through her fingers and landed on his feet.

"Thank you," she said, grateful that she affected a somewhat lofty tone.

He bent his head toward her, his eyes intent on the book. Long, slightly calloused fingers reached toward her bodice but stopped short to trace the embossed title stretching across the cover.

She hoped her barely audible gasp went unnoticed by him.

He chuckled low and deep in his chest. "*A Detailed History on the Production and Use of Cannons and Muskets.*" He straightened to his full height, a rare smile playing with the corner of his mouth. "I would never suppose that a woman of your sort would be all that interested in the tools of war."

My sort? Whatever did he mean by that? "Well then," she said pertly, "perhaps a man of *your sort* ought to cease making unfounded assumptions."

He tipped his head in a conceding gesture, a curious warmth in his gaze.

She fought the nearly overwhelming urge to ask him what he was thinking. "If y-you'll excuse me, I have a book to purchase." What a coward she was turning out to be.

He stepped aside, extending his arm to allow her the way.

Chin lifted, shoulders back, Rosalind passed him and strode toward the front desk, willing herself to keep her pace steady and unaffected.

Out of the corner of her eye she noticed that he wasn't that far behind, about three feet back to her left. However, just when she believed he was going to follow her, he turned and strode toward the exit.

The pretty shopgirl from before approached the door at the same time, her arms full of novels. Tipping his hat to her, he smiled as he opened the door for her.

Rosalind let her giant book slam on the counter. He *smiled*? He hardly ever smiled.

"My lady? Is something amiss?" A very concerned-looking Mr. Thwaites peered at Rosalind from behind tiny, round spectacles.

"No, Mr. Thwaites," she said flatly. "I am perfectly content this morning."

He visibly relaxed, though he appeared not to believe her. "Good to hear. Good to hear, my lady." He gestured to the book. "Will you be purchasing the book?"

Rosalind pushed it toward him with a sigh.

"Shall I list this on your credit, my lady?"

She nodded absentmindedly, her eyes drifting back to the door. After Mr. Thwaites finished recording her transaction, she mumbled her thanks, politely inquired after Mrs. Thwaites, then yanked the book into her arms before shuffling to the door.

She sighed, hefting the book in her grasp. Glaring down at it, she had the fleeting thought that should she meet Nicholas Kincaid on the street, she'd very gladly wallop him with it.

What a smashing day it was turning out to be. She had become the object of an idiotic wager that was nothing more than a flagrant waste of time, she had an appointment with her brother that most likely included dire warnings about meddling, she'd made a fool of herself in front of the man she loved—who'd admonished her as if she'd been but a child, and now she found herself saddled with a two-stone book that she had to carry all the way home and would most definitely never read.

As she neared the windows of the shop, a splattering of raindrops dotted the glass. Outside, her maid, Alice, appeared to be choking their umbrella. In another second, the thing fell apart in her hands. The girl looked up to see Rosalind through the window and lifted her shoulders in a helpless shrug.

Wonderful. The day couldn't possibly get any worse.

Chapter 2

"You've hired me a nursemaid?"

Using every ounce of self-restraint, Rosalind managed to remain seated across from her eldest brother—and not surge upright and stomp her foot like the child he clearly believed her to be.

Gabriel leaned back in his chair and eyed Rosalind with a gaze as frosty blue and unyielding as her own. "Not a nursemaid *exactly*."

"Then tell me, what is the difference? You say I am to be watched, looked after, that if ever a circumstance arose in which I need assistance, I am simply to call out and some unnamable brute shall spring forth from the shadows to come to my aid."

"He is to be your guardian," Gabriel replied in his usual impervious manner. "Unseen and unheard. There will be no contact, unless of course a predicament occurs."

"I've managed to survive this long on my own."

"That was before the damnable wager," he nearly shouted.

Grabbing the folded copy of the *Morning Post* from his desk, he tossed it in her direction, where it flopped open of its own accord to the very page that had managed to send him into a near rage this morning.

Rosalind turned away from the article. She had no wish to read it again. "The feeble minds of men," she muttered with distaste.

Gabriel shook his head, his smile grim. "To think before this came about, I worried about your meddling—or *matchmaking* as you call it—getting you into trouble. And now this monstrosity rears its head."

She rose to her feet, refusing to sit meekly any longer. "Am I not only to be pitied for my unmarried state but considered utterly helpless as well?"

"See here, Rosie. You make it sound as if I think of you as a child."

"Is it not obvious that you do?" Crossing her arms over her chest, she strode to the window overlooking the bustling street. The rumbling carriage wheels and clomping horse hooves were muffled behind the glass.

Soon, a steady stream of carriages would be arriving, spilling scores of guests upon their doorstep. This evening's fête marked the unofficial opening of the season and her new sister-in-law's introduction as a duchess. It also boasted to include a newly titled and highly available bachelor, the Marquess of Winterbourne, to be exact. The name sounded familiar, but she couldn't recall where she'd heard it before. Rosalind expected it to be quite the crush.

She ought to have been thrumming with barely contained excitement. But the news of her hired protector, coupled with the chance encounter with Nicholas in the bookshop, had tied her thoughts into knots.

Two more carriages passed by, and Rosalind wondered fleetingly if Nicholas was ensconced inside any one of them.

During the last two years, his presence at Wolverest had been rather scarce. According to Gabriel, Nicholas was simply busy managing his lands, overseeing the yield of livestock and timber. And it was undoubtedly true. Nicholas was known throughout the countryside for not hesitating to toss his coat aside, roll up his shirtsleeves, and assist in the repair of buildings, birthing of sheep, and digging of drains. His tenants revered him.

Rosalind only wished Castle Wolverest had been in need of a drain to be dug. Perhaps several.

And now this man of the country was in London?

She hadn't had the opportunity to inquire. She'd only returned home to have her brother inform her that he'd hired a guardian for her.

Rosalind appreciated her brother's protection over the years and often felt she knew the value of a doting father, as she had very little memory of their own. However, this was a matter of pride.

"I am four and twenty . . . soon to be five and twenty. If it wasn't for my station and wealth, I'd be considered on the shelf. I am not a little girl anymore. This is absurd, Gabriel."

"It is all perfectly logical, given the circumstances." His slow inhale told her that the threads of his patience were beginning to unwind. "And I do not, of all people, pity your unmarried state," Gabriel pointed out, his deep voice resonating within the room. "A woman of your distinction, superior connections, pristine reputation, and wealth need not be ashamed of being unmarried. You are, at all times, perfectly respectable. In fact," he continued wryly, "I should be completely happy should you never decide to take a husband.

In such a case, I needn't entertain the fear of accidentally throttling the idiot should he ever make you frown."

"You are ridiculous, Gabriel," Rosalind muttered with a smile.

Though truthfully, other than this singular instance, she couldn't blame him for being overprotective. The wager notwithstanding, the very second Gabriel and his new bride left Devine Mansion for their much-anticipated wedding trip, the floodgates would open indeed.

A flood of men. Men by the dozens. Men who would otherwise stay far away from the Devines' doorstep should Gabriel be in residence. His intimidating presence kept them at bay. Even now, as angry as she was at her brother, she was grateful for his diligence when it came to keeping men of questionable character and motives away.

Men acted like simpletons, or, worse, devious fortune hunters in her presence. All the attention was rather embarrassing and unwanted.

It was for these reasons that every single gentleman's intentions were always held suspect. And Rosalind, not at all the rebellious sort, was in perfect agreement. Until now.

Secretly, she had been anticipating Gabriel's departure as soon as he had announced his plans in the country. She was old enough and wise enough to juggle the foreseeable deluge of hopeful men ready to break down the door and test their wiles on her.

Besides, none of them would ever win her—she had already given her heart away.

But what she did not want, simply could not bear, was some strange man following her in and about Town, gauging her every move. And for heaven's sake, she'd have a chaperone with her at all times. Was he really needed?

"Well," Gabriel offered, "there is another solution."

"And that is?"

"You could simply return to the country until I return."

"That will not do."

"You'll not be running and hiding," he replied, reading her thoughts. "It's prudent."

"I intend to enjoy the season as much as I have any other."

"Then you shall have an appointed guard. It is done."

This was preposterous and she would have none of it.

"And what of Tristan?" she suggested, turning to face him fully now. "Why cannot our brother do the job?"

Gabriel merely raised a brow. "Tristan? You cannot be serious."

She lifted one shoulder. "Whyever not? He'll be two and twenty this summer. He knows the ways of wicked men, well, because he is one. Surely, he—"

"Needs his own nursemaid."

"So you admit to thinking of me as a child."

"Ye—no!" He stood, clearly frustrated, and ran a hand through his hair. "I think of you as my responsibility, my beloved sister. I will not have you in danger. Not now, not ever, and certainly not while I'm thoroughly and happily preoccupied with my wife. I cannot be in two places at once."

A resigned acceptance was creeping in. True, Gabriel tended to be a touch overbearing and vigilant when it came to those he loved, but Rosalind would feel immeasurable guilt knowing he wasn't enjoying himself on his wedding trip because he worried over some idiotic wager. She must relent.

Or at least allow him to believe that she had.

Pivoting on her heel to face a spectacular tapestry depicting a panoramic view of the family estate, Rosalind tapped her finger against her chin in thought as she paced the length and back again.

First, she must glean whatever information she could about this person in order to gain clues to determine his identity.

Then, once Gabriel and Madelyn were far and away, she'd discreetly approach him and pay him double whatever Gabriel had promised if he'd agree to go away.

It would be rather simple, really. She ought to ask a few questions before she quit the room. Why not be direct?

"Well then," she said, affecting resignation. "Who is he?"

"God willing, you will never need to know. I just want you to feel safe."

"All right," she said tightly. "What of this . . . this . . . *protector*. How sure are you of his moral standing? Your circle of trust is diminutive, indeed. How can you be so sure he'll not, oh I don't know, snatch me up himself and run away with me?"

Gabriel threw back his head and laughed. "He is not the sort to be swept away by romantic notions. I can assure you his only interest is to keep you safe until I return."

She doubted that. "His objective may be chivalrous at first, but the true intentions of men always reveal themselves eventually."

"You shall be safe," he insisted.

"How can you be so certain?" she asked, hoping Gabriel would think she was still trying to change his mind and therefore allow some clues to slip about her guardian's identity. "Have you known him long?"

He nodded. "Since I was a young man."

Her curiosity was piqued. "Have I met him then?"

"Perhaps. Perhaps not."

"Did you meet him at Eton?"

"No." His eyes narrowed. "Although he is well educated and attended a well-respected school in . . ." He allowed his words to trail off, apparently seeing the trap she was setting and thinking to take a step away from it.

"He is a gentleman, then? Not some Bow Street Runner?"

"His family and the Devines have known each other for quite some time. That is all I will say."

"How long has he been watching me?"

"He'll be discreet," he said, deliberately evading her question. "Aunt Eugenia needn't know his identity either."

41

"When does he begin watching me?"

Again, he admitted nothing, but he did look down at a paper on his desk, running his finger across a line as he read.

Before she left this room, Rosalind silently vowed, she was going to snatch that sheet of vellum from his desk. She believed it to be the guest list for this evening. And one of those guests, she supposed, was her guardian.

"He has been equipped with a directory of your acquaintances. Activities you usually participate in for the entire season," Gabriel continued. "Your shopping habits, et cetera."

"I don't follow a strict routine," she remarked. If she couldn't pay the goon off, she would shake him off instead. All she had to do was alter her schedule.

"I am certain he'll be able to conform to your changes."

Distinctive, feminine murmuring came from down the hall.

Gabriel's head jerked up at the sound, his gaze softening.

Madelyn. No one but Gabriel's wife could redirect her brother's attention so quickly and completely. And it greatly pleased Rosalind. She'd known they were perfect for each other from the very first moment Gabriel had spied Madelyn hiding in the garden last autumn.

Rosalind had had a small hand in bringing them together. After all, it was she who had insisted Madelyn ought to be invited to her brother's ball. Gabriel had originally deemed the former Miss Haywood too clumsy, too imperfect.

But she was absolutely perfect for him.

It didn't surprise Rosalind at all that Gabriel had fallen for Madelyn so hard and fast. Rosalind simply possessed a talent for knowing when two people belonged together. And she couldn't have been more right.

An adorable vision in a white satin slip over a light blue net frock, which complemented her dark-red hair to dazzling perfection, Madelyn stopped at the door frame and smiled at Gabriel. "Your *lovely* aunt . . ." She poked her head in. "Oh! Rosalind! There you are."

Amazing. A minute ago her brother had looked like a stuffy, arrogant duke. Now he smiled at his wife quite like a wolf who spied a plump bunny that had unknowingly wandered into his den.

A white lace ribbon that had been weaved through Madelyn's coif had come partially loose, which allowed a big coil of dark cherry hair to slide free. It dangled near her ear. Somehow it wouldn't be right if every hair was in place.

"I'm sorry. I don't mean to intrude," she said softly, "but your *aunt* and her cat have arrived, and they have both become rather *terse* over her 'less than hospitable' welcome into your home."

He exhaled wearily.

"She's upset because you have yet to make an appearance in the morning room."

"She can wait," Gabriel grumbled.

Rosalind closed her eyes on a slow blink. She had forgotten that since Madelyn and Gabriel were leaving early tomorrow morning, Aunt Eugenia must temporarily move in to act as chaperone.

Usually harmless, the crotchety old spinster had yet to give her approval of her nephew's choice of bride and liked to remind everyone of that fact every now and again. Gabriel would just as soon forbid the woman from entering the house, but Madelyn insisted he allow her to visit. Rosalind didn't think she would have been as gracious if put in the same situation.

"Madelyn and I will be leaving early tomorrow," Gabriel reminded her. "I expect you to exercise caution and keep your little nose out of everyone else's love affairs. Don't make this any more difficult for your guardian than it needs to be."

"Very well," Rosalind replied noncommittally, trying hard not to smile like an imp. Her gaze slid to the paper Gabriel had read from just a moment ago.

Clearing his throat, Gabriel motioned for Rosalind to proceed to the doorway.

Smiling innocently, she skirted around him, letting her arm trail behind her. If he would just turn his back for a second, she could just reach over and make a grab for . . .

Anticipating her thoughts, he snatched up the sheet of vellum and tossed it into the grate. The low flames flashed, and then curled around the edges, turning it into ash.

His brow lifted. "Think I don't know my own sister?"

Rosalind merely shrugged and walked out of the room, smiling at Madelyn. "Quick. Tell me who it is," she whispered out of the corner of her mouth as she passed.

Madelyn gave her head a slight shake. "I can't. He made me promise. He used . . . ah, persuasive tactics." She blushed and patted imaginary wrinkles from her bodice.

"Move along, Rosalind," Gabriel ordered.

Madelyn gave her an apologetic smile. "It's for the best."

"I understand," Rosalind answered. Despite the undue aggravation, she really wanted the two of them to have a lovely, worry-free trip. "If this brings Gabriel some peace, so be it. I'll manage it."

"That's exactly what I fear," Gabriel remarked, giving his wife a wink before Rosalind walked out the door.

A sudden thought, outlandish as it might very well be, sprouted in her mind. "Gabriel? I saw Nicholas Kincaid at the bookshop today."

He nodded, looking mildly surprised.

"Is he . . . ?"

Gabriel's mouth turned down at the corners. "Nicholas is here on business."

"I see," she muttered and turned away, her curiosity piqued. It had to be true. Gabriel wouldn't lie to her.

Halfway down the corridor, Rosalind realized the happy couple had not followed her. Her steps slowed and she looked over her shoulder, wondering what had held them back.

Gabriel must have caught sight of that loose coil in his wife's coiffure. He lifted his hand. For a second, Rosalind thought he would fix it for Madelyn, but she was wrong. Bending forward, he tipped it close to his lips with a single finger and kissed it.

Feeling a trifle embarrassed for having witnessed such a gentle, sweet gesture, Rosalind whipped back around, a touch of a blush heating her cheeks.

A second emotion resided in her heart as well. Envy.

Part of her knew that she would be just fine on her own. There would be joy to be found in observing the happiness of others. But it wasn't that simple—she loved someone.

An image of dark-brown hair kissed with gold by the sun and tousled around a supremely handsome face sprang to mind. Back home in Yorkshire, seeing Nicholas, having him visit or having him stay for supper—it had been the best part of her day. But *she*, apparently, hadn't been the highlight of *his* day. If she had been, then he surely would have made an offer for her by now.

A wave of uneasiness roiled through her. Rosalind already knew what a lifetime of indifference could do to a woman's spirit, her soul. To love someone who would never return the affection. Her mother had been such a woman. Was she destined to suffer the same fate? To make the same mistake?

The sting of unshed tears surprised her, but she banished them back to the depths of her heart. She needed all her wits about her if she was going to unveil this guardian of hers.

Rosalind looked back to see Gabriel slide his arm around Madelyn's waist and steer her down the opposite way.

"Wait, please!" Rosalind called out, hoping he'd be so distracted that he just might tell her more than he wanted to. Plus, she reminded herself, she did have another brother to try and glean information from. "Does Tristan know about this?"

Gabriel shook his head slowly. "No more questions, Rosalind. Just let the man do his job."

"Am I the only one not to know? You're not being fair."

"Now," he remarked pointedly, "you sound *exactly* like a child. Come now, you and I both know that should I give you one scrap of information on the man, you will use it to discover his identity and then try charming him to leave off."

"Don't be ridiculous." She gave a short, disbelieving laugh. "I would *never* do anything of the sort."

Charm him? Imagine!

If he was anything like another friend of her brother's, her wiles ought to have no effect on this guardian at all.

"Just don't cause trouble, Rosie," Gabriel warned.

"Trouble?" She scoffed. "I don't know the meaning of the word."

Chapter 3

Trouble had lively blue eyes and sleek sable tresses.

Her lips curved upward faintly at the corners even when she was at her most somber, giving one the misguided impression she knew all of your secrets . . . or she was about to tell you one of hers. And she had the longest legs he'd ever seen for someone who barely reached his shoulders.

Nicholas made a point to avoid Trouble, but he hadn't expected the slow burn of desire that had tugged at him when he'd stood so close to her in the bookshop. It had been so sudden, so unforeseeable in its power, that it had left him feeling shaken. And here he had thought that spending less time at the Devines' would finally free him from her effortless enchantment once and for all. What a fool he was.

He assured himself that she hadn't noticed—

Rosalind might be perceptive, but she couldn't read minds.

When they'd parted, her arms laden with a book her pride wouldn't allow her to put back, he hadn't been able to keep the grin from spreading across his face.

Good Christ. What a pitiful guardian he was turning out to be. After spending the last seven years successfully keeping the woman at arm's length, he'd almost buckled after being within two feet of her in a public place.

And she'd done very little to provoke him. She'd simply been herself, looking up at him with those big eyes as if he was responsible for hanging the moon.

He rolled his shoulders. It was only a twinge of attraction, he told himself. Nothing more. It wasn't as if he'd never felt it before when he'd been around her.

Aye, but all those times in the past you could just walk away, leave if you had to.

Indeed, but he didn't have that option anymore. At least not for the next three months. The thought made him deuced uncomfortable.

Slipping two fingers into the top of his cravat,

he tugged twice, willing all desirous thoughts of his charge to the back of his mind.

"Stop fidgeting," his sister chided from the foot of the stairs.

Standing in the foyer of his newly rented town house, Nicholas stretched on his leather gloves and grumbled, "Can't help it. The blasted thing is choking me."

Clasping her hands before her, Francesca made a wide arc around him. "You look quite dashing, Nicholas." She cleared her throat meaningfully. "Even despite the absence of proper breeches."

Nicholas shook his head slowly, a derisive smile lifting a corner of his mouth. "Ashamed of your ancestry, are we?"

"Of course not. But I daresay you're trying very hard not to fit in with your surroundings."

He leveled a stare at his sister. "It is only because I owe Gabriel a favor that I must refrain from my dearest wish. And that, wee sister, is to return to Yorkshire and keep pretending Lady Rosalind Devine doesn't exist."

"Nicholas," Frannie admonished, "we owe so much to His Grace. You should not speak of his sister as if she is some vexing creature."

He dipped his head with a reluctant nod. "Aye, I should not speak of her at all."

Frannie's eyes narrowed. "I cannot help but be curious as to why you feel you must pretend she doesn't exist. Does she threaten you in some way?"

When he didn't answer, she crossed her slender arms over her middle and nodded knowingly. "Very curious, indeed. Especially for someone who has shown nothing but passing interest in his admirers. Does this one have some hold over you?"

"No," he said, his tone cold. "The only thing she holds is the means for me to satisfy my need to repay her brother's generosity."

"And that is the only need worth satisfying? With you, there is always work, responsibility. What of love?"

"What of it?"

"Criminy, Nicholas. You act as if you don't know what it is."

It wasn't like that at all. He revered it for the powerful force that it was—and vowed to avoid such a miserable emotion until the day he perished from the earth.

An image of his father, grief tearing him apart, day after day, sprang unbidden to his mind. If he concentrated hard enough, Nicholas could still hear his father's whispered prayers in the dead of night, begging for the Lord to take him from this earth so that he could be with his wife once again. His father's nightly pleading would eventually break into deep, soul-wrenching sobs. Eleven years old at the time, Nicholas would stuff his pillow around his head, his own tears spilling — not just for the loss of his mother but for the horrible, unending pain his father endured.

Five years later, Malcolm Kincaid's prayers were finally answered. Nicholas could not deny the odd sense of relief he experienced. His father's everlasting suffering had come to an end.

"Why will you not take some happiness for yourself?" Francesca asked, breaking his stream of thought.

Nicholas's laugh was quiet and held no humor. "You imply love and happiness are companions."

"And you do not?"

Nicholas gave his head a slight shake. "Are you happy right now?" he asked, regretting his words as soon as he said them. Francesca had lost her husband two years ago. "Christ, Frannie, forgive me. I should not have said it."

She closed her eyes briefly, then said, "It's all right, Nicholas."

He was quiet for several moments, then muttered quietly, "I appreciate your thinking of me, but I'm perfectly satisfied with my life."

"But you must be lonesome. Was there no one in all of Yorkshire that piqued your interest? Scotland?" He didn't answer, so she continued unabated. "If not, I daresay, you might find her in London."

"Don't depend upon it." He plopped his hat atop his head and the butler opened the door. The Winterbourne carriage waited at the end of the walk. "Good evening, dear Frannie. It's getting late. And I'm on duty." With that he turned and strode out the door, a waft of cool, night air racing up his thighs.

"Rosalind! Let me not suppose that you're daring to open those doors. Come away, gel. Come away."

"Yes, Aunt Eugenia," Rosalind said dutifully, pasting a serene smile upon her lips. "Is your kitty safely ensconced inside your bedchamber?"

"I'm not worried about Oliver," her aunt replied, giving Rosalind a scathing look. "He's shy around people and would never run freely with so many strangers wandering about. What are you thinking?"

Oh, Lud. It was going to be a long season. "Can I get something for you?" Like a carriage ride back home.

"Upon my honor," Eugenia proclaimed in a hushed voice. "Who has a dance with the doors wide open so early in the spring?"

Those who do not wish to pass out from the stifling heat, perhaps.

Her aunt patted at her stiff collar, as if to make certain not a whisper of air could slip through the high neckline. "We could all catch a chill. It's rather cozy in here, and I should like it to remain that way."

"Then we shall all melt right along with the candle wax," Rosalind murmured.

Aunt Eugenia's head jerked up. "What was that, child?"

"I said, I think I just saw Miss Marianne Fairfax."

"Ah She's the harpist, is she not?"

"The cellist, this evening."

"That's what I said. Cellist."

"Yes, ma'am."

"Chubby girl, what a shame," her aunt said with a cluck of her tongue. "She'd be quite pretty if it weren't for that."

Rosalind's eyes opened wide. What a ridiculous

thing to say. "Miss Fairfax is lovely." The. End.

Her aunt simply shrugged. "You have your opinion. I have mine. She's not spoken for, is she? I daresay she is not. And probably never will be unless she does something about that figure."

Rosalind let out a breath of frustration to quell the urge to shout at her aunt for being so callous.

However, she must remind herself that she wasn't here to defend nice young women against bitter spinsters, nor was she here to play cupid. She wanted to discover the identity of her guardian.

Expose him, and then dispose of him.

Her pride depended upon it.

An oppressive heat seemed to suddenly surround her, and she found herself glancing longingly out the French doors. Being so newly returned to the city, Rosalind ought to feel jubilant. The shopping, the parties, reacquainting oneself with friends, they were all things she had come to anticipate while residing in Yorkshire.

Tonight, however, she felt an unusual pang for home. For routines and spending time outdoors. To be able to see the clear, blue sky without the blanket of yellow fog that seemed to hang over the city. To be able to watch Nicholas covertly from behind a book she'd pretend to read while he feigned losing a game of chess to Tristan.

Ah, yes, Nicholas was her own private temptation—though in her daydreams he thought she was irresistible. He'd toss her younger brother out the door, cross the room, sink down next to her on the sofa, and then pull her onto his lap—all of which he would do bare-chested, of course.

Swallowing, Rosalind opened her fan with a snap and began fanning herself. She really needed to stop looking for romantic reading materials in Tristan's private library.

She gave her head a tiny shake. What was the matter with her? She loved the city. She loved the shopping, the museums, the theater, the bustling about, and the endless parties. Yet the truth was that no matter how many friends and gentleman admirers surrounded her, no matter how many places she visited, she was always alone . . . and always daydreaming about *him*.

And he was here now.

Well, not *here* at this ball, but in London. She still hadn't figured out why, but she felt confident that she would eventually.

A group of young men, all of whom she had already danced with at least once this evening, sauntered by. After a quick check over their shoulders (no doubt looking for her eldest brother), they all smiled and gave her a friendly nod.

She smiled back, not coyly, nor invitingly. Just a smile. A hostess smile. A "please call on me tomorrow so that it may draw out my guardian" sort of smile.

If her plan was to work on the morrow, she had to sow the seeds now, and plenty of them, too.

Rosalind knew tonight would be a crush. It seemed nearly all of society was attending. To be sure, most had come to see the new Duchess of Wolverest, who was standing at the top of the room with Gabriel greeting some newly arriving guests. However, by the sheer volume of debutantes in attendance, Rosalind rather thought that many had come to get a peek at the new Marquess of Winterbourne.

And he wasn't even here yet. Rosalind wondered if he was late by design. Perhaps he wanted to make a grand entrance. Noblemen were notoriously arrogant.

"Lady Burberry!" Aunt Eugenia suddenly exclaimed, waving her closed fan slightly. "Pleasure to see you! Come sit!"

Rosalind smiled politely at the older woman as

she ambled past to plop down in a chair against the wall next to her aunt. Ah, the spinster corner. Every ballroom had one.

With her aunt occupied with genial conversation, Rosalind took a backward step, and then another, and then another, until she was far enough away that she could slip away.

Sliding her gaze over to her aunt, she was relieved to see the woman hadn't noticed. She seemed to be craning her neck in order to look toward the front of the room.

Rosalind supposed she ought to be standing near her brother, but she could inspect the faces in the crowd much better from the back of the room. If her guardian was here tonight, he'd be watching her, wouldn't he?

A smear of red hair caught her attention. Lord Stokes, the very man Rosalind imagined would someday make a declaration to her friend Lucy, was slowly walking the perimeter of the room. He seemed to be watching everyone carefully. Perhaps he was looking for someone in particular, but then again . . . perhaps *he* was her guardian.

Her lips lifted in a small, secret smile. Nothing was going to distract her from her mission. If she were to slip away from the ballroom, perhaps he would have no choice but to follow her, and then she'd know for certain.

She turned to do just that when the butler's flat voice resounded throughout the room. "Presenting the Marquess of Winterbourne."

Hissing whispers, giggling debutantes, the jovial mumblings of men—all of it lowered as heads turned to the front of the room.

Being short, Rosalind couldn't see a thing. For a fleeting moment, she toyed with the idea of standing on a chair but decided her aunt might have an apoplexy if she did.

All thoughts of her guardian flew out the doors at her back in the face of discovering why this new marquess held the guests in such a state of open curiosity.

As she threaded through the guests, whispers surrounded her.

"He's a Scot, eh?"

"He's a handsome one."

"God's truth, that isn't a padded jacket. That's him!"

"Did you see those legs? Now there's a man who needn't employ false calves."

"Stand straight, Mary, or else his lordship might not ask you to dance."

"Formidable-looking fellow. Kincaid's the family name."

Rosalind's head snapped to the right. Did someone just utter "Kincaid," or was she simply going mad? Her heartbeat tripped and her breathing quickened.

She rushed ahead, desperate to see what held everyone so spellbound. But the crowd seemed to close in around her as others shuffled closer to the top of the room. She looked to the right and left, but there was no escape.

Her shoulders heaved with a sigh and she relinquished the fight.

Perhaps if she feigned a swoon, a space would be cleared. She gave her head a slight shake. No, that would never do. At least not right now. Everyone was so distracted that they'd probably step over her.

Squeezing past the back of a portly gentleman, Rosalind thought she heard someone say her name.

"Pssst. Rosalind."

She turned to see Lucy Meriwether slide up to her.

"We're thinking about calling him 'Lord Sin,' "
Lucy whispered in delight. She did a little excited
hop. " 'Lord Winter' doesn't sound half as exciting,
though his stare is rather frosty."

"Who are you speaking of?"

"Why, Lord Winterbourne, of course."

"Already?" Rosalind gritted her teeth.

"Already what?" Lucy even had the nerve to
look perplexed.

"Already," Rosalind repeated with an agitated
nod. "I can't even get to the top of the room in my
own house and you've all made a nickname for
him?"

Lucy looked taken aback. "Well, it's not our fault
you're lollygagging."

"Lolly—" Rosalind cut herself off before she
lost complete control of her temper. She paused
and breathed deeply. In and out. In and out.
"Now," she said, feeling infinitely more at ease.
"Why are you all calling him Lord Sin? Is his
name Sinclair?"

"La, I am not aware of his family name."

"Is he a rake?"

Lucy shrugged and shook her head.

"A scoundrel?"

"Well, no one knows. He's only just arrived."

"Then why are you all calling him 'Lord Sin'?"

Lucy looked flummoxed. "Well, you've taken a good look at him, haven't you?"

"No. No. I have not," Rosalind said, noting that she sounded a little shrill. "I have been fighting to move an inch. Break it to me, I implore you."

Lucy bent her head close as they shuffled across the room. "Well, he just . . ." Her words trailed off as she turned an alarming shade of crimson. ". . . he's tall and scandalously tanned by the sun. And his evening clothes!"

"What could be so remarkable about his evening clothes?"

Lucy sighed like a girl fresh out the schoolroom who was seeing her first well-dressed man. "He's simply *sinful* to look at."

"Oh, how preposterous," Rosalind exclaimed. "Really, Lucy, you cannot be serious."

"I'm dancing the minuet with him first," Lucy blurted, counting off on her fingers. "Jane Locke is next for a country dance set. Clara Hopkins promised him the quadrille. Oh, and Mary Chambers was asked for the Scottish reel. And . . . is there to be a waltz this evening?"

Apparently, Lord Winterbourne did not hesitate in the filling up of dance cards.

"How did you all acquire dances with him so quickly?"

"Well, he asked us, 'tis all." Lucy eyed her speculatively. "I say, are you jealous?"

Rosalind leveled a stare at Lucy. "How on earth can I be jealous of the fact that you all have dances with someone I have never met?"

Lucy's brow puckered in confusion. "But you said you knew him."

"I did?" Now it was Rosalind's turn to look confused. "When did I say that I knew him?"

"In the bookshop," Lucy muttered, "this afternoon."

Rosalind's heart dropped down to her stomach.

"And you said he was a farmer." Lucy snorted. "A farmer, indeed. Admit it. You just didn't want me to set my cap for him because you wanted him all for yourself."

"It cannot be," Rosalind murmured.

But it was.

Before her, the crowd thinned and parted, revealing her eldest brother and Madelyn. Next to them stood Kincaid himself, tall and arrogant, looking like the handsomest devil in all of England, bare knees and all.

"It cannot be," she repeated.

Nicholas Kincaid was *Lord Winterbourne*? Nicholas Kincaid was a *marquess*? Which meant . . . she knew exactly why he was in London.

He had come for a wife.

Nicholas wagered that most observers, upon entering the Devine ballroom, would describe it as a gilded nest for the social elite. A prestigious affair, where the privileged could frolic, twitter to their hearts' content, and proudly puff out their feathers to display to all.

Nicholas saw it as a den of horrors.

Aye, it was beautiful, with its gleaming parquet floors and glimmering chandeliers glowing with hundreds of beeswax candles, but it was also stifling, crowded, and if one more lady's jaw dropped at the sight of his kilt—and his legs, for that matter—he would surely bend over and flash her something truly shocking.

Dressed in formal Scottish evening wear, Nicholas, for the most part, looked like an English gentleman from the waist up, and a Scot from the waist down. Apparently, it wasn't an everyday sight, which was fine, really. He was probably making them feel about as comfortable as he felt himself.

But he was nothing if not responsible. He would

do his duty. And then he was going back home to the country, where a man could walk across a room without getting four separate embroidered handkerchiefs discreetly stuffed in his palm—all of them accompanied with whispered invitations that would make a naval captain blush.

Three out of the four handkerchiefs were from married women, the fourth from a widow who couldn't have been a day over twenty. And if he wasn't getting offers for carnal companionship, the marriage-minded mothers were brazenly thrusting their daughters at him as if they were sacrificial lambs.

He couldn't believe his sister thought he might find a bride here among these duplicitous women—not that he was looking for one.

There were exceptions, he thought, thinking of Gabriel's Madelyn, but she was indeed a rare creature, and Gabriel's loyalty to her was rarer still.

He looked over at his friend and conjured up a grin that most likely looked like a grimace. He was appreciative of their friendship, of their alliance. The duke didn't trust many, and Nicholas echoed that feeling.

They had met when they'd both been lads, exploring the high country where they'd lived. Despite the initial difference in their social classes, they had become fast friends, intuitively recognizing similar dispositions and codes of conduct. Over the years, their relationship had grown on a solid foundation of mutual respect.

But there were things Gabriel had done for Nicholas's family—hell, for him, for that matter—which could never be repaid.

Nicholas firmly believed that if it wasn't for having a duke in his corner in Parliament, the individuals in the courts who had challenged his recent inheritance would have drawn out the battle until he would have been obliged to sell all the land that he had acquired on his own just to pay the legal costs. As it was, he had been able to keep all the estate properties that enabled his income.

Indeed. He owed much to the duke—none of it repayable, in Nicholas's estimation. And the man had never asked for anything in return. Until now.

Back in Yorkshire, he'd asked Nicholas to watch over Rosalind while he was away. Nicholas was, in a word, astounded. This man trusted—well, practically no one, in Nicholas's estimation. And yet he entrusted Nicholas with guarding something so dear as a sister. Someone as precious and exquisite as Rosalind.

Certainly, it was easy enough to keep his thoughts from straying to Rosalind in the country when there was plenty of work to distract him . . . but now that he must watch her every move?

Three months, he reminded himself. Three measly months and that was it. Nicholas would uphold his promise to Gabriel and keep an eye on her for the extent of the season. Of course, he'd see to it that she returned safely to Yorkshire to rusticate, but then he would go on with his life.

But Christ above, did ever a man see such an alluring sight?

She stood about twenty feet from him, dressed in a dark red gown that hugged every gentle curve, elongated every line, and accentuated all her feminine wiles. His eyes dropped down, momentarily, to a diamond-shaped, silver brooch that was pinned in the center of her bodice, directly under the deep cleft between her breasts. Wasn't the perfect symmetry of her lovely curving bosom distraction enough?

Her obsidian hair was upswept into a simple coiffure, dotted with tiny red flowers that matched her gown. A few inky coils dropped like precious jewels to dangle near her ears and down further to skim the porcelain-like skin of her neck and collarbone. All of that, he had gleaned from a hundred discreet glances flicked in her direction.

Tonight she reminded him of a bloodred rose against a clear night sky. A quiet, regal beauty, who—he flicked a glance over her head—was currently looking at him as if she wanted to a sink a dirk in his chest.

Aye, the lassie was a beauty. And meddlesome, and stubborn, and quite possibly spoiled. And, most assuredly hard to please. She was in her what, *seventh* season, was it? Surely that meant she was just as fastidious in love as the Devines were reputed to be.

He wouldn't look at her directly, not while she was looking at him. Not when they stood this close and there wasn't anything to distract him.

And yet he sensed something had changed. It was as if her mind had grown even sharper. He no longer held any doubts that she might not recognize his attraction for her reflected in his eyes. But he still wouldn't give her the satisfaction of adding himself to her bevy of admirers. He was her protector, her guardian. She had enough admirers.

Gabriel had warned him of how bad it would be, but Nicholas was still amazed at how these men followed her around like pups everywhere she went.

She seemed completely oblivious—or completely accustomed to it.

Whatever the case, Nicholas had first noticed the extent of her widespread appeal at the bookshop this afternoon while he had waited outside for her to leave. Once she'd come outside, he had watched her and her maid return to their carriage, which had been waiting for them across the park. Five other men had watched her progress as well.

One of them, a tall, lanky fellow with a shock of red hair, had followed them all the way from the bookshop and had even watched their carriage until it had pulled out of sight. Afterwards, the red-headed man had slipped into a carriage marked with a family crest: a falcon with a dove clutched in its talons. Nicholas hadn't recognized it (he knew very few family crests by sight), but it had been disturbing enough that it stood out to him.

He didn't know how Gabriel managed to keep his temper in check or even relax, for that matter.

Placing his hands behind his back, Nicholas took a deep breath and shook his head slightly.

"You look like you've swallowed a bad oyster," Gabriel grumbled from next to him.

"I feel like it, as well."

Gabriel clapped him on the back. "I know what will help." He nodded to the musicians at the top of the room. "After the minuet, meet me in the library and I'll pour you a brandy. Rosalind will be safe enough here."

"Make it whisky and I'll have two."

"Agreed."

"Good. I'll look forward to the short respite."

Gabriel chuckled. "Don't worry. The season will be over before you can blink."

Nicholas eyed the crowd warily. "Aye, and then I'm returning to the country, and that's where I'll stay."

The duke nodded. "Madelyn and I will most likely stay away from the city as much as we can once we return. At least, I'm not ready to share her with everyone else yet, and I know she has a project back home." He nodded in Rosalind's direction. "I appreciate your coming here."

"I know," Nicholas said quietly, daring a quick glance at Rosalind.

"You are the only one I trust. And she shouldn't be too much trouble."

Nicholas raised a dubious brow.

"Well, I must concede she was rather . . . concerned

about the entire affair, but she relinquished in the end," Gabriel replied.

From the corner of his eye, Nicholas watched Rosalind approach slowly from the side, her hands behind her back and her head turned in the opposite direction.

Just what was the wee beauty up to? More snooping?

Eavesdropping, he decided. She was eavesdropping.

"Let me warn you again," Gabriel said sotto voce. "If you can help it, don't let her know it's you. I'll reintroduce you so she will not find your presence suspect."

Nicholas nodded.

"Ah, Rosalind," the duke remarked as she drew nearer still. "Come, you remember my friend, Nicholas, recently the Marquess of Winterbourne."

With a slight nod, she looked up at him with those summer-blue eyes of hers. She held out her hand, watching him closely the whole time.

There was a single beat of hesitation before he took her gloved hand in his and bent over it. She dipped in a shallow curtsy at the same time.

"My lord."

"My lady."

There came an awkward silence wherein they both stared at one another. He'd never met with her before as her social equal. Undoubtedly, the gentry mixed with the aristocracy, but now that they were to blend in the same circles, he felt himself losing his footing. He'd always used their difference in social standing as a means to keep her at arm's length—at least in his own mind.

No matter, he assured himself silently. He rather believed he could resist her charms easily enough—he had done exactly that for years.

" 'My lady'? 'My lord'? Such formalities between old acquaintances?" Gabriel remarked, one side of his mouth pulled into a grin.

Nicholas hadn't a notion why it seemed the duke was teasing them, but he shrugged it aside.

The small quartet struck up a chord, signaling that the first dance of the evening would be commencing. Guests not obliged to dance were heading either toward the edges of the ballroom or slipping into the banquet room next door for light refreshment.

He would have to search for . . . who was it again? Ah, Miss Perimuther. Murrayleather? No. *Meriwether*. Wasn't that it?

And wasn't it impolite to hastily retrieve a lady for a dance?

Truthfully, he didn't care for dancing overly much. But he figured he might as well play the part. Hell, if all he did was stare at Rosalind all night long, she'd discover who her guardian was in no time at all. In fact, he honestly didn't think he'd get away with it for very long. She'd figure it out, and heaven help him then.

For now, he would be polite, dance a few times with a number of different women, and promptly forget each of his partner's names. After all, he must play the part of a wife-hunting marquess, if only to keep her from guessing his true purpose.

The cellist played a series of notes to signal the dance.

Nicholas bowed. "If you'll excuse me, I have promised this dance to a Miss Hairyfeather."

"Meriwether," Rosalind corrected flatly. And then those rosebud lips twitched with a smile, her eyes daring him to laugh at himself, he suspected.

And with those warm blue eyes twinkling up at him, Nicholas felt something inside him crack a little, and he almost smiled, too.

But instead, he gave her a stiff nod, then turned to melt into the crowd.

Chapter 4

"**O**h! Find him! FIND HIM!"

One hour later, Rosalind found herself on her knees, peering under her aunt Eugenia's bed while scores of guests yet danced, conversed, and made merry below stairs.

"I shall not sleep a wink unless he comes home," Eugenia exclaimed, pacing the length of her guest bedchamber, a soaked handkerchief pressed under her nose.

"I cannot see how you can sleep with a house full of guests," Rosalind mused before straightening. She dusted the wrinkles from her scarlet gown, then crossed the room to examine the wardrobe again.

Eugenia shook her head, clearly unnerved. "I always retire early." She paused to sniffle. "And Oliver always nests upon my covers. He's a great comfort to me, and now . . . and now . . ." Eugenia collapsed in a chair, the back of her hand pressed to her mouth.

Having turned to her aunt, Rosalind now averted her gaze. She'd never seen her aunt so upset. Apparently, this Oliver was very dear—he'd have to be to move a rather cantankerous, impassive old woman to tears by his absence.

"Perhaps he's in the garden," Rosalind suggested.

"No, not with all those people about," Eugenia muttered with an agitated flick of her handkerchief. "He's a bit skittish."

"Then, that's it. He's probably hiding somewhere in the house. Somewhere quiet and warm." Rosalind moved to stand before her aunt. "He'll come out when everyone's gone home, I'm sure of it."

"But what am I to do until then?"

Rosalind blinked, speechless for a second. Her aunt seemed a little lost, and it pulled a bit at her heart. "Margaret will help you ready yourself for bed while I delegate some of the staff to help locate Oliver. I'll continue to look for him as well."

"You ought to be enjoying yourself at the ball. Your brother will become agitated at your absence."

"I daresay he will not," Rosalind replied with a grin. "He's happily doting upon his wife and most likely thankful that he need not scowl at any of my dance partners."

Eugenia nodded solemnly, wiping her nose. Her next words stopped Rosalind at the door. "You'd do well to stand clear of that Scot."

"I'm sorry?"

Her aunt's red-rimmed eyes centered knowingly on Rosalind. "You know who I'm talking about. He might be a marquess and he might be acquainted with your brother, but I don't like the way he looks at you."

Rosalind swallowed, suddenly feeling a bit warm and stunned by this information. "He—he looks at me?"

"Indeed, he *looks*," Eugenia informed with a raised brow, "while trying very hard to appear *not* to be looking."

"That made absolutely no sense."

Eugenia's posture became rigid. "It's deceitful and misleading. It makes me wonder what depths he would sink to if there was to be no repercussions for his actions."

"Let me assure you," Rosalind murmured, "that man holds no interest in me."

"All right," Eugenia nearly barked, holding up a hand. "I confess I know little in the ways of men, but he's powerfully handsome. And those sorts of men are good for nothing but mischief, mark my words."

Rosalind gave a small laugh. "Do not worry. He's quite occupied this evening. In fact, I believe he has already engaged a partner for every dance." Indeed, except for the waltz.

Eugenia's gaze was unusually shrewd. "Do I detect a note of disappointment?"

Rosalind merely shook her head, not trusting herself to speak.

"Good."

At her aunt's satisfied nod, Rosalind quit the room with promises of retrieving the errant Oliver.

Halfway down the hall she encountered a maid, to whom she imparted the news of the missing cat and the need to have every available hand searching for him. As most of the Devine staff were busy in the kitchen and ballroom, Rosalind knew that the number of hands available to search was small. No matter, she would aid in the search, as well.

With the girl dashing down the corridor to inform others, Rosalind chose to use the servant's staircase, thinking it was dark and the perfect place for a timid kitty to hide.

She descended the steps and meandered down

the sparsely lit corridor, her gaze skimming the floor as she went, but Oliver had the misfortune of being a dark gray cat, she reminded herself; he would match the shadows perfectly.

After a couple of turns, the sound of voices raised in merriment grew as each step brought her closer to the ballroom. Turning the second to last corner, she spied Gabriel's retreating form. He must have come from the library, she mused.

She spied the open door ahead and the twitch of what looked like a tail just before it slipped inside the room.

"Ah-ha," she whispered. "Oliver, kitty, come here."

Creeping to the door, Rosalind made little noises with her tongue, pressing it on the roof of her mouth, in an attempt to call the cat to her.

She crossed the threshold, her gaze darting back and forth across the dark room for some sign of him. "Oliver," she whispered. "Come on out, Oliver, and I'll take you upstairs."

A small branch of candles had been lit and set upon on a sideboard equipped with a row of decanters. The soft glow of light did little to lighten the deep room.

Determined to find the cat, she ignored a twinge

of foreboding, blaming it on the dark silence of the spacious room.

And then a sound that could only be described as a soft growl emanated from a circle of chairs and sofas across the room. She ambled toward the center, mindful of the legs of the furniture.

"Ack!" All right, perhaps not so mindful. She bent to rub her sore ankle, which had had the misfortune of whacking the corner of an unseen footstool.

Oliver sat under a small oval table, tail flicking, eyes glowing yellow and huge in the dark.

"There you are," she whispered, bending to reach under the table.

The cat let forth a sudden, vicious hiss, swinging needle-sharp paws at Rosalind's outstretched hands.

Startled, she lurched back in reaction. "Why, you and Aunt Eugenia are a perfect match."

And then Oliver shot out from the table, springing toward her.

Rosalind shrieked and jumped back again. The backs of her thighs hit the arm of a wingback chair and she tumbled backward, landing, to her surprise, not on the plump seat cushion but instead upon the hard lap of the unseen occupant of the chair. "Oompf!"

Stern gray eyes met her startled gaze.

"Nicholas," she breathed.

"Oliver is the cat, correct?" Nicholas asked, his deep voice vibrating through her. "Or are you looking for one of your suitors?"

She chose to ignore his taunt. For whatever reason, her gaze was drawn to his neck. "Your cravat is crooked," she blurted.

"Thank you," he murmured grumpily. "I shall endeavor to straighten it as soon as possible."

"Good."

"Fine."

They stared at one another through several beats of silence, some sort of tangible tension building between them. And truly, she couldn't remove herself if she wanted to. The chair was deep and she was nearly folded in half.

She swallowed hard, suddenly acutely aware of every inch of her that happened to be touching him—her backside in between thighs that might very well have been made of granite, her breasts pressed against the heat of his chest, her fingers nestled into the fabric of his frock coat.

She had imagined such a scenario at least a hundred times before, but nothing had prepared her for just how *good* it felt to be so close to him.

Nicholas swallowed heavily, and Rosalind watched his Adam's apple bounce between the corded muscles of his throat.

"You should get up now," he said quietly, his gaze never leaving her face.

"Really?" She heard the disappointment and gave her head a small shake. "I-I meant, yes. Yes, of course I should." The room felt overly warm. If she didn't know better, she'd think there was a roaring fire in the grate.

Letting forth a rather unladylike grunt, she tried to scoot off the way she'd come, but her knees were hooked high on the arm of the chair and the silk of her dress was too smooth. All she managed to do was wiggle back and forth.

Nicholas did little, if anything, to help her.

Her position forced her to face him or lie back. She tried rearing back, but something tugged at her bodice.

She looked down the same time he did, their foreheads brushing.

"Damn and blast," he muttered.

For a second all Rosalind could see—and feel, for that matter—were the stiff lapels of Nicholas's coat brushing against the swells of her bosom. She tried hardening herself against the sensation, but as she stared down, his warm breath feathered over her sensitive skin. Thousands of tiny shivers raced down her arms, goose pimples rising across her flesh.

"We're stuck," he growled.

"Stuck? Stuck how?"

He half sighed, half growled again. "Your brooch. My tie pin."

Rosalind blinked, willing her eyes to focus. "How did that happen?"

He picked up his head and delivered a sardonic glare, but said nothing.

A sudden spurt of raucous laughter echoed from the corridor.

She inhaled sharply. "Someone could be coming."

Her movements quick, she braced her hands on the arms of the chair, which made it look, at least for the barest of seconds, as if she was trapping him in the chair on purpose. Using her hands as leverage, she pulled her legs in, then twisted to slide them to the floor.

Awkwardly leaning forward with one hand at her back, Nicholas moved with her—his cravat pin was stuck to her bodice, after all.

In the end, no one came to the door, but Rosalind found herself kneeling between Kincaid's legs, a knee on either side of her breasts. Her hands braced his rock-hard upper arms. He looked incredibly uncomfortable leaning forward as he was. And incredibly handsome.

A thick, dark brown lock had slid out from the queue at his neck and half-covered one gray eye. "What the devil did you do that for?"

She looked at his lips as he spoke and became momentarily mesmerized by their sculpted shape and a peek of white teeth.

"I-I'm sorry." She gulped. "Here . . . let me . . ."

"I wouldn't think it was possible," he said as he looked down briefly, an odd light in his gaze, "but I think you've made things worse."

"Surely you don't still think I did this on purpose!"

"I'm not certain," he said quietly, his brogue sounding thicker now for some reason. "And you should quiet down."

"Not certain! I was trying to collect my aunt's atrocious cat. Just what were you doing in here, sitting in the dark?"

He didn't answer her.

"What then?" she pressed.

"Well, I wasn't waiting for a certain clumsy female to land upon my lap."

"I am *not* clumsy," she intoned, affronted. She straightened a bit, which brought them eye to eye. And mouth to mouth.

He raised a dubious brow but did not pull away. Their lips were so close that they might as well have been kissing. But they remained thus, almost as if testing—or perhaps challenging—the other to take action.

"Were you *hiding* in here?" she asked, her words mostly air.

His silver gaze dipped to her mouth before returning to meet her stare. "Why the hell would I hide?"

"Hmm. Gabriel said you had come to London on business. Perhaps your business has something to do with being in this room." *Like, having a romantic tryst with a potential bride, perhaps.* The flare of jealousy didn't surprise her.

He looked down and began fumbling at her bodice, twisting her brooch and causing her to become acutely aware of the weight of her breasts. "If it will get you to hush that bonny mouth of yours to know, I was having a dram with your brother."

"*Hush*?" she blurted, positively perspiring over his use of the phrase "bonny mouth." Still, she tried to hold on to her senses. "No one has ever *'hushed'* me before."

"Aye. If you keep talking so much, I'll hush you again."

She wanted to pinch him . . . really hard.

"Come closer," he commanded.

"If I come any closer, I'll be in your lap again." More precisely, she'd be further in between his thighs.

"Just shift . . ." He reached around her back and place his warm hand in the middle of her shoulder blades. Then he pushed her slightly toward him, arching her back. Once he got her in the position he wanted her in, he went back to work on his task.

She looked about herself, noting the way he loomed above her, around her. He radiated heat and smelled marvelous.

"Someone could walk in at any moment," she murmured. "Look at us. Do you think they'd believe that we came about our position by happenstance?"

He merely grunted.

Her chin dropped to watch his long fingers maneuver her brooch this way and that. "What are you doing?"

"Trying to discern the best way to disengage ourselves without ripping your gown."

A thought occurred to her then. What if her guardian were to walk in just then? It was possible his "watch" had begun this evening. And she didn't know anything about this person. What if he was the sort to jump to conclusions? What if he carried a pistol? What if . . . ?

"Hurry, then."

Briefly, Nicholas looked up from his work, his gaze intensely annoyed. "Believe me, I am hurrying."

Their breath mingled between them for a moment, then he looked back down. A strong pull, that same thrumming vibration, seemed to hover around them. She tried to ignore it, but it occurred to her at that moment that for two people doing nothing more than trying to extricate their accessories, they were both suddenly breathing quite hard. And Nicholas's hand seemed to be trembling.

"Nicholas," she whispered.

His fingers stilled and his gaze traveled slowly upward from her brooch, to her bodice, to her neck, to her mouth, and then finally her eyes.

Rosalind licked her bottom lip, thinking she ought to say something, when one of his hands lifted to cradle her chin between his fingers. Shivers danced down her spine. He applied light pressure with the pad of his thumb, and she felt her lips parting. He looked at her mouth so intensely that her eyes drifted shut and her head tilted.

And then suddenly, Nicholas's hand dropped away. She opened her eyes in just enough time to see him give his head a quick shake. Then he closed his eyes and took a long, deep breath before opening them again.

"You were . . . ," she began breathlessly, ". . . you were about to . . ."

Reaching down, he removed his tie pin, disrupting the simple knot of his cravat. "There," he said quietly. "We are free." He leaned back in the chair, his strength surrounding her.

He had been about to kiss her, she was sure of it. But why had he stopped? Oh, she could scream. Why did he hesitate?

There was some desperate, discontented part of her that flirted with the idea of grabbing him and kissing him herself, but she resisted.

"You can stand now," he pointed out rather gruffly.

She nodded, staring up at him, trying to figure him out.

Sighing, he reached out, grabbed her at the waist, and practically shoved her up before him.

"My, you're as gentle as a lamb," she muttered, straightening.

He nodded his thanks, a half smile upon his lips.

"I did not intend that as a compliment," she said, her tone stern.

Nicholas chuckled. He couldn't help it. And he hadn't wanted her to move. The thought shook him. If he could do whatever he wanted at that moment, hang the consequences, he would want nothing more than to wrap his arms around her and drag her back down onto his lap and pin her to his shirt for good.

For safekeeping, of course. It would be a lot easier to watch her, wouldn't it?

Ooh, what was he thinking? He had almost kissed her. Hell, he had practically invited her to do so should she have the desire. And the equally terrifying thing was he rather thought she desired—just as much as he did.

And just what the hell had he been doing with the tie pin? He could have disengaged them within seconds, but instead he'd tarried, lingered, savored. The view, dear Lord, the view . . .

"Christ," he muttered under his breath.

He stood and crossed the room with brisk strides. The further away she was from him right now, the better.

Standing in the same spot he'd put her in, Rosalind brushed at her skirts. Her head jerked up at the sound of raised voices floating in from the hall.

"It's one of my brothers," she announced, her slightly alarmed gaze sliding to meet Nicholas's.

He nodded to the cat that was currently trotting his way to the door. The thing looked positively harmless now.

"Go," he ordered quietly. "I'll wait until you've moved on before I leave."

She nodded, following the cat from the room.

As Nicholas looked down to refasten his tie pin, he swore he heard Rosalind whisper, "Thank you, Oliver, for being such a naughty kitty."

Rosalind didn't think it could be possible, but three hours later, her mood had darkened considerably.

Her guardian was here tonight, she was sure of it, and she had failed to reveal him. However, it was possible that he retained his cover so well for the simple fact that there hadn't been any real danger here at Devine Mansion.

Or, perhaps, if her ears hadn't been abused with constant blithering speculations concerning the new marquess in their midst, Rosalind would have been able to concentrate.

If they only knew she had sat upon his lap in a room down the hall, she'd be delegated from respectable almost-spinster to a hoyden in the course of a single evening.

"I heard the Scots have insatiable carnal appetites," someone whispered from behind a fan, which caused someone else to gasp.

"Truly?"

"How frightening!"

Rosalind flicked a glance toward the small grouping of women on her right, her brow rising in wonder. A seated young lady seemed to be sliding out of her chair. Had she fallen asleep?

Strangely, several other ladies seemed to have an odd tilt to their heads. What was happening to their necks?

Rosalind turned to look past the dancers at the other side of the room. Even the women over there seemed to be suffering from the same peculiar head tilt.

She followed their gazes . . . directly to Nicholas's kilt. Her mouth opened on a small gasp. Apparently, the sly creatures were all trying to get a peek.

A new surge of jealousy sprouted within her. She didn't begrudge him his inheritance. She was delighted for him. But life had seemed so much simpler when he had been her own little secret.

Rosalind smirked. Could she blame them? He was rather breathtaking.

But she'd had about enough of all these women ogling Nicholas and his bare knees. And his sculpted calves. And his trim waist.

Seven dances. Seven! And he had not asked her once.

"Rosalind."

Blinking out of her musings, she turned to find Gabriel standing before her.

She smiled in greeting, her brows lifting. "Yes?" Another minuet had ended and some guests were marveling at the grace of the dancers.

"As the last dance of the evening is approaching, I wanted to give you one last instruction."

"What is it?"

"It was not below my notice that you danced with a number of gentlemen this evening. More than usual, more than you ought to have."

She sighed quietly.

He ran a hand through his hair. "Tomorrow,

after Madelyn and I depart, when *they* come calling, and you and I both know who I'm talking about, you are to inform Briggs to tell them that you are not at home. They will insist on leaving cards, I realize, but then they had better get the hell out of my house. It's not safe. Not with that damnable wager setting fire to their heels. "

Rosalind blinked slowly. He had just given her a splendid idea.

"Please, do not fret," she said simply.

The chords signaled that the waltz was about to begin. It was the only waltz of the evening.

Gabriel gave her a nod, then strode across the room to retrieve his wife for the dance.

Tomorrow, Rosalind would welcome the deluge of men coming to call. Perhaps with a houseful of male visitors, her guardian would have no choice but to lurk about the windows—or perhaps he'd be bold enough to come to call himself.

And once the matter of dismissing her guardian was settled, she could focus all her energy on an entirely different matter.

Season after season she had concentrated on other people's happiness in matters of love. And now with Nicholas in London, it was time for her to make her own match.

He had wanted to kiss her, she was sure of it. And yet, he'd hesitated. She wasn't certain why, but she knew without a doubt that if Nicholas Kincaid had come to London to find a bride, that woman was going to be her.

Her plan set, Rosalind couldn't help but smile with proud satisfaction as she watched her brother sweep his wife into his arms, gliding her effortlessly onto the dance floor. They looked perfect together, quite like they completed each other. No one could deny their being in love.

It occurred to Rosalind then that no one had asked her to dance. She looked about, spying Nicholas sauntering in her direction.

Her heart skittered. It was the last dance of the evening, the only waltz, and very fitting that he ask her. He neared, his paces slowing.

Lifting her chin, she straightened her spine and took a deep breath, her acquiescence poised on the tip of her tongue.

And then he passed her by and walked out of the room.

Chapter 5

Long walks in the countryside had never failed to clear Nicholas's head in the past.

Unfortunately, he was currently traversing a crowded, sooty city, and any thought-clearing he managed amid the clattering of wagons, carriages, and bustling people only seemed to make more room for all things Lady Rosalind Devine.

And when it came to that particular woman, his imagination often wandered into dangerous territory.

As he turned the corner that would bring him to Hyde Park and closer to the Devine residence, he told himself he was only a man. A man attracted to his charge.

He hadn't wanted to hurt her last night, but maybe it would do the proud lassie a wee bit of good to be brought down a peg or two.

However, his mind kept replaying the way her shoulders had lowered, the way she'd twisted her hands in the folds of her gown, when he had passed her by.

She hadn't stood alone for long, however. Some gangly, young lad had approached her, and, after gracefully accepting his offer, she'd allowed him to twirl her enthusiastically around the ballroom floor. She had smiled graciously, all infallible politeness.

He had gone to bed last night, his mind replaying the events of the evening: the look of open interest gracing her features when Gabriel had introduced them, the way his blood had surged at the sight of her kneeling on the floor between his legs, the smell of her. And once Nicholas had managed to fall asleep, she'd haunted his dreams. In his uninhibited imaginings, it was *he* who had swept her up into the dance.

He had clutched her tightly to him, his fingers sliding roughly through her hair. He had bent down and plundered her rosebud mouth until she'd surrendered and sunk into him for support and more of his kiss. Right there in the middle of the ballroom for everyone to see.

He had woken sheathed in sweat, the sheets twisted in his hands. It surprised him that just the idea of this particular woman engaged so intimately with him in the dance was enough to set his blood to an immediate boil.

Aye, it was wise of him not to dance with her. After that dream, he wasn't so sure that he would have held her respectfully nor kept the secrets of his mind so easily hidden.

Especially from her brother.

And Nicholas wanted Gabriel to know she was safe with him, *from him.*

Her brother placed his rare trust in him. As Gabriel's friend, Nicholas had to uphold a certain code of conduct. And that included keeping his eyes, hands, and mouth from roving over Gabriel's sister.

"Pardon." Nicholas muttered to a group of ladies as he stepped around their meandering gait in order to pass them.

They lifted their noses at his words. He sighed. So lofty and unforgiving. Perhaps they'd heard about his choice of attire the other night and feared he was indeed a real-life Scottish beastie.

Smothering a grin, he strode onward through Hyde Park, aiming for Grosvenor Square and Devine Mansion.

The decision to walk was made in part by a stubborn horse who was proving to be the biggest, hairiest bairn when it came to the distractions of the city, and partly because it wasn't that far from his rented town house.

Accustomed to much more strenuous exercise in the country, it was really just a small trek to their home, and he needn't fight with the congestion of the streets either.

Was it really midmorning already? It felt as if he had just left Devine Mansion.

He pulled out his pocket watch. "Twelve o'clock." Well, it was some ten hours ago.

City hours for the ton were vastly different. As they attended ball after ball, partygoers kept "town hours"—sleeping until noon, some of them. He hoped Tristan was awake or, at least, home.

He needed to speak with the lad. He needed to tell him that he'd be watching the back of the house this evening.

Upon leaving Devine Mansion late the night before, Nicholas had been about to mount his jittery horse when he'd noticed the redheaded man—the same man from outside the bookshop. He'd been standing near a shadowed row between houses across the lane.

Nicholas had approached the man and shouted a greeting.

Well, to be honest, it had been less a greeting and more specifically, "What the hell are you doing over there?" Subtlety was never his forte.

The man had run. Nicholas had chased him for half a block before the stranger had become winded and able to run no more. Reaching him, Nicholas had grabbed him, but the lanky man surprised him by wresting free enough to slip out a small dagger.

Nicholas had managed to dodge the blow aimed at his face, but he'd lost his hold. The vermin had scurried away, disappearing down another alley like a rat slipping into some invisible crack in the foundation.

That creature could be anywhere, Nicholas thought grimly with a narrow-eyed glare as he scanned the people milling about the streets and surrounding park, his gaze snagging on the unsuspecting women in particular.

Dangers lurked everywhere.

Take that situation just over the rise, for instance, he pondered.

A young, bespectacled, flaxen-haired lass sat on a bench nestled under a tree with a book. Next to her dozed a woman he guessed was her mother, her head slack and resting on the back of the bench.

Unbeknownst to the sleeping woman, her charge was being watched by a man atop a glossy black stallion.

As Nicholas passed, the man never took his eyes off the girl, and she seemed completely oblivious to his half-adoring, half-ravenous gaze.

A lion nearly salivating at a dainty mouse.

Just what were this fellow's intentions? Nicholas found himself wondering. It looked nefarious to him, but then again, Nicholas was admittedly more suspicious than most.

Shaking his head, he crossed the crowded street and quickened his steps. Before long the Devines' town house came into view. He looked up, noticing a commotion near Rosalind's front door. Och, were they hosting another party, and in the middle of the day?

The front door open wide, three men were coming down the steps as two more were trying to get up, their arms laden with blooms of every color and various wee, prettily wrapped packages.

Nicholas squinted. Was that a horse tethered to the railings, ribbons and small flowers twined through the beast's mane and tail? What the devil was going on?

"AAAAAAA-CHOOOO!"

Nicholas nearly jolted out of his skin as a sneezing man sped past him, holding the largest bouquet of roses he'd ever seen in his life.

"You there! Sir!" Nicholas shouted. "Hold!"

With a sigh, the man came to an abrupt stop and turned around. His eyes were red-rimmed and weeping, his bulbous nose shiny and damp. He looked miserable. "Yes?" he asked, sounding nasal and rather irritated.

"What is this all about?"

"Well," the man started, looking peevish and sounding much like he was explaining something to a dull-wit, "these are flowers and I'm delivering them."

"To whom?"

The man sighed. "To Devine Mansion. Again. And I suppose once I return to the shop other . . . ah . . ."

Nicholas took a step back just in time.

" . . . ACHOOOOOOOO!!" The man wiped at his nose with his sleeve. "When I return to the shop," he began again, "I suppose there will be more . . . ah . . . ahhh . . ."

"Here." With one hand, Nicholas took the tall vase of pink roses from the man. "Allow me." Reaching into the inside pocket of his coat, he grabbed some coin and handed it to the man.

He looked affronted for a moment, then glanced at the money, and then back at Nicholas. "How do I know you'll not steal these for yourself?" His question was laced with suspicion. "We have a reputation to uphold—"

Nicholas held up a hand. "You can watch me deliver it from over here. And," he added with a grin, "you might want to think about another line of work."

"I'll say," the man agreed, swiping at his sweaty brow.

"Christ, Rosie! The front hall looks like a bloody jungle."

"Don't I know," Rosalind cringed from behind an enormous bundle of bright red tulips before dumping them in a vase brought by a maid. "And poor Briggs," she continued, speaking of their butler. "I sent him off. He couldn't stop sneezing."

"Ah," Tristan said, shrugging out of his cloak. "That would explain his absence." He glanced behind him before tossing the garment on the chair to the right of the door, then ceased abruptly once he realized the seat was already occupied by a large potted fern.

"Bloody bounders," Tristan growled. "Gabriel's been gone a whole of five hours and they're upon you in an instant."

"Shh! They'll hear you."

"Have you gone mad? Now you believe flowers have feelings?"

"Not the flowers, dunderhead. The gentlemen inside the morning room," she muttered with a point in that direction.

"Gentlemen?"

She nodded, adjusting the arrangement of a small bouquet of wildflowers.

"Inside our morning room?"

Her lips flattened. "With Aunt Eugenia."

"With Aunt . . . what the devil is going on?"

She shrugged innocently. "Every girl receives a few gentleman callers the day after a ball. It's perfectly normal."

Tristan shot her an incredulous look. "Normal is one or two, or hell, even ten! This place resembles a hothouse, Rosie." He stared down at her with eyes the same frosty blue all the Devine siblings shared. "And what the hell is *that*?"

Rosalind followed his appalled gaze to a portrait propped up against the wall near her feet. Someone had had her likeness painted and sent it as a gift. She hoped it wasn't an accurate likeness. She rather looked like she was part horse.

Tristan shook his head. "As you well know, I am not so overbearing as Gabriel, but you are my sister. Please, do not tell me the number of men in the next room surpasses the number of bouquets in this one."

"They've been coming and going since eleven. However, rest assured, there are only two now. No, no. There are three. Or was it four?" She scratched at a tickle near her ear and mumbled, "No, Lord Dalhousie already left, that's right. So that makes . . ."

"How many?" Tristan nearly growled.

"There are three," she murmured very quickly.

He sighed and ran a slow hand through his tousled auburn locks. "Listen carefully. I'm going to allow them —"

"Now wait just a minute, *little* brother," she warned.

Tristan halted her puny threat in its tracks with a hardened jaw. "*I'm* going to allow them to stay until I change my clothes and I—"

"Are you going back out?"

"Later, but if you must know I've just returned from Angelo's—"

"Fencing again?"

"Yes," he answered with a slow blink. "Now will you cease interrupting me?"

She held her tongue.

"When I come back down, which will probably be in"—he glanced at the long case clock near the door—"a half hour, I want all of them gone. Whoever is still in that morning room when I come down will find themselves thrown out on their posterior."

Rosalind couldn't help but smile cheekily. "Does that include Aunt Eugenia?"

"Oh, yes," he replied with a grave nod and a sparkle in his eye. "Indeed, it does."

Turning, he shook his head and bounded up the steps, taking three at a time with ease.

There came a shuffling at the door, which was left open to accommodate the wealth of flower deliveries.

Rosalind turned to see a pair of long, male legs topped with the most enormous vase of pink blooms she had ever seen. The flowers must have numbered at least two dozen, but what was even more astonishing was the legs that had carried them in here. This was no delivery boy.

Snug, biscuit-colored breeches hugged every sinewy muscle of his thighs to sheer perfection.

Tall, polished boots shown glossy in the light pouring in from the open door.

My, her newest caller possessed such dashing attire. And must favor physical activity, as well, for no man looked that muscular and virile without it, she was sure.

The soft heels of her kid boots made not a sound as she approached this new visitor. Reaching forward with both hands, she grasped around the middle of the wide vase, her fingers coming into brief contact with warm hands covered in smooth leather.

"Thank you," she said politely, glancing down at the nest of blooms before looking up at the man. "I'll put them . . ."

"Rosalind," Nicholas said, his tone stiff, his gray eyes sparkling like jewels.

A shock of surprise burned in her chest. "Oh," she said, affecting indifference. "It's just *you*."

Her feelings were still smarting from yesterday's ball. The constant swaying of his indifference to interest to slighting her for a dance grated on her mind. Years of being able to read the behavior of individuals in order to gauge the level of interest—or lack of—in others had not prepared her for Nicholas. He was a conundrum.

She walked away from him, scooting a fat pot of begonias out of the way to make room for the roses.

He took off his hat as she did so and hung it on the rack next to the door.

"Those," he said as he gestured to the roses with an indolent flick of his wrist, "are not from me."

She smiled stiffly. "I would never dream that they were."

She hated to admit it, but the fickle-hearted buffoon that he was, he still looked gloriously attractive. And had he cut his hair?

"Is that someone coming up the walk?" She made a show of appearing to look past him and out the open door at his back. No, he hadn't cut his hair. All those silky brown locks were pulled back and tied with a leather queue.

A peculiar slow heat crept through her. Last night he'd looked half gentleman, half wild and wonderful Scot. To her irritation, she hadn't been the only one who'd noticed. However, amongst all the sighing and wistful looks he'd received from the younger set, Rosalind had also heard some older women mock his physical stature, claiming his muscles, strength, and tanned skin marked him as a common laborer.

Rosalind didn't believe there was anything common about Nicholas.

Indeed, it had been difficult not to stare at him last night, but today was even worse. Today he looked every inch the cultured nobleman with an undercurrent of virility and restrained wickedness. And had she ever seen another man fill his clothes so well?

Her gaze scoured over his form. She couldn't seem to stop herself. His black coat was expertly fitted, stretching across his shoulders as if it had been stitched while on him. His waistcoat was also black, but it had threadwork of a pearly blue that swirled in a lazy design across the flat expanse of his stomach.

She had the sudden urge to fan her hand against it, test its resistance.

Finally, she looked to his face and found his own gaze was just returning from his own languid perusal. Of her.

But she couldn't be quite sure, could she? Perhaps she had a petal or a leaf sitting on her skirt or in her hair. She patted her dark blue skirts down and swiped at her shoulders.

She looked up to find him looking at her quizzically.

"Is something wrong?" he asked, raising a brow.

"Is there a leaf or a flower petal or something?" she asked, twisting left and right.

He stepped forward suddenly and, reaching out, gently pinched at the fabric of her right sleeve, which sent a thousand shivers racing down her arm. A tiny leaf floated to the floor.

"Thank you," she murmured.

He dipped his chin.

They stared at one another for a long minute, the only sounds that of the ticking clock and the bustling street scene behind him.

Sudden sniffling came from the back of the house. Rosalind turned to see Briggs returning to his post.

"My apologies, my lady," he intoned, wiping at his nose with a handkerchief before stuffing it in the front pocket of his livery. He closed the door behind Nicholas.

"No need to apologize, Briggs," she replied with concern. "I understand. It is the flowers, yes? Had I known they caused you trouble, I would have had them placed in another room."

Briggs waved away her concern. "No, my lady. I suppose it is a bit more from this dreadful head cold."

Rosalind dipped her head. "Perhaps you ought to retire early, then." When the loyal servant shook his head, she insisted, "Yes, you should. I'll have Cook make soup, and Jenny will bring it up to you."

"My lady is too kind," Briggs intoned.

Her attention returned to Nicholas.

He was looking about the room, seeming to notice only now the plethora of blooms in which they stood. "For the love of God, woman," he murmured. "Is this normal?"

She lifted her chin. "I'll have you know that it is *quite* normal for gentlemen to send flowers to a lady after a ball."

"Aye, but of this magnitude?"

"There are some things which I cannot control."

"Like your appeal, is it?"

"That's not what I meant at all," she answered testily. "I cannot help it that they were so generous—"

"Flamboyant," he interrupted, gesturing to the rather poor, but quite large, watercolor of her likeness.

"I did not ask for any of this," she said defensively.

"Oh, you did," he murmured darkly. "Just by walking into a room."

Her brow quirked at that, but she recovered swiftly.

"Some *gentlemen*," she stressed, "find it is the proper thing to do after an evening in which he shared a dance with the lady. I can only assume by your remarks that you did no such thing for the long list of ladies who accompanied you on the ballroom floor yesterday evening."

"One should never assume."

"So you did send them flowers?" she blurted, then wished she'd had the forbearance to bite her tongue.

He was quiet for a moment, and then a broad smile crept over his mouth. "I'm curious to know why you find the subject of such interest."

"I don't."

"But you asked," he said, gazing down at her intensely, the smile turning lopsided.

She blushed hotly. "So, I did," she conceded. "There is no reason for you to answer me. I reckon it is none of my business."

Another long pause, and then he finally replied, "I did not send flowers. I'm sure that marks me a savage in your eyes, but there you have it. Next, I presume, you'll think I like to swing from trees and eat soup with my fingers."

She pressed her lips together, smothering a smile. "Very well," she managed after a moment. "I was only curious, I imagine, not *jealous*." Oh, dear God, why had she said that?

A muscle in his cheek twitched. "I didn't say you were." He walked around her and headed for the double doors of the morning room.

She followed the insolent man.

The distant murmurings of the gentlemen ensconced in the room reached her ears. Aunt Eugenia's perpetual disapproving tones were loudest of them all. One of the doors was open a crack. Nicholas tilted his head to peek through between the doors.

She took a deep breath, then whispered harshly, "Why are you here?"

He looked down at her, those devastatingly gray eyes twinkling. "Are you up to something? I ask because you seem guilty. Are you meddling? Eavesdropping? Matchmaking?"

"Indeed, I am not."

"You could be," he said quietly. "Your aunt is a single lady, and there are"—he glanced around the door to look inside the deep room once again—"three men present."

"Those three gentlemen are old enough to be her sons."

He shrugged one shoulder while he continued to spy on them. "It would not be unheard of in your circles."

"Just what is that supposed to mean?" she asked, eyes narrowing.

"Oh, I think you know."

"I'm afraid I am at a loss. Explain."

"I'd rather not," he mumbled.

"*You* are stubborn."

"And *you* are surprisingly astute."

"Well, thank . . ." Her gratitude died on her tongue. "Your insult was poorly veiled as a compliment."

"As I said, astute."

She nearly gave a small scream of frustration. Instead, she asked through a tight smile, "What, pray, are you doing here?" When he failed to answer her directly, she gave his back a poke and couldn't help but notice her finger met steely resistance. Was every inch of him covered in muscle? "Perhaps you were lost?"

"Very funny. I'm here to see Tristan."

Her brow quirked at that. Although he and Tristan were friendly, they weren't close.

"I was hoping he could lead me in the direction of a gambling club."

"I see," she said tartly. "Well, if you're looking for a night of prowling for feminine distraction, I'm sorry to inform you that you'll have to do that on your own. Tristan has been engaged since last autumn."

"I do not intend to take the lad with me."

Something inside her crumbled a bit. It displeased her to realize that Nicholas was looking for a night of carousing and sordid female companionship. She hadn't thought he was like that.

She blinked rapidly, trying to keep disappointment from her expression. "Shall I ring for him, then?"

He nodded without moving his assessing gaze from the occupants of the room.

Rosalind turned to a young, freckled maid who was passing down the corridor in the direction of the front door, a large carrot in her hand, presumably for the horse tethered outside—a gift Rosalind could not, in good graces, accept. The horse, that is. Carrots she liked just fine.

116

"Maria? Will you inform his lordship's valet that he has a visitor?"

The maid curtsied. "Yes, miss."

Rosalind turned back to Nicholas. "You can wait for him in the study. It's down the hall on the . . ."

He was gone.

" . . . right."

But gone he was not. Heavens, no. That would have been too easy. The stubborn man was now standing in the middle of the morning room as if this was *his* residence.

As she watched, he spoke to her trio of male visitors, who, in turn, regarded him with the flare of competition in their eyes.

She would like to blame his brashness on his newly titled status, but he'd behaved in much the same manner that day in the bookshop. At least he was consistent in that.

She crept inside the room, her dark blue skirts swishing on the Aubusson carpet. The seated men instantly stood, greeting her with wide smiles.

"Please, gentlemen," Aunt Eugenia implored haughtily. "Do sit. The gel is likely to stand all day. I'm not sure what's wrong. She's been rather fidgety, peeking around the drapes to look outside. I can only presume you've all spoiled my niece with the attention and she's grown bored."

Rosalind nearly groaned aloud.

Slowly, the men complied, looking for a moment as if they'd like nothing better than to jump out the window to freedom themselves.

Rosalind wanted to feel sorry for them, but she didn't. None of the men who had come to call today possessed an ounce of sincerity between them. But they never have, she reminded herself, even without the dreadful wager.

Part of her wanted to toss them out, just as her eldest brother advised her to do, but she couldn't. She needed them. Their presence here today served a purpose. She hoped to draw out her guardian.

"Who's this?" her aunt asked rudely, gesturing to Nicholas with a lift of her chin.

A warm blush crept up Rosalind's neck as she realized she had been standing behind him. She stepped forward and made the proper introductions.

Now that Nicholas was here, that made four eligible males in her town house. What sort of guardian could resist such a situation? But she was beginning to believe that the man, whoever he was, was either really good at keeping his distance or incredibly lax in his duties. Perhaps he hovered outside for some reason.

She flicked a glance over to the window overlooking the street. The action was not missed by Nicholas.

"Are you looking for someone in particular?" he asked from beside her.

She pressed her lips together and shook her head.

He gave her a skeptical nod and one of his disarming grins.

Heat infused her entire body. Clearing her throat delicately, Rosalind moved over to the settee against the wall, thinking Nicholas would take the empty chair near the others. She offered it in passing with an open palm and a polite "come and sit."

However, once she sat down, she realized he had followed her. Flipping the tails of his jacket out of the way, he sank down next to her, his long legs stretched out before them.

It was a big enough seat . . . for two women, but with a man of Nicholas's size, there was no helping their touching each other. From thigh to knee.

A path of fire seemed to smolder at that seam of contact.

"You there, young man," Aunt Eugenia replied,

gesturing to Nicholas. "You were at the ball last night, were you not? I saw you talking to my nephew."

"Aye, madam."

"Weren't you wearing a skirt?" Eugenia asked, giving him a once-over, the number of her chins increasing as she dipped her head.

Rosalind sighed softly.

"It's called a kilt, madam. But I thank you kindly for noticing." And then he winked.

"Such arrogance," Aunt Eugenia croaked, her wrinkled forehead furrowing further with her indignant frown. "I cannot believe Rosalind let you in the house. Such talk from one of her admirers!"

He cleared his throat. "I am not one of her admirers. I'm here to visit with Tristan."

Eyes widened, Aunt Eugenia's wide nostrils flared at the insult she apparently thought was aimed at Rosalind.

"If you've come to see to my nephew, what are you doing in here?"

Rosalind looked at Nicholas, curious to what his answer would be to her disapproving aunt.

His gray gaze flicked to her, and then back to her aunt. "Well, you must realize I could not resist ensconcing myself in the company of such fine women."

What a flirt—and an excellent approach at befuddling her aunt, Rosalind mused, noting that Aunt Eugenia was now blushing like a green girl.

"Shall I ring for a fresh pot of tea, my lord?" Rosalind interjected quietly before her aunt regained her sense.

When he didn't immediately answer, she turned to meet his gaze. What a mistake. He was too close. And the silver glints in his eyes seared a path straight to her belly, which made her squirm slightly.

"No, thank you," he answered just as quietly, his gaze dipping to her lips before returning to meld with her own gaze.

He had never looked at her like this before. He looked . . . hungry. Quite like she was a tasty morsel of . . . something, and he couldn't wait to sink his teeth in her.

For five seconds she forgot to breathe.

"Your eyes," Lord Bates suddenly proclaimed from across the room.

Blinking out of Nicholas's surely accidental enchantment, Rosalind wasn't sure who Bates was talking to, or about, for that matter, until she managed to turn her head in his direction.

"Pardon?" she asked.

Lord Bates gave her a completely besotted—and completely feigned, she was sure—glance. "I noticed them while we danced last night. They're the bluest I've ever seen."

"Thank you," she mumbled, feeling quite awkward. "But I must say I've seen many women with blue eyes just like mine."

"I wanted to remark upon them at the time, but it slipped my mind," he continued, flushing.

Lord, this was terribly strange.

"I second the notion." Lord Wells straightened in his chair. "I daresay, they're not frosty like your elder brother's, but alluring. Quite like a bright summer sky."

Nicholas shifted next to her, crossing his arms over his chest.

"No, that's not it," Lord Morton replied. "They're more like sapphires, I say."

"Sapphires?" Lord Bates scoffed. "Her eyes are too brilliant to be described as such a deep blue. Now, what they are is sparkly. Like a winter morning sky—"

"Gentlemen, please!" Aunt Eugenia proclaimed.

"Listen to yourselves. Arguing about the gel's eye color! Preposterous. Next, you'll all come to blows on the street over the exact hue. Let it rest. Upon my word."

The gentlemen quieted their ridiculous debate only to begin marveling over what they deemed was Rosalind's talent for dancing.

Rosalind pressed her lips together, wanting nothing more than to crawl under the settee. She wasn't *that* spectacular a dancer. Only passable at best. Oh, how she wished they would cease.

Nicholas tilted his crossed arms, gently brushing against her upper arm in the process, presumably to gain her attention.

She turned to look at him and nearly sighed with thankfulness for his surly expression. He was looking not at her but at the hopeful suitors.

"Is it really always like this?" he said softly, barely moving his lips.

"Yes. And no," she replied just as quietly. "When Gabriel is here, they aren't permitted in the house."

"I see."

She wondered if he truly did see. Was he aware of how unsettling and downright ridiculous their behavior could be? And she was to think she would find a husband among these men someday?

"You don't like it," he stated, and she could feel his gaze upon her.

She looked up at him. "Can you blame me?"

"Do you have high standards of conduct for prospective husbands?"

"Indeed. I suppose there are some women who would be ecstatic to have such enthusiasm in her suitors. However, I would much prefer sincerity over anything else. True affection."

"Love?" he asked, the timbre of his voice coaxing an unexpected shiver to spark through her.

She could only nod, hoping she didn't look as vulnerable as she felt at that moment.

"And you don't think you'll ever find it," he finished for her.

She gave him a small smile but was unable to hold his gaze. The truth was, "love" was sitting next to her, but of course she wouldn't say that aloud. Not when he continued to confuse her about how he felt about her.

"What I think," she began, still speaking in low tones, "or rather, what I *know*, is that I will not marry unless my prospective husband surrenders his entire heart to me. If I can't have it all, I want none of it."

"Some men might find that prospect frightening. Loving completely. Relinquishing."

"But why?"

"Perhaps they believe love makes one vulnerable. It weakens you. Opens you up to pain and fear." He closed his eyes slowly, briefly. "For some, love is like death."

She straightened. "But love is life."

"To you, perhaps."

"Not to you?"

When he didn't answer her, she forged onward with her point. "My father charmed my mother at the very first ball she attended, and they were married soon after. She was twenty, romantic, and longed for a love match. She thought she had found that very thing with my father and grew to love him deeply. But my father never reciprocated those feelings. Sometimes there would be a gesture or a kind word, and I believe it was those things that kept her hanging on to the hope that he would one day declare his love. I was thirteen years old and even I knew—"

"He toyed with her feelings?"

She shook her head, the thought that Nicholas seemed genuinely interested in what she was saying warming her heart. It did not escape her notice that she'd never spoken to another man about her parents' relationship before—besides Gabriel, that is.

"Perhaps he was toying with her," she said. "He was rarely home, but my mother lived for those times. As time went on, he came home less and less. News of his mistresses traveled to Wolverest and it devastated my mother. Tristan was too young and too much of a free spirit to notice such things, but Gabriel and I watched her slowly waste away."

Frowning, Nicholas shook his head. "Her love for your father destroyed her."

"My father's love would have brought her back to life." She sighed. "I don't want to make the same mistake. I don't want to be in love with someone that feigns his affection. I'd rather be alone."

He stared at her, his firm, expertly sculpted lips opening slightly as if he was about to say something more but thought better of it. His gaze dropped to her lips and he leaned slightly toward her.

For a moment, she thought he was actually going to kiss her, right here in the morning room, but then she felt his breath at her ear.

"I don't think you were made to be alone," he whispered hotly before pulling away.

Her eyes fluttered. She hadn't expected him to say something like that, and she wasn't sure she understood his meaning. Was he flirting? Was that some sort of twisted compliment that circled back to his earlier insinuations that she enjoyed the attention from men?

Before she could ask him what he'd meant, her stomach gave a sudden, horrific growl. The spell between them broke and she patted at her skirts, hoping the swishing masked it.

She had been so busy at the door (and at the windows) and in the morning room that she hadn't eaten a morsel since very early this morning, and it had only been a slice of toast with a drop of honey.

Licking her lips, Rosalind glanced longingly at a plate of chocolate cake.

"Do you want some, lass?" Nicholas drawled from beside her.

She looked over to find him staring at her mouth intently. "Ah, no. No, thank you. I'm fine. Really."

"I could get you a nice, thick slice. You would like it."

Her gaze flicked to the plate, then back to Nicholas's face. "Oh, I would. I would."

"Then let me get it for you."

"Winterbourne!" Tristan shouted from the

doorway. "Sorry to have kept you waiting."

Rosalind's breath shuddered. Just what was going on here? All the man was doing was asking if she wanted some cake, but it somehow felt much more intimate in nature.

Frighteningly, she wanted it to continue. She wanted cake. She wanted him to feed her cake. In truth, she didn't even care if he ate the cake himself just so that he'd keep talking to her in those dark tones while looking at her mouth like he wanted to kiss her.

"If you'll excuse me," Nicholas spoke to the room at large.

Rosalind watched him leave, marveling at his size. She inhaled the hint of his cologne and mourned the warmth he took with him.

Why did he have to be such a confusing, beguiling beast?

As soon as Nicholas was out of the room, Tristan gave her a pointed look, then threw one that held considerable more heat at the grouping of men.

"Gentlemen," he said, affecting Gabriel's dark baritone precisely. "My sister has had a very busy afternoon."

Surprisingly, they all stood and made their hushed excuses.

Twenty minutes later, Aunt Eugenia rose and declared she was to return to her rooms. "I've eaten too much cake and talked to too many idiots for one afternoon," she said.

Which left Rosalind alone with her thoughts—and the last slice of luscious chocolate cake.

The house was incredibly quiet. Nicholas had probably left, as well.

She strained to hear his voice down the hall, but she perceived nothing but the ticking clock and the occasional sniffle from Briggs.

Silent, like a cat, she stole across the room. Sucking in her lips, she plucked the moist wedge from the plate, and then, opening her mouth wide, she shoved the entire thing in her mouth all at once.

It was heaven. It was divine. It was . . .

"Impressive."

Cheeks full to bursting, she turned her head to find Nicholas leaning inside the doorway, a grin slanting across his handsome face.

She froze, but only for a moment. Her cheeks probably looked as plump as a cherub's. She ought to be mortified, but she wasn't.

Undeterred, she finished chewing, dabbed at the corners of her mouth with a linen napkin, and then, of course, took an exaggerated bow. She came up smiling broadly, knowing that chocolate most likely stained her teeth, making it look like she was missing a few.

Nicholas pushed off the doorframe, clapping politely. He knew that it would be an infinitely wiser choice to turn around and make his exit, but his feet were apparently paying no attention at all to his thoughts. Before he could stop himself, he stood before her, the small table with an empty cake plate squatting between them.

His eyes followed the path of her pink tongue as it peeked out to lick her lower lip. Sweet Christ.

"Has Tristan given you a sufficient supply of the best gaming hells, then?" she asked, a bite to her words.

"Adequate, I suppose." He hated having to lie to her, but he couldn't very well tell her he'd had to tell Tristan that he would be watching the house this evening.

"Nicholas?"

He inwardly cringed. He knew that tone. He had a younger sister, after all. That pitch in her voice meant she was about to ask him a question she suspected he wouldn't want to answer.

"At the ball the other night," she said, skirting around the table to step closer to him.

He took a backwards step.

"I noticed you danced, oh, seven sets—to the delight of the debutantes in attendance." She took another step, the hem of her dress brushing the toes of his boots.

He gulped.

"Why did you not waltz?"

For a moment his mind froze. He hadn't expected her to ask him that question. "Well, I-I . . ." Damn, but she had him blubbering like a schoolboy. He cleared his throat. "I cannot waltz."

Her chin dropped.

There. He'd said it. It wasn't true, but he was quite proud of himself for being so very clever. Three wee words and now he was neatly exonerated from ever having to dance with her at any of the numerous balls she would undoubtedly be attending. The dread that hovered in his dreams, whispering warnings that he wouldn't be able to control himself, hide his attraction if he was forced to hold her in his embrace, evaporated in an instant.

"You cannot waltz?"

He grinned wide and sanguine. "No."

Her azure gaze narrowed on him as a slow smile curled her lips.

A sense of foreboding as heavy as an anvil dropped in his stomach.

Before he could react—and truly, he didn't know what he would have done if he'd had time—Rosalind did a little hop where she stood and grabbed his hand.

"Then I shall teach you," she chirped, pulling him with her.

Chapter 6

❦❦

"Teach me? Now? Here? Where are you taking me?"

"To the wilds of South America," she intoned dryly, rolling her eyes. "To the middle of the room, Nicholas." Letting go of his hand, she scooted a chair to the side. "Sheesh, you act as if you fear I'll ravish you."

Quite the reverse, I fear I'll ravish you.

"All right," she declared, holding up her arms as if an imaginary man stood before her. "This shouldn't take too long, seeing as how well you danced the other night. And you did watch the others dance, I presume." She smiled at him. "Come on. I promise not to stomp on your toes. Seven seasons and not a single victim to date."

Like an imbecile he just stood there, frozen at the prospect of holding her in his arms. Sitting next to her on the sofa had been one thing—there had been other people in the room, after all. But

133

they were most definitely alone now. Alone and unchaperoned. Clearly, she had no idea at all about how attracted he was to her, which was a good thing, but he suspected the threads of his restraint were popping free, cord by cord, each time he had to touch her.

It's only lust, he kept telling himself.

His every step measured, Nicholas came before her, resigned to her little dance lesson.

"Now," she said, her tone befitting one of his old mathematics tutors. "You do know the waltz time? The music for the minuet last night was in waltz time . . . one . . . two . . . three."

He responded with a grunt.

"Good." She smiled. "Now hold me."

"What?" he asked a bit loudly.

She sighed, though he detected a shakiness to her breath. "Encircle my waist with your right arm. Keep your posture firm."

Hardening his resolve to behave, he closed his eyes and slid his arm around her. He felt her shiver.

"Now, hold my right hand with your left," she said softly. "Keep your arm bent at the elbow."

On purpose, he held it too high.

"Lower. Almost to the height of my waist."

And then, because Nicholas was a little bit

wicked, he let the hand that splayed across the base of her spine lower inch by glorious inch until his thumb rested at her waist, his fingers at the top of her backside.

She did not correct him.

He opened his eyes, knowing full well he could not keep the heat from his gaze any longer.

She stared up at him and swallowed. "You are responsible for guiding me across the dance floor."

He nodded slowly and began to move, hesitantly at first, but soon in perfect time.

Rosalind was impressed. It took skill to traverse the room—and furniture—without whacking into something.

"How am I doing?" he asked, his gray eyes alight with unmistakable heat.

"Wonderful," she choked out, suddenly breathless. Truly, she'd never had a more capable partner. She supposed it helped that she loved this man and might very well be a touch biased, but he was marvelous, masterful.

He was either a quick learner or she was a brilliant teacher.

Or he had been lying about not knowing how to waltz in the first place. She could not dismiss that possibility.

Rounding the sofa they had sat in earlier, he came to an abrupt stop. She had not expected it. Her skirts swished between them and she started to slip sideways.

Nicholas grabbed her fully around the back and twisted their positions, presumably so that he would feel the brunt of the fall and not her. As he tripped backwards, Rosalind was helpless but to go along with him from the momentum. He landed in a sitting position on the sofa with Rosalind sprawled on top of him, straddling one of his thighs.

Breathless, she gazed into his hooded eyes. "Are you all right?" she asked.

Panting himself, he shook his head.

His gaze lowered to her neck. His head tilted. His hot mouth fastened tenderly to her throat.

Rosalind shuddered with a moan. It was as if she had been starving for this moment. Her head lolled to the side and she straightened, undeniably giving him the signal that she wanted more.

His tongue lapped at her skin. His teeth grazed her. His sculpted lips soothed the bite and suckled her. It was as if she was this delicious treat that he hungered for and now savored every taste. And she wanted Nicholas to devour every inch of her.

Soon, his lips feathered across the swells of her bosom and she shivered. When his tongue stabbed into her cleavage, she inhaled sharply and writhed upon his hard thigh, every nerve alive and superbly sensitive.

As he nipped and nuzzled the tops of her breasts, one of his hands sat heavy on her back, keeping her close, while the other was sliding up her arm, his fingers curling into the cap sleeve of her dress.

He trailed his intoxicating kisses upward. Their open, panting mouths met, hesitated, and then joined. He kissed her ferociously, gently, his tongue sweeping inside again and again. Waves of sensation buffeted her.

She should have been shocked. She shouldn't have known how to respond, but it all seemed so natural to her, like she was born to love this man, to be made love to by this man.

The hand at her back lowered to her bottom and squeezed, rolling her hard onto his thigh. She moaned as unspeakable pleasure throbbed at the apex of her thighs. He buried his head against her chest, and she could feel him trembling.

And then his hands slowed. And then he stopped.

His hands fell away and he closed his eyes with a sigh.

Gradually, her senses returned. She blinked open her eyes and looked about the room. The door to the hall was open. Tristan and her aunt were home—not to mention the fact that Briggs was in the hall and the maid could have come to take the empty cake plate away.

She looked over her shoulder, slightly relieved that it sat there untouched.

Grabbing her skirts, which had rucked up to her thighs, she slid off of Nicholas and stood on shaky legs.

What was she thinking? That was just it. She wasn't thinking. By luck alone no one had walked in on them. If someone had, she'd be considered compromised and would soon find herself married to a man that quite possibly only wanted her but didn't love her.

"Nicholas, I—"

He held up a hand and stood. "You needn't say a word."

"But—"

"No. My actions were reprehensible." He wouldn't look at her.

She took a step toward him and he jerked away.

"I apologize. It should not have happened. I don't know what came over me." Holding out his hands in front of him, he looked at them. They were shaking slightly—almost as much as her legs.

She reached out a hand to still them.

He evaded her touch with a backward step. "I-I'm going now. We shall pretend this never happened." He turned, striding to the door.

Rosalind could have sworn she heard him curse himself.

Would she ever see him again? Given his past history of making himself scarce of late at Wolverest, it was a possibility. "Nicholas, wait."

She didn't expect him to listen, but he surprised her by halting at the doorway, although he didn't turn around to look at her.

"Tomorrow afternoon is the Fairfax musicale. Did you, by chance, get an invitation?"

He was silent for so long that she thought he wasn't going to answer her. "Are *you* going?" he asked, his deep baritone clipped and cold sounding.

"I attend every year."

"Then I shall be there as well." And with that, he stepped out into the hall and let himself out.

Despite his apology and promise that nothing like that would ever happen again, Rosalind smiled to herself. Perhaps the gentleman in him was embarrassed by his attraction. In truth, she was a little shaken by the strength of the passion that had ignited between them, as well. However, one thing was perfectly clear in her mind: Nicholas seemed to be spending a lot more time in her presence, and that could mean only one thing—he liked her.

Chapter 7

⁓∽◯◯∾⁓

Inside the Devines' octagonal summerhouse, which was tucked inside a half-circle of Italian cypresses in the rear yard of Devine Mansion, Nicholas shifted his weight yet again on the stone bench. Och, his arse was sore.

The time was nearing ten o'clock in the evening, and he had been sitting here since just after sunset, watching the house, waiting for some sign that the redheaded man he had seen the night before had returned.

He'd wait another hour or so, then take a trip to the front of the house and watch from over there for awhile. He couldn't risk walking back and forth. Rosalind might spot him.

However, blanketed in shadow with a sliver of a moon as his only light, there wasn't any way for her to spy him in the garden.

But what would she do if she knew *he* was guarding her?

Speaking with Tristan today, Nicholas had learned that Rosalind and Gabriel had debated at length about her need for an appointed guard.

Nicholas wasn't surprised. She was a strong-willed and stubborn woman, and if it hadn't been for the fact that he'd been entrusted with her safety, if it hadn't been for the fact that she was his friend's little sister, he just might have pulled her to him again and kissed her until she was senseless.

Damn, but he rather thought that *he* had been the senseless one this afternoon. He'd thoroughly enjoyed every moment of it, but hell, he had nearly ravished his best friend's sister in the very room where her brother probably drank his tea. What the devil had come over him?

He ran a hand through his hair. It mustn't ever happen again. It was, no, *she* was unbelievable. Having her in his arms, the taste of her—it was better than he ever dared to imagine. It mustn't ever happen again. And for a myriad of reasons.

The most pressing at the moment was that he knew he mustn't allow himself to be distracted by her. He had a duty to protect her. He'd given Gabriel his word. In addition, according to Tristan, the amounts in the betting books at White's were nearing record-breaking sums. The eager bachelors' wager to win her was turning into a frenzy fueled by foolish pride. Men were capable of taking dangerous risks in the name of competition.

He needed to stay focused. Sighing, Nicholas pushed all thoughts of Rosalind aside. Should be easy enough. He'd managed it for years, hadn't he?

He just kept telling himself that she was nothing but a spoiled society lass with a penchant for snooping, meddling, and occasionally glaring at him like she'd love to see his head on a platter one day. Or his heart.

But he would never give her the opportunity. He had vowed to never let a woman get under his skin. It had been an easy vow to keep. Until now.

He smiled to himself as a sudden image of Rosalind, chocolate teeth and all, sprung to mind. How curious it was that she was able to laugh at herself after being caught stuffing the biggest slice of chocolate cake he'd ever seen into her mouth.

Oh and Christ, what a sweet mouth she had.

It was getting harder and harder to dismiss her physical effect on him. And had that been a hint of jealousy he'd spied when they'd spoken in the foyer this afternoon?

At first he'd thought it was only her pride that made her angry that he had danced with others but not her. Would it be such a stretch to imagine she was jealous?

Or was he merely hoping? And why *was* he hoping?

He let forth a long, frustrated sigh. It would be so much easier to forget about her if she resented him for some reason. Hell, perhaps he should march up to her front door right now and confess to being her guardian. She'd surely hate him then.

And just as certainly, she'd make the act of protecting her a living hell. And he could never back down. No, Nicholas thought, it was better that she didn't know he was her guardian.

He yawned and stretched out his legs. Damn, but it was a chilly night.

Having rid himself of his jacket a long time ago, he snagged it from next to him on the bench and proceeded to cover himself with it.

There was no sign of her. Except for a glow through a window set in a door that led to the kitchen entrance, no other candlelight beckoned from the windows. Perhaps she had already fallen asleep or was reading in the study.

He yawned again, thinking he'd best get up and go to the front of the house now, before he fell asleep himself.

A flicker of light glowed from an upstairs window. A short but shapely silhouette came into view, fumbling with the latch.

A second later the pair of windows creaked open, revealing Rosalind, her sleek, black hair unbound, racing down bare, slender shoulders to curl seductively around her breasts, which looked to be covered with a noticeably thin white shift.

No maidenly robe. No prudish heavy night rail, but a threadbare shift?

Bloody hell.

Incredibly warm and completely wide awake now, he slowly sat forward, his coat falling to the floor, his mouth watering for another taste of her.

He gulped like a schoolboy. And though the spark of desire was unmistakably instant, he couldn't help but wonder aloud, "It's a damnable chilly evening, what the devil are you thinking, woman?"

"I can't believe I shoved an entire piece of cake in my mouth in front of Nicholas." Rosalind leaned on the windowsill of her bedchamber, hoping the chill air would somehow clear her mind.

When he *wasn't* near, her manners, speech, and poise were utter perfection. She rather thought she could balance a stack of books on her head, twirl across a crowded room, and tip nary a one. But around Nicholas . . . the books would undoubtedly tumble down.

Just like the rest of her. Truly, had he tried to take other liberties with her person yesterday afternoon, she didn't think she would have had the forbearance to stop him.

She was weak when it came to Nicholas, and she'd be lying if she didn't admit that it frightened her a little. She did not want to end up like her mother, who'd spent the majority of her life in misery, pining for a man who would never, ever love her.

And wasn't Nicholas carousing this evening? She tried not to think of it or else she'd feel ill.

She sighed, her eyes scanning the velvety expanse of the sky. Her guardian was out there, too, somewhere. And here she thought it would be so easy to find out who he was. With the distraction of Nicholas that afternoon, she had even forgotten about her goal to ferret the mysterious man out.

"Come away from the window, my lady," her maid implored. "You'll catch an ague!"

"It would serve me right," Rosalind said pensively, gazing out into the garden.

What a waste of a day. All those gentlemen callers—she ought to have been watching for some sign of a man lurking about, or she should have paid stricter attention to her callers, looking for odd behavior.

Instead she'd hung on every word that had spilled from Nicholas's lips. But she really couldn't blame herself.

Yawning, she raised her arms above her head, stretching long and sleepily.

An odd sound came from below.

She froze in the pose, listening. When no other sound came, she planted her hands on the sill and leaned far over to gaze into the dark garden, inhaling sharply when her bosom met with the cool stone.

She heard it again.

Her brow furrowed. It sounded like a man cursing softly. Or groaning, she wasn't sure.

She stood by the window for a couple of minutes more, but when she didn't hear it again after several moments, she shrugged, deciding to dismiss it.

This particular set of windows faced the back garden. The landscaping was designed specifically to afford privacy, so none of her neighbors could have seen her standing at her window in her favorite night rail.

Alice hated that Rosalind wore the well-worn garment, but Rosalind refused to relinquish it. She certainly had a plethora of newer, finer sleeping garments, but this shift was incredibly soft and smooth. Besides, it had been her mother's, and wild boars couldn't rip it from her.

Closing the window, she latched it, then shuffled over to her bed.

Alice finished stoking the fire and wiped her hands on her apron. "If you won't be needing me, my lady, I'll be leaving, if you please. I'm to go spend the night at my Nellie's, if you remember. And I'm also to remind you that Briggs is here, but sick in bed."

Rosalind crawled onto her bed and slipped under the bright, white counterpane. She yawned. "I remember. I'll be jush fine," she mumbled sleepily. "Go and enjoy that new grandchild of yours. I'll see you late tomorrow."

She heard the click of the door, closed her eyes, and fell asleep.

She dreamed of moonlit gardens, floating plates of chocolate cake, and Nicholas sitting in her morning room wearing nothing but his kilt.

* * *

Rosalind gasped and jolted to a sitting position in bed.

As her heartbeat slammed inside her breast, it took her half a minute to realize that a loud crash had startled her from her sleep.

Her eyes flew to the mantel clock. The fire in the grate had burned low, the glowing embers giving her room a haunting glow. The faint trill of a single bird told her dawn was near.

There was a chance it was only Tristan coming home, but he was never disruptive.

A loud thump and a startled shout sounded from below stairs.

"Oh, dear heaven." Was there an intruder?

The rumbling of masculine voices reached her and much shuffling about ensued.

Rosalind swung her legs down from her bed. Her hands shook as she reached for her shawl, which was draped over the end of the bed. Tossing it over her shoulders, she wrapped it tightly around herself.

What should she do? Should she hide? Should she scream for a neighbor? Where was Tristan? Should she alert Aunt Eugenia? No, unless the thief had an aversion to surly spinsters in mob

149

caps, she was useless to help her. Besides, her aunt was hard of hearing on one side (Rosalind always forgot which side it was), but if the woman slept on her good ear side, she'd sleep through a burlesque show going on in her very own bedchamber.

Rosalind had only herself to rely on. Heaven help her.

She clutched at the heavy, white shawl covering her shoulders and launched herself across the room. Grabbing a fireplace poker, she held it high above her head and crept to the door to wait and listen.

Her frightened pants slowed as seconds stretched into minutes without further disruptions from below.

She knew she hadn't imagined the sound, but whatever had made it seemed to have gone away. Or . . .

The corridor outside her bedroom creaked in a lumbering, rhythmic pattern. A walking pattern—as if someone had finally reached the top of the steps and was now creeping down the hall toward her room.

"Let go of me, you bloody oaf!"

"Tristan!" Rosalind yelled. Someone must have accosted her brother as he was coming in the house.

Without thought or consequence, Rosalind opened the door and flung herself into the corridor, brandishing her makeshift weapon high above her head.

Nicholas Kincaid stood before her, half-carrying, half-dragging a boneless-looking Tristan.

"Hullo, sis," Tristan drawled drunkenly.

Her chest rose and fell with her rapid breathing. "Nicholas," she exclaimed breathlessly, her shawl sliding off her shoulders to pool at her feet.

Hard gray eyes instantly softened and hungrily raked her entire body from top to bottom and back again.

She shivered visibly.

Nicholas's arms went slack, sending Tristan sprawling to the floor.

"Bloody hell!" Tristan exclaimed, holding his head.

"Nicholas. What are you doing in my house?" Her tone was plain astonishment.

His eyes still roving all over her form, he opened his mouth to speak, then closed it, then opened it, then closed it—and this time, his eyes as well. He gave his head a quick shake.

"What's wrong with you?" She lowered the fireplace poker, her brow furrowed.

"You're standing in front of the man in your blasted shift, you addle-pated pea goose," exclaimed the drunken sod sprawled on the floor.

While Rosalind resisted the urge to step on Tristan's fingers, her senses seemed to finally converge. Lud, she was practically naked. She dropped down to retrieve her shawl, glancing at her brother in the process.

She inhaled sharply at the sight of his eye and the great big purple splotch surrounding it. "Who did this to you?"

"He did," Tristan squeaked, raising a wobbly finger in the air. And then, he muttered, "Dropped me on the floor, 'e did." But Rosalind didn't hear him.

Chin set, she whipped her shawl around her shoulders and stood up. She met Nicholas's gaze. "*You* did this?" she accused. "You gave him a blackened eye."

He crossed his arms over his chest and shook his head. "The only thing I did," he said forcefully, "was pick your brother up from the front steps and bring him in the house."

"We broke your lovely, lovely picture," Tristan muttered from the floor. "You know, that one some bloke had painted and brought here this morning? Yesh, put my foot right through it, I did. So sorry."

"It was hideous." She dropped another glance at her brother. "But what the addle-pated pea goose wants to know, Tristan, is how you acquired your black eye."

With some great difficulty, he managed to pull himself up to rest on his arms. "Well, there were these four men who came out of the alley and jumped me from behind. I fought off one and . . ."

She raised an eyebrow. "Are you trying to tell me you fought off *four* men in the condition you're in?"

He was quiet for a moment. "All right, there were three."

She narrowed her eyes.

"All right, there were two." He smiled up at her. "One?"

"Tristan," she warned.

"Oh, all right. I hit myself in the eye with the toe of my boot as I was trying to pull it off."

She put a hand over her mouth to smother her laugh and failed miserably. Her laughing eyes met Nicholas's.

He looked incredibly serious despite the absurd things coming out of Tristan's mouth.

"Did you witness his . . . unfortunate circumstance?" she asked, her voice laced with amusement.

His mouth twitched with a ghost of a grin, almost as if he wished he could laugh but something kept him from giving in to it. "Your brother, it seems, thought the front of the house was his bedchamber. After tripping up the steps, he took hold of the railing as if his very connection to the earth depended upon it." He paused as Rosalind laughed again. "After he realized he could let go and not fly into the sky, he plopped down and proceeded to relieve himself of his boots."

"Oh, dear," Rosalind breathed, wiping tears of suppressed mirth from the corners of her eyes with the fringe of her shawl.

"Let's get your brother to bed," Nicholas said, his voice sounding tight.

"Come along, Tristan," she said, kneeing down to pull up on his arm.

Nicholas joined her and shook his head. "The lad walks like a one-legged sailor abroad a boat in a turbulent sea. It'll be much easier if you let me do it."

She nodded and stepped aside.

Nicholas scooped up her brother fairly easily

and half dragged, half walked Tristan into his room.

Once inside his room, Rosalind fetched the chamber pot, just in case he was ill, and slid it to the side of his bed. She brought over a cloth and a small bowl of water from the washstand, as well.

She turned to find that Nicholas had propped up her brother on the bed. Tristan's head was leaning against the headboard.

Mutterings came from the hall. Nicholas became instantly alert, jerking his head toward the noise.

"Perhaps it's Tristan's valet or some other servant," she placated.

Nicholas left to apparently investigate, although judging by the set of his jaw, he looked a lot angrier now than when he'd come in.

"Tristan, scoot down," she ordered.

He did as she directed, sliding down on his back.

"No, not on your back." She grabbed hold of his shirt and pulled him so he was on his stomach. "If you get sick, you'll choke."

"Lovely thought," he mumbled. "Now I remember why I don't do this very often."

She made a sound of agreement and sat down next to him on the edge of the bed. Dipping the cloth in the cool water, she pressed it gently to his blackened eye.

"Rosie, I got myself leg-shackled—"

She froze. "Tristan, please don't tell me you married someone in this condition."

His head bobbed, and she realized he was shaking it for no.

"How would I have done that? Don't have a special license. I meant tap-hackled."

"Well, that's very different. That's means you're drunk." She tucked the blankets around him, sniffing daintily. "However, anyone with a nose could tell you that," she mumbled.

"Thank you."

"It wasn't a compliment," she pointed out.

"I know."

"How much did you drink?" she asked, sitting back.

He opened one blue eye and looked at her. "I'm not telling you."

She almost smiled. "Whyever not?"

"'Cause it's a trifling amount. Rather embarrassing."

"All right," she said, tossing the cloth on the table to cross her arms over her chest. "*Why* did you drink a 'trifling' amount?"

He turned his head slightly, which put his face in the pillow. "In celebration," he said, sounding muffled.

"May I ask, in celebration of what?"

"The end of my engagement."

Rosalind gasped. "Miss Harriet Beauchamp cried off?"

He nodded into the pillow.

She gasped, a hand cupped over her mouth. "I had a feeling she'd do something like this!" She stood and paced the room. "As soon as I realized Gabriel was going to marry Madelyn, I *thought* she might reconsider. I *knew* from the start you didn't suit. And if anyone would know, it would be me. Please, I mean no offense to you, but I believe we all realized her affections resided solely in the fact that she believed Gabriel wouldn't marry, and that by marrying you, she might one day produce the Devine heir." She looked down to see his shoulders shaking.

A mortified shock ran through her. Was he . . . crying?

"Tristan, I'm so sorry. I hadn't realized that you'd grown attached."

He turned his head from the nest of the pillow and smiled.

He wasn't crying, he was laughing.

"I said, 'celebration.' " He tried to roll on his back. "Hell, Rosie, I'm the one who's foxed."

She pushed him back over and sighed with some relief. Twisting, she looked about the room to see if Nicholas had returned. "Wherever did he go?"

"Who go?"

"Nicholas."

"How the devil should I know? You won't let me roll over."

"Did you meet up this evening? Go to the same club?"

"No."

Disappointment had her shoulders slouching. Had he gone? And without saying good-bye? She wanted to thank him for helping Tristan, at least. It was the polite thing to do.

With feigned casualness, she stepped to the door and looked up and down the empty hall before creeping ahead.

Her bare feet swished softly on the red and gold carpet. Up ahead she spied Tristan's boots, which sat slumped over against the wall opposite her bedchamber door.

"I guess you had gotten them off after all," she murmured, picking them up.

The sound of shattering pottery disrupted the silence of the corridor. Her head snapped to her open doorway.

A tall, masculine shadow stood at a side window of her bedchamber, which looked between the houses. Kincaid. He had gone into her room.

His back was to her as Rosalind stepped soundlessly inside the room. Her gaze slid down from tousled dark locks resting on the back of his neck, down his broad back covered in white lawn, and down further to his firm backside. Lord, she was truly wanton.

Her writing desk crouched under the high window and she bit her bottom lip as she took in the sight of his muscular thighs, the tops of which pressed against the wood as he peered out into the predawn.

He must have sensed her presence. Slowly, he straightened from the window and turned to regard her, her desk at his back. A mischievous glint in his eyes simmered to a heated smolder.

"What was that sound?" she asked, crossing the room. A smart woman would admonish his sheer audacity to enter into her private chambers; a wise woman would cast him out. But Rosalind loved this man. The strong, sensual pull compelled her forward, as did the curiosity about the crashing sound she had heard.

His grin was lopsided and hardly innocent. "Your flowers . . . they had an accident."

Her mouth opened. "That lovely pot of begonias I brought upstairs?"

"That would be them." He smiled wide, flashing straight white teeth and a dimple in his cheek that she'd never known he had. His eyes dipped to her toes and back again.

She was suddenly acutely aware of her state of undress. She loved this night rail, but she'd bet it was fairly see-through, if the look on Nicholas's face was any indication.

Glad that her unbound hair was tucked under her shawl—otherwise she'd feel incredibly shameless—she closed the space between them, one fine brow arched.

Only now did she notice that his waistcoat was unbuttoned and his cravat was tied loosely, offering her a small glimpse of tan skin. The queue that held his hair back had loosened, and some of his mahogany locks had slipped from its hold to brush against his cheekbones. He looked slightly rumpled, so strong and masculine and very wicked in the dark.

"What are you doing in my room?" She gulped, then lifted her chin in hopes that he hadn't noticed.

He leaned his weight on her desk, crossed his arms over his chest, and stated calmly, "I heard a noise."

"What sort of noise?"

"Ah, hell," someone yelled from outside her window. *"Now where the devil did you go?"*

Her brow furrowed. "What in the . . ." She made to take a step around him, only to have access to her view denied by Nicholas as he slid to block her.

"There's nothing to see," he said, looking down at her, his gray eyes glittering in the low light of the fire.

She dropped her brother's boots to the floor.

It was probably a would-be suitor. Occasionally, one would get drunk and come to sing or shout poetry at her window. It was embarrassing and unwanted, and she just hoped her neighbors slept through it.

"Let me see who's down there," she said in her most threatening tone, which wasn't, admittedly, awfully intimidating.

161

He pressed his lips together for a moment, as if in thought, and then grinned. "No."

She tilted her head, eyes narrowing. "How dare you," she breathed, not daring to speak louder than a whisper. "It is *my* window and *my* bedchamber. And *you* shouldn't even be in here." She did a little hop, thinking she could see over his shoulder. It didn't work, however, but it made him chuckle, low and deep in his chest.

The sound made her feel like she'd just swallowed a glass of sherry in just one gulp.

Glancing around his trim waist, she saw that her lamp was missing its candle. Her eyes quickly scanned what she could see of the desk. Missing as well were her inkwell, three candle stubs, and a wooden duck paperweight that Gabriel had carved for her when she was a little girl.

"Where are all my things?" she asked, her voice soft and bewildered.

"Well," he said, his brogue more pronounced than usual, "I spotted a wee pest outside your window and I thought I'd scare him off. But don't fret your bonnie head, I'll retrieve them for you."

"A *wee* pest?" she repeated. "What sort of wee pest?"

"I had to toss your hairbrush, as well. I almost got 'im with that one."

She looked over her shoulder to her dressing table. There was a soft swoosh near her feet and she turned back around to witness Nicholas tossing one of her brother's boots out of the window.

He turned to face her, leaning his weight on the desk once again. "Damn, I missed again."

"I cannot believe you," she muttered, grasping her shawl tight with one hand.

"What would you have me do? Gifts, pictures, flowers, hell, even the horse makes some sense, but Shakespeare at your window near dawn? Will they stoop to anything?"

"Well, I don't like it, but at least I don't throw objects intended to knock people unconscious like some . . . like some uncivilized beast."

"My country manners must offend you, your royal highness," he mocked. "What is the proper etiquette when one wants to rid a star-eyed drunken sot at one's window? Shall we write him a letter?"

Her chin lifted and she stifled the urge to laugh. "All right." She'd take his suggestion.

She reached out to open a drawer next to his thigh. He twitched. Paying the action no further heed, she removed a tablet, flipped it open, picked up her quill pen . . . and paused.

That's right. Her inkwell was on the lawn. Throwing Nicholas a glare, she snapped the pen down and rummaged through the drawer until she found a charcoal pencil. She scribbled the words, "Please, sir, do go away." Pressing her lips together, she handed it to Nicholas. "There. Just tear out the sheet—"

He tossed the entire tablet over his shoulder. It flapped straight out the window.

"You are abominable. What a waste . . ."

"I agree. I should have looked before I threw it and I would have got him."

She shook her head slowly and readjusted her shawl. "I can't believe your nerve."

"My nerve? I can't believe the bollocks—excuse me—the impudence of these foolish whelps."

Nicholas's chin dipped as his gaze swept her from top to bottom in a quick, thorough sweep.

Rosalind followed suit.

Oh, Lord, she hadn't realized she had been standing between his legs until just that moment.

With a muffled oath, he slid away from her with a brisk, sliding step. Rosalind took a step back at the same time.

Embarrassment flooded through her. "So sorry," she mumbled. "I hadn't realized . . ."

He disregarded her apology with a quick shake of his head, his lips in a hard line.

He took a deep breath and ran a hand through his hair, dislodging the leather strip that tied his hair back. It slid soundlessly to the floor. Rosalind realized that he didn't seem to notice.

After a long pause, he said with a note of distaste in his tone, "Did you know, that arse down there, I saw him in the park early this morning—"

"Yesterday morning, now," she corrected.

"—and he was staring at a tiny blond lassie wearing spectacles like she was the empress of his dreams." He shook his head and slowly paced the room, lingering in the shadows. "And now he's here, blithering drunk, and professing his love to *you*. Fickle lad."

Her eyes widened. She knew the man—*and* the "tiny blond lassie"—he spoke of. She had been trying to get those two together for years, but the man, a Lord Rothbury, was as stubborn as a mule when it came to admitting his feelings. Adding to his resistance, undoubtedly, was his belief that the girl was infatuated with none other than his friend Tristan.

She turned her back to the window and rested her bottom against her desk like Nicholas had done earlier, although when he did it, it was the backs of his thighs that touched.

He seemed to disappear for a second in the shadow near her bookcase.

"His words hold no truth for me," she said simply and without remorse. "He is in love with the woman whose family rents the town house next door. I wager he thought to confess his love for her and lost his courage along the way."

"One of your matchmaking schemes gone awry," he stated darkly. With his hands behind his back, he approached her with slow, measured strides.

Moonlight from the high window at her back slanted across his face until he stepped even closer and back into shadow. Her pulse skittered. In that brief flash, she realized he looked grim, dangerous, his jaw tight.

What was he up to? "Thank you for helping my brother," she blurted, surprised that her voice shook a little. "You should go now. "

When the tops of his thighs brushed against her shawl, he came to a stop. "And leave you here all alone to deal with your admirer down there?"

She swallowed. *No, stay*, she wished she could say. Just stay.

And it was shameful and wrong for her to feel that way, she knew. He was in her room, for goodness' sake, but she wouldn't lie to herself. She wanted him to stay a bit longer, she wanted him to like her, she wanted him to . . . to . . . to not throw *A Detailed History on the Production and Use of Cannons and Muskets* out the window!

"Stop," she whispered harshly, flipping around to make a grab for the book.

But it was too late; the book had already dropped. And by the sound of it, it had hit its mark.

Rosalind stilled, sprawled across her desk on her stomach, the coolness of the wood seeping through her flimsy night rail. Her shawl had bunched around her shoulders and neck, leaving her thinly covered bottom exposed to the cool night air . . . and Nicholas's gaze.

His breath hitched loudly.

He saw.

A delicious heat spread over Rosalind right before she peeked over her shoulder to find Nicholas standing oh-so-close, his open palm just inches from her bottom.

Chapter 8

Sweet Christ, why was he being subjected to such decadent torment?

Surely, Nicholas would never claim to be a perfect man, but for the love of whisky and Robert the Bruce, did he deserve this torture? Did he have to have such a delectable sight a mere inch from his fingertips?

To hell with his fingers. The desk was the perfect height, her lovely, gently curving backside at the perfect level. Should he grab her by the waist and angle his hips barely a notch, he'd be able to sink his . . .

His fingers clenched into a fist. A long exhale blew from his lips. Whatever his deepest, wildest wishes were, he reached up and pulled her shawl back down to cover up her exquisite derriere instead.

What a shame. What a damn shame.

"Get up," he ordered, his voice gruff with suppressed desire.

Quickly, she shimmed down and off her writing desk. Grasping her shawl closed, she poked him hard in the chest. "You probably killed him," she whispered harshly.

"I did not," he said, looking over her head and out the window. "See, that wee blond has come out and is tending to him."

Rosalind didn't turn to look but glared up at him instead.

"She is," he assured her. "Look, he's moving now."

Shaking her head in slow disapproval, she poked him again and took a step toward him. He took a step back.

"I may not approve of his conduct, but your conduct is equally appalling. Lucky for you his neck isn't broken. And what about all my things," she said, lifting an arm and making an arc, "scattered across the lawn? It'll be dawn soon, and what will the neighbors say? And the inkwell . . ."

As she continued her stream of complaints, Nicholas's attention was drawn to the sound of a door opening from down the hall.

Could it be Tristan?

" . . . ink everywhere, I daresay, spotting the grass, dotting the flowers, staining the brick . . ."

Nicholas turned his head toward her open door to better listen. Was that footsteps?

" . . . they'll see the objects, know they're all mine and they'll think I've gone completely mad. Nicholas? Are you listening to me?"

"Hush."

The floor creaked and an older female cleared her throat.

Rosalind worked her jaw. "Did you just 'hush' me *again*? In all my life, I've never been hushed once, and you've managed to hu—"

He clamped one hand to her mouth, the other to the back of her head. "Someone is coming," he rushed out in a whisper.

Rosalind's eyes widened in revelation. Nicholas nodded gravely.

Shuffling footsteps neared. "Rosalind? Rosalind? Are you awake? Such a clamor in this house!"

Nicholas's gaze darted to her wardrobe, and he quickly assessed that he'd never fit. There simply wasn't any time to find a proper hiding place.

Swinging a startled Rosalind into his arms, he threw her roughly on the bed. She landed with a bounce and a squeak, but, quick-thinking lass that she was, she lifted the covers up, inviting him inside. Without a moment's hesitation, he dove under them.

He couldn't see a thing, thank the good Lord. He did not forget—indeed, how could he?—that Rosalind wore next to nothing and her face was above the covers. If there was a smidgen of light, he could feast his eyes upon her without her ever knowing. And judging by the heat generating under the blankets, she was positioned very close to him.

Golden light pervaded the coverlet, and he swore under his breath. Her dotty aunt must have been carrying a lamp.

"Margaret, build a fresh fire for my niece."

"Yes, ma'am."

She must have brought her maid with her. Ah, hell. Now the room would be awash with light.

Flat on his stomach, Nicholas kept as still as he could and closed his eyes.

"I needn't a fire," Rosalind remarked softly. "It's rather warm in here, is it not?"

Indeed. Sweltering. Jasmine and cream. Lord, he could smell her, and he had to bite the sheet to keep from reaching out and sinking his mouth onto whatever part of her body he came into contact with first. He'd lick and suck . . . and she'd taste as good as she smelled. He winked open one eye and spied the gentle curve of one bare shoulder, the capped sleeve of her night rail having slid off. Oh, yes. He swallowed, his mouth watering.

"Drafty is what it is," he heard her aunt say. "Though I do suppose you have such a heap of blankets upon your bed, you wouldn't feel it. Shall I have Margaret remove some?"

"NO!" She cleared her throat, then added more calmly, "I mean, no. It's not necessary. I quite like the heap and want it to stay." She patted the blanket atop him.

"Whatever you wish, child, but you ought to have your maid keep your door shut through the night."

"I shall remind her," answered a sleepy-sounding Rosalind.

"Did the noise awaken you, as well?"

A very real sounding yawn emerged from above his head. "What noise?"

"I was startled awake by a thump."

"That's strange. I didn't hear anything."

"Hmph."

"I suppose it could have been Tristan coming home from a late night about Town."

"I suppose." Her aunt sighed. "Hurry up, Margaret; I'm going back to bed." Quick footsteps moved across the room, followed by slower ones. A minute later the door clicked shut.

The lovely body next to him shifted. "They're gone," Rosalind whispered.

Nicholas gave a sigh of relief. "That was a close one, lass."

He peeled back the coverlet to find Rosalind eyeing him curiously, a small smile playing upon her lips. Or, he supposed, she might not have been smiling at all. Those damn, tempting lips of hers had that disarming habit of curving up at the corners. He wondered how her brothers ever knew what she was thinking. Maybe they always assumed the worst.

A sudden yawn overtook her and she settled her cheek against the pillow, gazing at him sleepily.

He liked this Rosalind. She was soft and tender and he just wanted to pull her into his arms. It had been a long night . . . and morning for her. She must be exhausted. Aye, and he was as well.

"You must go," she said huskily. "The servants will be stirring and I've been scandalous enough for one evening, I suppose."

He nodded, oddly tempted to sleep with her.

Honestly, just sleep with her. What the devil was wrong with him?

"I agree," he said, slipping reluctantly from the bed. "And I've had my share of fighting off your zealous suitors for one evening."

"Me, too," she said around another yawn.

He came to her side of the bed and, before he even knew what he was about, began tucking the blankets around her.

She sighed, snuggled deeper in the blankets, and closed her eyes.

Trust. She trusted him. She might not realize it yet, but she trusted him. This sought-after woman, plagued with dodging a plethora of bumbling suitors, felt comfortable and safe . . . with him.

He should go. Right now. *Creep to the door, listen for the aunt, and slip out and into the night while shadows yet cling to the earth, you great big buffoon.*

But he didn't. Not yet. For whatever reason, he wanted nothing more than to take advantage of her current, appealing state.

"Thank you," she mumbled, "for helping Tristan up the stairs."

Leaning down, Nicholas let his lips hover above her forehead for five whole seconds before sinking down for a brief kiss. Her skin was soft and cool, her exotic scent pervading his nostrils and sinking straight to his heart, where he committed it to memory.

Before he could pull away, however, she surprised him by slipping her warm hands around the back of his neck, keeping him close.

Delicate fingers slid into his hair. He licked his lips, unable to tear his gaze away from her sleepy eyes. And then, before he knew what she was about, she raised her head and pressed her lips softly to his cheek.

He stiffened, her scent washing over him and sending heat straight to his loins. He wanted nothing more at that moment than to kiss her, to plunder her mouth until she sighed with pleasure and pulled him down atop her.

But he wouldn't.

First, he wasn't so arrogant to believe that the lass would welcome his kisses again. And secondly, this was Gabriel's sister. He was to guard her, not ravish her.

But he was left little choice in the matter when her soft, rosy lips whispered across his cheek and down his jaw to settle at the corner of his mouth.

His lips sought to feel hers more fully, feathering across hers back and forth. It wasn't a kiss. It was slow, scorching, openmouthed exploration.

He inhaled her scent, reveled in the heat of her soft breath on his mouth, and tested the plumpness of her lower lip with the edge of his teeth. He heard her breath catch and his responded in kind. The intensity was almost unbearable. He went to pull away, but the pressure of her fingertips at the nape of his neck increased, telling him she wanted him to stay right where he was.

"No, lass," he drawled.

She nodded.

He couldn't stop his smile. "No."

"Why?" she whispered. "I want to and I think you want to, as well."

"You do not know what you ask of me. I have a respon—" He closed his eyes briefly and swallowed. "We mustn't."

She nodded as if she understood. A ghost of regret swept across her features. She looked away, hurt by his refusal.

"Ah, lass. You'll be the death of me," he groaned, sinking to his knees beside her bed.

Cradling her face in his hands, he brushed his lips across hers in an achingly slow rhythm until he felt her lips blossoming beneath his. As soon as she opened to him, he sunk his mouth fully onto hers in a gentle caress.

She was soft and warm, and he couldn't stop himself from taking a quick taste. Strawberries and . . . a hint of chocolate. "Mmm," he said against her lips.

A small sound came from the back of her throat, and it called to him like a sea nymph beckoning him to his doom. Without a whisper of warning, the pressure and rhythm of the kiss escalated—openmouthed and wet and addictively erotic.

She arched upwards, pressing her soft breasts against his chest. One of his hands held the back of her head; the other slipped behind her back to hold her even more tightly against him.

He thought he could take a sip of her and stop. How foolish. He kissed her like a man starved for her. Shyly, her tongue flicked his, coaxing him, encouraging him. She gave an impatient whimper, and he suspected she didn't know what she wanted, she just *wanted*. He sank his tongue inside her welcoming mouth with lazy sweeps and she moaned, threading her fingers through his hair. Holy hell, this had to stop.

Shakily, he pulled away.

Reaching back with both hands, he gently—regretfully—pulled her hands away from the back of his neck. They felt so delicate in his own.

"I'll see you later this afternoon," he said quietly, "at the Fairfax musicale." Bringing her hands to his mouth, he kissed her knuckles.

Still panting, she nodded, gazing up at him as he stood.

"Sleep well, Rosalind," he said, turning to head for the door.

"Sleep well, Nicholas."

And then he forced himself to steal out of her room and out of her house. He retrieved his coat from the summerhouse, then collected all of her things from the lawn and placed them near the door to the kitchen for some servant to find and return to their mistress.

As Nicholas winded his way through the darkened streets, he was grateful that he had remembered his coat, but he chose not to wear it. He needed the harsh chill in the air to diffuse the heat of desire that thrummed through his veins.

He must banish the memory of her scent, her warmth, and the feel of her lips pressed gently to his bristled cheek. The taste of that kiss. Christ, how he wanted to go back to her room and make love to her.

She claimed she wanted to marry for affection, love even. She was not impressed by her tactless suitors, nor did it seem as if she appreciated all the attention. In fact, she seemed to despise them for their insincerity. She wanted loyalty, honesty, and love. She didn't put it in those exact words, but there it was.

He would want—no, *demand*—those same things from a wife should he allow himself to be the sort of man who wanted to marry, to fall in love.

But he was determined not to. If he avoided love, he avoided pain. It wasn't that difficult a task.

As he walked onward, he told himself that Rosalind would not, *would not*, get under his skin.

Perhaps by the time he reached his town house, he'd believe it.

Rosalind snuggled deeper into her blankets, replaying the events of the past hour over and over. Mostly, that kiss.

She sighed, pressing her fingertips lightly to her lips. Since her debut, there had been a couple of gentlemen—their names escaped her now—who had surprised her with a kiss in a dark garden at a ball. They'd been short, unmemorable busses that had made her blush, nothing more.

But Nicholas's kisses made her forget she was a lady, made her think, if only for those precious moments while his lips and tongue tended to her mouth, that rules and strictures of society weren't important. All that mattered was that he must do it again and take all that he wanted.

His hands had felt so delightful upon her skin, and he'd smelled so good and felt so wicked stretched out next to her under the covers.

And if he had been like her other suitors, he would have revealed his presence to her aunt, thereby forcing their union. A compromising situation. But he hadn't. A little voice told her that he hadn't because he didn't like her and wouldn't want to marry her, forced or not, but Rosalind promptly crumpled up that thought and threw it from her mind.

She smiled and sighed instead, thinking he must be warming to her.

He had even made a point to tell her that he would be seeing her later today. Much later, after they all slept, of course. She wondered if he would steal a kiss at the musicale. She rather hoped he would. It wasn't the sort of thing her brother attended, so perhaps they could slip away . . .

Rosalind froze. How had it come to pass that Nicholas had found Tristan this evening? She had asked her brother if Nicholas had gone out with him, but he'd said no.

Tossing back her covers, Rosalind charged across her room, flung open her wardrobe, and put on a proper robe.

She carefully opened her bedchamber door—the last thing she wanted was to reawaken her aunt—and crept down the hall to Tristan's room.

Dawn was fast approaching, streaking pink and blue light through her brother's windows.

Standing in the doorway, she regarded his prone form. Was he asleep?

"What do you want, Rosie?"

She nearly jumped a foot. "Are you asleep?"

"Ah, yes. I'm supremely talented and can hold coherent conversations whilst I'm dreaming." He sighed. "Come on, what do you think?"

"Do not most people, after a night of imbibing heavily, fall into a deep slumber?"

"I suppose most do." He hiccupped. "However, I am, apparently, not most."

Rosalind could tell by the tone in his voice that

her brother was still quite inebriated. Cranky clearly, but inebriated. Good, then he would answer her questions without any filtering. And there was also a good chance he wouldn't even remember talking to her later on today after he had slept.

"Did, ah, Nicholas join you in your 'celebration' this evening?" She'd already asked the question, but she figured it couldn't hurt to do so again. Maybe she'd get a different answer.

"No," he answered impatiently.

She swallowed hard. "Then how did you come about him?"

"Where did you think, Rosie?" Tristan mumbled, sounding exhausted. "He was guarding the front door."

Chapter 9

The following afternoon Rosalind swept inside the gold-and-cream dining room and found Tristan seated at the head of the table, his forehead in his hand. A large glass filled with a thick red liquid sat before him, and a stick of celery sat on a linen napkin to his left.

"That cannot possibly taste good," she said, breaking the silence of the room.

"Rosalind," Tristan replied a bit desperately, "must you shout?"

"Sorry." She pressed her lips together as she took the chair to his left.

He waved away her apology with a flick of his fingers.

"I will not ask how you're feeling, as it is obvious."

"I would nod," he said quietly, "but then my head might roll off my neck."

"I see. Can't have that." She twisted her hands in her lap.

Part of her wanted to just come right out and ask Tristan if Nicholas was her guardian. She needed to know whether or not Tristan's drunken admission was indeed the truth. However, part of her wanted to pretend that the mounting evidence didn't exist.

Certainly, it was odd to see him in London, but he had inherited a lofty title. He was at least thirty and unmarried. It made perfect sense that he should come to Town for the season and look for a wife.

And he had come to call yesterday afternoon to speak with Tristan—not to scare off her gentlemen callers, although he had forced his way into the morning room and made himself quite comfortable by squeezing next to her on the settee. But then again, if he was her guardian, wouldn't he have stayed until they'd left? But wait . . . hadn't he? Or had it been coincidence that his meeting with Tristan had ended soon after her callers had left?

And surely it was pure happenstance that he had heard Rothbury slurring Shakespeare at her window, although Nicholas's behavior did border on protective, didn't it?

Lord, she was confused. She did know one

thing for certain: if Nicholas was her guardian, she would find out today. All she had to do was change her plans.

"Are you still going to Angelo's to fence?"

"No," Tristan groaned. "I'm going to crawl back to bed, actually."

"That doesn't sound like the Tristan I know." Indeed, it did not. He was physically active almost to a fault.

"Yes, but I was not myself last night," he murmured before bringing the glass to his lips with a grimace. "I suppose you weren't either—being yourself, that is."

Her brow quirked. "Whatever do you mean?"

"Standing there, making calf-eyes at Nicholas." He took another sip and shuddered.

"I didn't make eyes at him!"

He closed his eyes briefly. "Rosie, the shouting..."

"So sorry," she murmured quietly.

"If it wasn't for my presence, I think you would have thrown yourself at him ... or kissed him, or something else foolishly dramatic ..." His mumbled words died away as he brought the glass back to his lips.

"Don't be absurd."

He raised a dubious brow. "Are you going to sit

there and tell me that you don't notice it? You, the little cupid, detecting attraction between man and woman before the poor souls even know for themselves?" He shrugged, nearly sending the slushy brew over the rim. "Perhaps that's it. You can see it in others, but not for yourself."

She took a deep breath, suddenly feeling befuddled. "What are you saying?"

"I haven't a bloody clue." He stared straight ahead, quite like he had fallen asleep with his eyes open.

It was definitely time to put her plan in motion. Tristan looked ready to be sick at the table or slump face first onto it. Delicately, she cleared her throat. "I've made a change of plans for later today," she announced.

"Hmm?"

"I've decided *not* to attend the Fairfax musicale this afternoon."

He turned to look at her with a serious expression. "You're not?"

She shook her head.

"Why? Don't you like the Fairfaxes?"

"I do. I simply decided that I wanted to attend the dowager Lady Beecham's annual garden tea instead."

He mumbled something that sounded quite like "The silliest chits in England can be found there," but then he cleared his throat and said, "you do know what her little parties are known for, don't you?"

Indeed, the dowager's gatherings were infamous among the younger set as a wonderful spot to mingle with friends and potential beaus without the pressure of dance cards and marriage-minded mamas. Plus, her gardens were extensive and had many hidden nooks to explore . . . and get lost in if one should desire.

Rosalind lifted a shoulder. "Lots of young women attend."

Tristan set down his glass. "She has the tiniest chairs in existence, Rosie. I daresay, she eyes everyone's bottom size before issuing an invitation."

Rosalind grinned despite her mood. "Stop. She does not."

He nodded knowingly, then grimaced, as the action must have pained his head.

"The dowager offers an open invitation. Guests come and go all day." She almost laughed to think of Nicholas at such an event.

"Well, go if you must, but I should think you'd enjoy yourself infinitely more at the musicale."

"That might be so, little brother," she said with a sigh.

Indeed, but if she was right about Nicholas, her brother would certainly inform him of her change of plans as soon as possible, and of course, her guardian would act accordingly.

And once she saw him at the dowager's, she'd know the truth once and for all.

Nicholas was willing to wager that surely there was a special place in heaven for those individuals who, when they had walked the earth, endured varying degrees of torture. Certainly heaven would offer some sort of solace for those souls who had suffered the unfortunate consequence of having to listen to an asinine argument between seven siblings.

All of them female. All of them flighty, pretentious, and loud. Each one sillier than the next. And all of them seated on chairs made for bunny bottoms, not human bottoms. Somehow that facet made having to endure their incessant prattling almost completely unbearable.

"Do you like the cobalt? I like the cobalt."

"Hmm. Cobalt. I shouldn't liken *that* to cobalt."

"What then?" another voice yelled.

"Indigo."

"Indigo?" This said with such vehement distaste that one would think someone had just disclosed she was going to elope to Gretna Green with Napoleon himself instead of simply describing the color of a new gown.

"No, no. Indigo is too dark."

Nicholas blinked a couple of times and gulped down his tepid tea in a single swallow. What was it about the color blue that confused these people?

"It's cerulean. I had a riding habit made up last fall for a party. It was the same color. Our modiste called it so."

"It can't be! Cerulean makes you look sallow. And since we have the same coloring—"

"Me? Sallow? Fine time to bring this to my attention now! You could have told me this before I wore it to the Montagues' soiree, walking around with pride, unknowingly looking like I had the plague."

"You have it all wrong, it's azure."

"Azure? Heavens, no. It's more like—"

"Blue!" Nicholas bellowed from his perch on the chair. And then with his temper in control, he placed his teacup on the ornate garden table

191

between them and calmly added, "The bloody dress is blue."

The walking plague harrumphed.

The other ladies stared at him mutely for a moment, then ducked their heads together in order to peruse the pages of their fashion page once again.

"Lord Winterbourne," the dowager Lady Beecham suddenly exclaimed in her singsong voice, "I cannot tell you what an honor it is to have you as a guest. It is my hope that more bachelors follow your lead. I do so love to see young people mingling about my gardens. Why, last year, a group of men played a game of rounders on the lawn. We had such fun watching them play."

The dowager was a genuinely kind lady, Nicholas conceded. Round and short, her face seemed to hold a perpetual smile, her laughter always at the ready for the slightest quip made by her guests. She seemed to want everyone to enjoy themselves and would feel deeply hurt should that not be the case.

"Would you like another cucumber sandwich?" she asked.

Nicholas eyed the tiny morsels. In truth, he could probably eat two hundred of them before feeling remotely appeased. "Thank you," he said, shaking his head.

"I've heard that Lady Rosalind Devine is coming today. She sent word earlier this afternoon. You're acquainted with her family, yes?"

He nodded and pasted a smile on his face that he hoped appeared sincere.

Aye, he had a hunch the sharp lassie had an idea that he was her guardian. Why else would she change her plans so abruptly after asking him pointedly if he would be attending the musicale?

Tristan had sent a note advising him of his sister's new intentions. Nicholas knew he was walking into a trap by her design. No doubt his presence last night had aroused her suspicions.

Christ, he was an arse. He should have left Tristan on the doorstep and let their butler or a footman find him in the morning. He might not be in this situation then.

And yet, he knew she'd find out sooner rather than later. Honestly, he didn't know how the hell Gabriel thought this would work.

She knew. Oh, dear Lord, she knew, and now she would make him pay. He didn't know how, and that's what he feared the most.

He shook his head. What a coward. Afraid of a wee lassie.

He forced a smile at his hostess. "I thank you for your hospitality, my lady," he replied. "And your gardens are lovely, indeed."

She nodded, her face brightening even more.

"And if you'll excuse me," he said, extracting himself from the torturously small chair, "I should like to take a closer look."

Actually, what he would like to do was to go back in time and tell Gabriel there wasn't a chance in hell he'd watch his sister for him. But that wasn't going to happen.

The Beecham gardens were split into thirds. On the left was an intricate maze comprised of towering yew hedges clipped to depict the crenelated walls of a castle fortress. Next to that crouched an expansive walled garden where pink climbing roses scrambled randomly over the brick and an iron gate marked the entrance. And to the right sprawled a bit of forest, only part of its neatly raked, winding path visible from his position.

Straightening his beaver topper, he headed for the path. It was the best option he had to ensure that no one would be able to hear an indignant Lady Rosalind shouting at him. But as he strode further into the woods, he couldn't help but realize the absurdity of what he was truly doing—hiding.

"How dare he," Rosalind said rather wearily.

"How indeed," Lucy agreed from her perch on the tiny chair opposite Rosalind.

"He tricked me."

Lucy raised a finger. "Not precisely. He misled you. Duped you. Withheld infor—"

"All right," Rosalind muttered testily, then mumbled a quick apology for her tone.

Having arrived moments ago, the two friends were now seated at a table separate from the others.

The dowager viscountess Lady Beecham had given them a warm welcome and then pointedly informed Rosalind that Lord Winterbourne was somewhere on the grounds and seemed quite eager for her arrival.

"I just bet he is," she had grumbled in response.

Rosalind squinted into the sunlight as she scanned the grounds for some sign of Nicholas.

"Can you believe this, Lucy? I'm so embarrassed I didn't figure it out right away." She shook her head derisively. "Stupid girl."

Lucy nodded in support, then plopped a square of plum cake in her mouth.

Rosalind leveled a stare at her friend. "You don't have to be so agreeable."

"Oh! So sorry." Lucy cleared her throat. "You're not stupid. You were just distracted."

"Indeed, I was."

Rosalind had, at first, hesitated to apprise Lucy of this personal matter, but the truth was, Rosalind needed to confide in *someone*. Her mother was gone, Aunt Eugenia was . . . well, Aunt Eugenia, and Madelyn was in Wales, or Italy, or who knew. Truthfully, she had forgotten at present. However, Rosalind hadn't told Lucy the entire story—she'd withheld that she was in love with Nicholas.

Besides, Lucy was a good sport and quite adept about keeping secrets. Well, most secrets. All right, Rosalind had threatened to tell Neville Nibbons that Lucy was madly in love with him if she happened to utter so much as a peep.

Neville Nibbons had long adored Lucy. Lucy thought Neville smelled of old cheese and had wooden teeth; hence, Rosalind's secret was safe.

Rosalind cast a brief, narrow-eyed glare over her shoulder to where a thin path snaked through a patch of forest. Oh, she couldn't see the infernal Scot, but she knew he was there. She could feel it right down to where her toes wriggled in her fine English-crafted leather half boots.

Turning her head, Rosalind took a deep, calming breath. "If it were not for the fact that I am a lady, I would not hesitate telling him to—"

"Take a trip to Hades?" Lucy offered with a wobbling half smile.

"No, no. That is not the thing at all." Rosalind tapped her fingertip to her bottom lip, searching for the perfect phrase that would describe how she was feeling.

Now that she knew he was here—and not at the Fairfax musicale—she knew he was her assigned guardian. How could she not have realized sooner?

Lucy cleared her throat delicately. "I think you should cease blaming yourself for not suspecting. After all, you asked your brother straightaway and he said no. I daresay you should be cross with him for lying to you."

But Gabriel hadn't lied. Again and again Rosalind had gone over their conversation in his study. When she had asked him, his response had been that Nicholas was here on business. That's it. He'd never said no.

She should have caught that. She should have realized that the reason he was paying her so much attention was that he was guarding her.

"He's coming this way," Lucy said with a nod in the direction of the woods.

"Ah. Hiding, is he?" Rosalind stood abruptly, nearly disrupting the table. "Lucy," she called without looking at her.

Her friend shot up as well, and together, arm in arm, they approached him.

His eyes centered on Rosalind, Nicholas tipped his hat and bowed his head in greeting but didn't say a word. She was quite peeved to discern that he did not look sheepish, or regretful, or guilty. He looked . . . like he wanted to throttle her right here in front of everyone.

Rosalind and Lucy dipped into shallow curtsies.

"How interesting to find you here," Rosalind murmured saucily.

He said nothing and gave her a barely perceptible nod.

"There you are, my lordship," Lady Beecham exclaimed, coming to stand next to their little group. "Did you enjoy your walk, sir?"

"Indeed," he nodded, bestowing a devastatingly

charming grin on the widow, the ring of silver in his eyes sparkling in the sunlight.

"Lady Rosalind and Miss Meriwether have only just arrived." She turned to give Rosalind's arm an affectionate squeeze. "And now that you're all together I should like to make a happy announcement." The last she said loudly and with a turn to address all of her guests.

"My son, Lord Beecham, has surprised us all yesterday morning and informed us that he has asked Miss Honeywell for her hand in marriage," the dowager beamed with barely concealed joy. "And the lady has accepted."

Gasps of delight and murmurs of congratulations trickled through the crowd.

"And I invite all of you to a small impromptu engagement ball later this evening. It'll be most fun! I daresay my staff is always at the ready to throw a party, are they not?"

After this she laughed uproariously, which prompted a few guests to laugh as well, which, in turn, prompted Rosalind to have the peculiar feeling she'd missed a joke of some sort. In truth, she had never attended one of the dowager's parties, but her curiosity was indeed piqued.

Smiling, the dowager turned back to look at Nicholas, and then said candidly, "I've to thank Lady Rosalind here for this outcome. I didn't think my son would ever remarry. Do you know she introduced them?"

Nicholas shook his head, pressing his lips together tightly in some semblance of a smile.

"She introduced them and encouraged them when she could, inviting them to join her and Lucy for walks and ices and such."

Someone beckoned the dowager and, still smiling, she excused herself from their company, giving Rosalind a wink.

Hmmph. And Nicholas thought her matchmaking was nothing but fruitless meddling that would do nothing but get her in trouble.

She turned to him with a smug smile, then remembered that he had tricked her. Well, not exactly tricked. He had misled her.

Because the truth was, she was hurt. If it wasn't for the fact that her brother had asked him to watch over her, he'd still be in Yorkshire, ignoring her, while she spent yet another season praying that she would return home in the fall to discover Nicholas hadn't married someone else.

She was tired of this game. If he had feelings

for her, why wouldn't he come out with them? She wasn't a vain creature. But she did realize he was at least attracted to her.

Was that it? Did he feel guilty for desiring his best friend's sister? But if he felt guilty, then that would imply that those were the *only* feelings he had for her.

That wasn't enough. She wanted his heart, too.

She was just going to have to come right out and ask him.

She turned her back to him and, without looking behind her, trudged to the iron gate of the rose garden, her strides angry and quick.

And he followed, albeit from a distance, just like she knew he would.

She flung a glare over her shoulder and noticed Lucy running up to catch her.

"Wait," Lucy breathed. "Lady Beecham might have slightly lax rules here, but you cannot go off with Lord Winterbourne alone. At least not so obviously."

Rosalind only huffed in response. She unhooked the latch and the gate opened with a groan.

Together they stepped inside the small garden. Green vines heavy with pale pink roses crawled over the brick walls, swelling near the top. A tall, silver-leafed pear tree punctuated the center of the garden, and several paths radiated from that focal point, rather like the rays of the sun.

Reaching the tree, Rosalind nodded to Lucy, who wandered down the path directly opposite the graveled path that Rosalind took. It would be a respectable distance from Lucy, one that would still provide privacy for her conversation with Nicholas.

Rosalind ambled toward the end of the path, which was marked by a stone bench, roses curling along its legs. With serenity she did not feel, Rosalind sank down slowly, adjusting the cream-colored skirts of her frock. She turned her head away from the sight of Nicholas's slow approach, his hands tucked behind his back.

When he came to a stop before her, she finally looked up at him.

It was a mistake. She ought to have continued to avert her gaze.

He was so achingly handsome. Broad shoulders, encased in an expertly fitted dark gray coat, effectively blocked out the sun. His cravat, for once, was straight, tied in a cascade of folds; the offending green-tipped pin from the evening before nestled inside.

His eyes, without the glare from the sun, were dark gray today, and there was a softness to them as well.

And presently, while he looked down at her quite like she was the executioner and he the brave offender awaiting his fate, she was almost inclined to forgive him. Gabriel could be heavy-handed, but her pride wouldn't let Nicholas off so easily.

Or her heart. It was what had prohibited her from falling back asleep this morning.

She had tossed and turned, finally finding comfort in the odd position of hanging half off her bed, her arms stretched downward to pull and tug at the threads of her carpet. Over and over, she'd rehearsed what she would say to him, but now that the time had come, a hollow ache settled in her chest and the cool indignation she had nurtured now smarted with an unexpected sting of wretchedness.

She took a deep breath, composing herself. "You are the man my brother hired," she stated simply.

"Aye," he said, his face an unreadable mask.

Her heart gave a little triumphant twist to hear it said aloud. She swallowed several times before she trusted herself to speak. "Why?"

"He trusts me. He needed my help. I reckon he

had no choice other than to force you to stay in the country. You and I both know he wouldn't do that."

"How much?"

His brow quirked.

"How much did he pay you?" she repeated a bit more forcefully. It was a guess. In truth, she had no idea if her brother compensated him or not.

At first he said nothing, and then, having come to some decision within his own mind, he muttered, "A crate of his finest Scotch whisky."

There, he said it. Now let her hate him. It was better this way. Easier. For Nicholas didn't think he could resist the need to kiss her, touch her, hell, just to be near her, much longer. Since coming to London, every time he thought of her, which was all the time, he could feel himself falling deeper.

When Gabriel had first introduced them when Rosalind was just seventeen, Nicholas had been immediately aware of a natural affinity between them. Not only had he been attracted to her but it had almost felt like he'd known her soul. It had frightened him.

Up until that point in his life, he had evaded love for fear of experiencing the pain his father had endured. It was the easiest task Nicholas had ever upheld, but then he'd never met a woman who threatened to topple it. Until Rosalind.

So he tried to dismiss her in his own mind. He told himself she was just a spoiled lass who would grow fickle and vain—those thoughts made him feel safe from her. But he was a fool. She was none of those things.

She was surprisingly giving, compassionate, loyal, humble about her appearance, and incredibly passionate. She was also the owner of his heart, he feared, but nothing would come of it. He wasn't going to let it. If he had to, he would force things to go his way.

Still, it pained him to see the hurt in her gaze. A gaze that had grown suspiciously teary. Christ, don't let her cry.

He hadn't meant for any of this to happen. From the look on her face, he now realized that in the guarding of his own heart, he just might be hurting hers.

She blinked several times, her head shaking slightly in apparent disbelief. "A-A case of whisky?"

He nodded. This would make her angry, possibly despise him, and he would, once again, evade her power over him.

Outraged vehemence replaced the hurt in her eyes. "I . . . am . . . worth . . . a case of whisky?" Her jaw worked, and then she blurted, "Whisky!?"

He closed his eyes on a slow blink.

"How lucky for the both of you to reach such an agreeable compensation." She shot up, the brim of her bonnet skimming his chin.

He did not take a step back and neither did she.

Her chin hardened and all he wanted to do was kiss it. Toss off her bonnet and bury his fists in her hair. He'd kiss her until she begged him to take her right here on the bench. He'd sit her down and duck under her skirts. He'd start at her ankles and bite and lick his way up to her inner thighs.

Although it was impossible for her to see his thoughts, something in his gaze sparked her to poke the middle of his chest with her finger and declare, "I am not afraid of you."

"I don't want you to be."

"I won't have you following me around."

"You don't have a choice," he said darkly.

"I don't need you," she said quietly, her throat convulsing. "I don't need any man."

"Well, then, that makes my job a hell of a lot easier."

"I'm fine on my own."

"The hell you are," he replied harshly.

She took a deep breath and the lapels of his coat brushed her bodice. He ignored it by grinding his teeth. What the hell was he doing? He couldn't seem to control his thoughts. She was upset, more deeply upset than he had anticipated. He had thought she'd screech at him for misleading her, tell him to bugger off, but it seemed something deep and painful had been brought to the surface.

"I'm fine on my own," she repeated. "I always have been. And it will always be as such."

Her voice seemed to break on that last sentence, and it undid him. He reached up to touch her cheek with the back of his gloved fingers.

She swatted his hand away. "Men. You are all the same." Her voice sounded husky to him now. "At least as you all pertain to me. And here I thought—y-you made me believe, if only for a moment last night, before you left, I had thought something was . . ."

"Rosalind . . ."

"Is there anything between us, Nicholas? Do you feel something for me?"

He remained silent.

"Nothing at all?"

He took a step back but held her indignant gaze. Silence stretched before them, the only sound the drone of a buzzing bee.

"For all my good intentions . . . how easily I see sincerity in the eyes of others . . ." Her voice trailed away and she shook her head.

Footsteps approached, softly crunching in gravel.

"Rosalind," Lucy whispered gently from behind Nicholas. "Rosalind, come away. Let us return to Lady Beecham."

Rosalind leveled a hard stare at Nicholas. "Stay away from me."

"I cannot."

"Just stay away," she warned in a beseeching tone that confused him.

"I will not."

She raised a haughty brow. "Will another case of whisky change your mind?" she asked, her tone mocking.

"I have enough whisky."

She stepped around him, her shoulders stiff, her posture ramrod straight. "Then I shall shake free of you," she vowed.

"Then I shall hunt you down."

"I'll run," she challenged with a lift of her chin.

"And I'll catch you."

"You'll regret that you agreed to do this, Nicholas."

"I already do, lass. I already do."

Chapter 10

The Beecham Engagement Soiree

"Do you know what he needs?"

"Certainly not whisky," Rosalind murmured, inspecting her glass of punch as discreetly as she possibly could. "What do you suppose is in here, Lucy? I thought it was simply punch, but there's a distinctive flavor that I can't quite identify." She licked the vibrant flavor from her lips.

"He needs a distraction," Lucy continued unabated.

Rosalind took another small sip, savoring the rich flavor before swallowing. The slow burn down her throat made her shiver. "It's rather like a dessert wine, but more pungent." She thrust the glass under Lucy's nose. "Here. Taste it."

Lucy shook her head, never taking her eyes off the guests ambling about the Beechams' gardens. Considering the spontaneity of the celebration, Rosalind was rather surprised to see such a crush.

The gardens were quite pretty by day but utterly dazzling in the evening. Gone were the tiny-bottom chairs and elegant teacups perched on delicate-looking tables. They had all been cleared away from the section of paved courtyard to make room for dancing.

A string quartet played from the terrace above, the honeyed music flowing gently throughout the gardens, where randomly spaced glass lanterns chased away the darkness.

And somewhere lurking in the shadows was her guardian, Rosalind mused with a rather unladylike scowl. What a little fool she was to believe that he harbored some sort of *feeling* for her.

Taking another inquisitive sniff of her glass of punch, Rosalind gulped the rest of it down.

"Just how many of those have you had?" Lucy asked, eyeing her curiously.

"Only this one," Rosalind answered. "I think it might be potent stuff. Look at that gentleman over there." She gestured with a nod of her head to a man standing to their far left. "I don't believe he realizes that the woman he was talking to has walked off. He has been conversing with that armless statue for at least ten minutes now."

Lucy laughed. "I do believe you're right."

Rosalind giggled along with her friend despite her sour mood, which was certainly from the effects of the suspicious punch she had been drinking.

"Now tell me," Rosalind began, clutching her empty glass on her lap, "what were you saying about what he needs?"

Lucy sat forward, her eyes alight with enthusiasm. "If you want to rid yourself of him you need to find him a distraction."

"Of what sort?"

"The female variety." Lucy waggled her brows. "With his focus redirected, he just might give up on his duty."

Rosalind blinked and gave her head a slight shake. She didn't want to do that, but Lucy didn't know that Rosalind loved this man.

"It really is a perfect idea," Lucy pressed. "Now, go find out what sort of woman he fancies."

"Right," Rosalind agreed with false enthusiasm. She stood and went to take a step, but her legs seemed to have grown heavier.

"What's wrong with you?"

"I think all that punch went to my head," she guessed, staring down into her empty glass. "Or my legs."

"I think you should stay away from that punch," Lucy said, plucking the glass from Rosalind's loose grip.

Rosalind nodded, feeling quite strange. Managing to smother it somehow, she smiled instead and scanned the gathering for Nicholas.

All swarthy good looks, he stood near the entrance to the maze, his scowl apparently keeping all the young ladies at bay.

Straightening her spine, she made no pretense to avoid him and headed straight for him. Despite the effects of the heady punch, she was determined to maintain cool poise.

Unfortunately, he got taller the closer she got to him, and all that determination she had felt began to falter. The thought occurred to her that she should turn back around and hurry back to Lucy, but she quickly dismissed the notion.

She stopped about two feet in front of him, her dark plum skirts swishing over his polished boots.

His gaze flicked downward before making a slow, measured ascent.

She shivered, ignored it, then cleared her throat delicately. "How strange it is to find you here, my lord."

His eyes appeared dark gray in the night, and they bore down on her with caged curiosity. "Not so strange, as we both know."

"Of course," she said. "The Beechams' fêtes always seem to draw such a young crowd. The perfect spot to search for potential wives, don't you agree, my lord?"

"I suppose."

She had no intention of finding him a "distraction," as Lucy had put it, but Rosalind was curious to know if Nicholas *was* looking for a bride. He had a new title. Marrying and producing heirs to secure the line was perfectly logical.

But the opportunity to engage in a conversation with him on the matter was lost when, behind her, a group of young men with whom she was mildly acquainted approached and soon made a semicircle around her.

"Lord Bradley," she said in greeting.

"My lady, you look lovely this evening."

"She looks lovely every evening," Lord Bentley drawled.

"Did you know," Lord Hamel chimed in, "there is to be another waltz this evening?"

"How scandalous," she remarked, to which all the men laughed in an exaggerated fashion.

"She already promised the next set to me," Lord Noble intoned.

Had she? She couldn't quite remember that he had asked her.

And then they all began speaking to her at once—or so it seemed. Had Rosalind a clearer mind she would have made sense of it all, but as it was, she couldn't separate their voices.

So she smiled and nodded, praying the punch would wear off already.

One of the men—the redheaded Lord Stokes—stepped in close to Rosalind.

"Lord Stokes," she called. "Have you seen Miss Meriwether this evening?"

He shook his head, then ducked close to her ear. Whatever he was whispering was lost on her, however, because Nicholas grabbed her by the elbow and pulled her away.

He didn't stop walking until they stood in a nook made by a half-circle of tall hedges.

Rosalind looked down at Nicholas's hand at her arm. "What was that all about?"

"They were becoming unruly."

"Indeed they were not."

"I thought you didn't like their attention."

"I don't. I like *your* attention, but you seem content to stand separate from me like some stone-faced sentry when we could be dancing." Good Lord, had she said that aloud?

A pair of young debutantes caught Rosalind's attention as they angled past the hedges, their eyes centered on Nicholas.

Rosalind couldn't help but wonder if he would have returned their smiles if it hadn't been for his obligation to watch out for her. Perhaps he would have followed them down the garden path. Oh, she despised this insecurity he evoked in her!

She turned back to him. "Do you know what Miss Meriwether thinks you need?"

"I haven't the foggiest."

Rosalind took a step closer to him. "A distraction."

A slow smile curved his lips. "Allow me to assure you, my lady, you are all the distraction I will ever need."

She was absurdly pleased at his words and smiled up at him.

Silver light winked in his eyes.

"Pardon?" a voice interrupted from behind her.

She turned to see Lord Noble, whose intentions reputedly never were, standing behind her.

"My lady, I believe the set you have promised me has begun," he said smoothly.

"It is to be a waltz."

"Indeed," Noble agreed.

She looked back at Nicholas. *Say it. Say "You must be mistaken, the lass is dancing with me." Say something.*

But he said nothing. His expression darkening, he gave her a slight shake of his head.

He wanted her to refuse. Quite honestly, she didn't harbor a pressing need to dance, but Nicholas's stubbornness, coupled with his silent order for her not to do it, sparked her temper.

She certainly danced with other men before she knew he was her guardian. Why should she stop now? Lord Noble might be a rake, but they were surrounded by throngs of people. She wasn't alone and it was just a dance.

"If you'll excuse me," she murmured, placing her hand on Lord Noble's arm.

She allowed him to walk her to the dancing area, but the crowd thickened the closer they got, slowing their progress.

"I've a better way." Reaching down, Noble grasped her hand and led her quickly through the throng. It wasn't until they broke free that Rosalind realized he had steered her directly toward the bit of forest. There was but one small lamp near the opening of the woods, the darkness apparently keeping the other guests at bay.

Foolish girl! To think she could trust a snake not to lead her into the brush.

She tried to pull her hand free from his grasp, but he held fast. "Stop it, your lordship, I implore you."

He ignored her request. She looked about, but none of the other guests seemed to be paying them any attention. It was too dark.

"Wait," she ordered again. "Stop." She dug her heels into the grass, but it did not impede him.

Once inside the woods, Rosalind jerked to a halt. Enveloped in near darkness, she twisted her hand free, only to find herself yanked hard against Noble. He bent his head, descending toward her lips.

She made a fist but never got to use it.

A second later, Noble simply disappeared.

Rosalind blinked, trying to get her eyes to focus in the darkness. Soon, she made out Lord Noble staggering on the path, his face pulled into a sneer. He made a fist, and then made the mistake of looking at it before taking aim.

Nicholas planted a powerful blow to the underside of Noble's jaw, sending the lanky man head over heels to land in a bush.

All tall indignation, Nicholas stood before her, the only movement was the angry rise and fall of his chest. Slowly, his shadowed gaze turned on her. Rosalind nearly shrank back.

"What spurred you to the depths of idiocy, my *lady*? The spiced rum in Beecham's punch?" A muscle twitched in his cheek. "Don't you *ever* do something so foolish as that again."

"All I did was accept a dance," she muttered in her defense. "It wasn't anything I've never done before."

Nicholas grabbed her arm and hauled her back down the path. His steps were purposeful, his hold gentle but firm. "Perhaps, but that was before there was a wager made by a bunch of wealthy, bored fools with entirely too much free time."

They seamlessly threaded back into the light with the other guests. The waltz had just begun, and many crowded near to watch the couples dancing.

"Where's your aunt?" he asked, letting go of her arm.

"She's in the house, playing whist with some of her acquaintances."

"Good," he said, taking up her arm again. "Then she can't protest should I occupy you for every dance at this ball."

"I did not agree . . . ," she stuttered.

But there was no time to talk. Her breath was nearly knocked out of her as Nicholas swept her into his arms and onto the dance floor. His rhythm was flawless, his hold shockingly possessive with a heavy hand low and hot on her waist.

What a good teacher she was.

Hardening her chin, she stomped on his foot. Hard.

"So sorry," she said demurely.

In answer, he took the next turn with a dizzying spin, which forced Rosalind to clutch at his arms for support.

Once they fell back into pace with the other dancers, he raised a suggestive brow. A challenge.

She made to stomp on his foot again, but he swirled her into a new direction, deflecting the blow.

Settling back into the undulating rhythm, he glared down at her while she matched his stare with a narrow-eyed frown of her own.

Atop the terrace, the dowager Lady Beecham stood next to Lucy Meriwether as they both watched the same couple with avid interest.

"My word," Lady Beecham exclaimed, waving her fan rapidly. "I don't believe I've ever seen the waltz performed so . . . so vigorously."

"Indeed," Lucy murmured. "They look like they want to murder each other."

Lady Beecham sighed, long and sad. "And here I had hoped they liked each other. Such a handsome couple. Shall I separate them?"

The strains of the waltz came to a flourishing finish—almost as if they played for Nicholas and Rosalind alone.

Lucy shook her head. "I don't think there will be a need."

Taking a step back from one another, Nicholas gave the customary bow, but Rosalind immediately presented him with her back and stalked off. She ascended the terrace steps at a near run.

Flushed and out of breath, she offered Lady Beecham a small smile. "Lady Beecham, it has been a pleasure to be a guest not once but twice in one day."

"You're always welcome, dear."

"Thank you. I trust my aunt is yet playing whist in the house?"

"Ah, yes, I do believe you are correct. Although I did hear her mention that she hoped you were ready to depart soon."

Rosalind smiled and gave her thanks again.

Lucy waited until the dowager had descended the steps before pulling Rosalind close.

"What were you doing?" she asked in a throaty whisper. "You were supposed to inquire what sort of woman he favors. You weren't supposed to dance with him."

"I wasn't given much of a choice," Rosalind answered, approaching the balustrade. "He's incredibly charming and I wasn't able to resist him."

"Truly?" Lucy asked, sounding surprised.

"No." Crossing her arms over her chest, Rosalind leaned a hip against the stone railing.

Nicholas stood slightly separated from the guests, his arms behind his back, his eyes trained at some point above her head.

223

Lucy gave Rosalind's skirt a twitch. "What are you going to do about him?"

"Shake him free." Rosalind's heart lurched as his eyes unerringly met hers. Her gaze narrowed. He winked.

"And how do you suppose you're going to do that?"

"I'm not sure," she answered, nodding. "But it'll be awful."

Chapter 11

"How could anyone spend three and a half hours picking out gloves?" Nicholas asked from atop a beautiful, friendly Friesian he'd bought yesterday at Tattersalls. His horse was still jittery at the sounds of the city and would only venture out to the stable yard and no further. And he couldn't very well track Rosalind around the city on foot.

He needed speed, agility, and a dram or three of whisky.

Closing his eyes on a slow blink, Nicholas shook his head. He shouldn't have told her that her brother had offered him a crate of his finest whisky in exchange for keeping an eye on her. It was cruel, yes, but it was also a lie.

He had said it because . . . hell, he didn't know exactly why he'd said it. All he knew was that while she'd looked up at him, he'd grasped at the opportunity to make her despise him.

The London season was short; the Devines were scheduled to depart for Yorkshire in three months' time. Surely he could manage this for a wee bit longer, and then his life could go back to normal.

His eyes reaffixed on the door to the shop she was currently in, presumably to purchase a new pair of riding gloves.

"Is one even allowed to spend that much time in one store? She couldn't possibly need more than twenty minutes to pick out a pair."

Standing next to the Friesian, Tristan nodded slowly, grimacing. "She's trying to bore you to death, my friend."

"*Bore* me?" He shook his head. "Your sister *astounds* me."

"Yes, she is quite astounding," Tristan agreed. "She also can be quite the pain in the arse."

Nicholas grunted in response. He hadn't expected Rosalind to take this approach. He'd foolishly thought she'd flounce across the city visiting legions of her friends in a maddeningly frantic pace in order to lose him.

Or perhaps she might be so daring as to take ride after ride in a crowded Hyde Park with any number of gentlemen just to make following her around nearly impossible.

But this—this was shopping.

This was *torture*.

At that moment, he saw her pass the window. His chest swelled with hope. Was she finally taking her leave? She must have acquired fifty pairs of gloves by now. He smiled, anticipating a nice cup of tea with a splash of whisky.

And then she disappeared deeper into the shop.

His smile fell. All right, maybe a nice cup of whisky with a splash of tea would be better.

He threw a glance at the family carriage waiting down the lane in front of a milliner's shop. They sold ribbons and bonnets and other such fripperies—Rosalind and Miss Meriwether had spent two hours in there.

Their driver was now fast asleep, his hat covering his face. Alice, her maid, stood in the shade chatting animatedly with Miss Meriwether's maid.

"What are your intentions?" Tristan asked, with a nod of his head toward the shop his sister was in.

Nicholas's gaze shot down to him.

Arms crossed, Tristan rolled back on his heels, looking at him expectantly.

"What do mean by *intentions*?" Nicholas asked cautiously.

"Are you going to marry my sister, or what?" Tristan deadpanned.

Nicholas opened his mouth to speak, then balked.

Tristan laughed. "Rest easy. I couldn't resist. I meant for tonight."

"What are her plans for tonight? She was supposed to be attending the Hazeltons' ball. Has that changed?"

"Unfortunately."

"I wonder . . . does she ever just stay home, Tristan?"

"Hardly when she's in London. And now that she has you to make miserable, I don't suppose she'll ever stay home."

"Why does she do this?" Nicholas heard himself asking before he had the sense to stop. "What I mean to ask, lad, is why isn't your sister married by now? She's"—he ran a hand through his hair—"clever, intelligent, beautiful, and just as stubborn as I. Why does she not marry? She could have anyone she wants."

His questions were met with silence, and Nicholas looked away, instantly regretting uttering them. What must Tristan think? The lad was barely one and twenty and had probably never thought of his sister's marriageable prospects before.

He looked down to find Tristan staring at him quizzically. "What is it?"

Tristan shrugged, and his expression faded away. "I don't know," he said noncommittally. "Gabriel's always chasing would-be suitors away—and rightfully so. Most of them are politicians or have aspirations of being one. They want the connection to a powerful family. Rakes see nothing but her beauty, bounders see nothing but the fact that she's of noble blood, fortune hunters see nothing but her wealth."

Over the years, Gabriel had rarely spoken of Rosalind with Nicholas. But Nicholas remembered every single sliver of information about the lass that came his way. He knew things about her that she had no idea that he knew.

"Once your brother told me that he feared her falling in love with a man who did not return her affections equally," Nicholas said, hoping Tristan would expound on the subject.

Tristan shrugged. "Something to do with our parents, I imagine. They had no love match. I believe our father harbored not the slightest affection for Mother and had her sequestered at Wolverest for almost the entirety of her life."

Nicholas nodded, his smile grim. "I think Gabriel's concerns have passed down to her, though that was not his intent, I'm sure."

"Or perhaps it was," Tristan injected, then sighed. "Whatever the case, she's very guarded about setting her cap for anyone. In fact, I can't think of a single gentleman that she's even spoken of specifically." He leveled a stare at Nicholas. "Except, of course, for you."

"For me?" Nicholas asked, straightening in the saddle.

Tristan cocked his head to the side and squinted down the lane as a small group of ladies turned the corner, heading for their direction. "I wager Rosie's looking for her own love match and is having a deuced time of it, is all."

"Perhaps she's not looking hard enough," Nicholas injected.

"Perhaps," Tristan muttered distractedly, "she's decided to never marry. What do you think of that?"

"I suppose with her position she could remain unmarried and be perfectly happy."

The group of women from down the lane ambled past them now. Tristan's sharp eyes followed them. "Good day, ladies," he murmured, tipping his hat.

They answered with a mixture of giggles and "Good day to you, Lord Devine."

Nicholas watched with half a smile as Tristan followed their retreating forms for as long as he could before they slipped into a shop.

"*Lord Devine*?" Nicholas asked, chuckling. "I thought 'Lord Tristan' was your courtesy title."

"Hmm. I suppose. But they've been calling me Lord Devine ever since news of my broken engagement." He gave his head a little shake. "Anyway, you'll have a hell of a time tonight."

Nicholas's sigh was heavy and resigned. "All right. Tell me. Where is she going to be instead?"

"She *is* going to the Hazelton ball, but not until at least ten or eleven. However, first, she's going to the pleasure gardens of Vauxhall."

Ah, hell.

True, part of the gardens were lit with thousands of oil lamps, but there were yards upon yards of dark, intertwining secluded paths surrounded by forest. There would be plenty of opportunities for her to lose him.

And without a doubt, she was going to try and make him earn every ounce of the imaginary whisky.

His temples started to pound. "It's going to be a bloody nightmare."

"It's like a wonderful dream," Rosalind stated with a smile at her surroundings. "You must admit, Aunt, there isn't anything quite like Vauxhall."

Moonlit groves, mazes of secluded arbors, decorated supper boxes graced with rural paintings, each of them unique. Music and gaiety all around and only for a shilling. And because of this, Vauxhall drew an eclectic crowd. The person standing next to you could be a duchess or a strumpet, the Prince of Wales or the stable hand's son.

Forgoing their supper box, they sat at a private table around the orchestra, the area bathed in the glow of the remarkable lamps. Their small party consisted of Aunt Eugenia, Tristan, who was currently holding up a rather delicate piece of ham to the light with his fork, and herself.

She didn't know what he was doing and she told herself not to care. She was upset with Tristan still.

She sighed, silently reminding herself that there was something rather peaceful about dining outside under the lamps, even if the food was not quite as appetizing as one anticipated.

Closing her eyes briefly, she took a deep breath

of fresh evening air. A fleeting thundershower earlier had left a slight breeze behind, and she shivered suddenly. Perhaps she should have been more prudent in her choice of gown for this evening.

She wore a dress of dark green muslin, which looked black in the dark. The vest laced across her bosom in a crisscross fashion. A matching cottage mantle lined with cream-colored silk flowed from her shoulders. At least she had listened to Alice when the girl had suggested she cover her nearly bare shoulders.

"Are you going to eat that?" Tristan asked from beside her.

"I'm not talking to you," she mumbled for his ears only. Even so, she nudged her plate closer to him.

He stabbed her barely-there ham with his fork, joining it with his own, and then spread it on a slice of bread.

He proceeded to cram the entire thing in his mouth, then chewed laboriously and swallowed. When he was done, he smiled at her. "Sorry. I was famished."

She hadn't realized food-cramming was hereditary. "Didn't you eat at home?" she asked, even though she wasn't supposed to be speaking to him.

He shook his head, watching the crowd promenade past. "I was busy keeping Nicholas company while you drove him mad."

His words had her sitting forward in her chair. "I drove him mad?"

"Indeed." Tristan stretched out his legs and crossed his arms over his chest. "You ought to have seen his face when you came out of that last shop three hours after entering it without having bought a single item. I thought he'd charge straight for you on horseback and pluck you from the street."

"And what, do you suppose, he'd do with me then?"

"Throw you in the Thames."

"He was very mad, then?" She eased back, satisfied. "Good." At least he felt *something*.

"It was a waste of time, you know. He is determined to fulfill his duty."

"He should leave off."

"He won't. Why don't you just go on about your season and forget he's around?"

As if she could. "Is he here?" she asked.

"Of course."

She deliberated for a moment, then sprung up from her chair. "Well, then that settles it."

"Settles what, Rosalind?" Her aunt had asked the question.

"I should like to go for a walk."

Aunt Eugenia grumbled something under her breath but stood as well. "Tristan," she exclaimed. "Shall I trust you not to lose me in the crowd?"

Her brother mumbled something that sounded quite like, "If only we should be so lucky." But Rosalind couldn't be sure.

"Actually," he said with a look to the orchestra, "I was thinking of sitting here for a spell and listening to the music. If that's all right?"

Eugenia's eyes narrowed as she gazed toward the musicians before returning her eyes to her nephew. "Very well."

Tristan, really, was being polite. At one and twenty he needn't ask permission to stay behind.

Now a party of two, they stepped away from the orchestra and wove into the crowd on the Grand South Walk.

Rosalind spotted him instantly.

A gap in the crowd had opened as a small crowd of people who had been admiring a fantastic marble statue of Handel moved along.

Starkly handsome in all black, except his simply tied cravat, Nicholas's intense gaze bore into her, causing an involuntary shiver to race down her arms and back.

And then he looked past her, which wasn't terribly odd, for he tended to do that quite often, but this time it was different—different because his facial expression changed.

He looked as if he saw someone he recognized in the crowd.

She followed his gaze to a small group of women. Upon closer inspection, Rosalind deemed three of the four women were around Aunt Eugenia's age, but the last one looked to be slightly younger than Rosalind.

A tall blond, young and fresh-looking with her short, cropped curls. Rosalind could not deny the girl's beauty. Her eyes were drawn to the simple cut of her pink gown, the material slightly worn—as if she had very few dresses and wore this one often. In deep discussion with one of the older women in her party, she was oblivious to Nicholas's notice of her.

Rosalind wished *she* had been. She suddenly felt ill. Her cheeks flushed with heat, and perspiration formed between her breasts and at the back of her neck despite the slight chill in the air.

She didn't know who the woman was, but it was apparent that Nicholas did.

It was only a look of recognition, she told herself. It wasn't a lust-filled stare.

No matter, she still felt sick.

Lord, what was the matter with her? It was just some woman with a tatty gown.

She was being spiteful. The girl was lovely, tatty gown or not.

She dared a quick glance to where he last stood, thinking he'd still be staring at the young woman, but his gaze had now returned to Rosalind.

Once their gazes met, Rosalind looked quickly away, fearing he'd spy the unbidden jealousy there. Her breathing quickened and her head seemed to spin a bit. She clutched at Aunt Eugenia's arm.

"Are you all right, Rosalind?"

She nodded, looking to the ground as they shuffled onward.

"Dear me," her aunt replied, "I think the crowd grows thicker still."

Rosalind managed to shake her head slightly, her thoughts slow to come back around. She looked up. The crowd had quite suddenly seemed to swarm around them now.

A face stood out from the crowd up ahead. Lord Stokes. The sight of him wouldn't normally cause her to feel alarmed, but he had a look about him tonight—like his eyes sparked with alertness once her gaze connected to his.

Perhaps she was overreacting, but an unmistakable sense of foreboding nearly overtook her.

"Let us break free," she intoned, suddenly feeling panicked.

"Don't lose me," Eugenia murmured.

Together they burst heedlessly into the throng.

"Damn these congested walks," Nicholas muttered. "There must be thousands of people."

Tristan nodded stiffly. "There's to be an exhibition this evening."

"What the hell was she thinking, walking off with her aunt in this crowd?"

"It did surge suddenly."

To make matters worse, Nicholas had spotted Lord Stokes in the throng, watching Rosalind's progress.

Even he knew that the tree-lined alleys of Vauxhall were known for sending mothers into frenzies over their daughters having wandered off.

Aye, the lass had tested his patience earlier in the day, visiting shop after shop thinking she'd eventually wear him down and he'd give up. But he would not abandon his agreement to her brother, no matter how easily she edged closer to

his heart, no matter how strongly he wanted her
to be there.

"Where the devil did she go?" Tristan muttered,
having stayed behind purposely so that he could
assist Nicholas.

"I don't know," he nearly growled. "Do you still
see Stokes?"

"Lost him. What if she became separated from
our aunt?"

Nicholas gave a curt nod. "Listen. Circle around
and head up the Druid Walk. I'll forge ahead."

Tristan nodded.

"The crowd is thinning," Nicholas went on.
"There are no lamps up ahead to light the path that
winds through the forest of elms and sycamore."

And Nicholas knew only too well that there was
nothing more that an opportunistic cur needed
than the cover of a dark forest to pounce.

As Rosalind dashed around another tree,
breathless and lost, she admitted that she had
made a terrible mistake.

She should have remained at their table by the
orchestra.

The paths were crowded this evening, more so

than she had anticipated, and it wasn't long before she'd become separated from her aunt.

Lord Stokes, for all his tranquil demeanor, had followed her. Grasping her arms, he had yanked her into the woods, claiming it was a shortcut, only to clutch her tightly to his lanky frame and beg her to go with him to Gretna Green.

And to think she'd once thought he would be perfect for Lucy.

She had managed to wrest free and then run blindly through a thick wood, which had seemed to grow denser with each step. At first, she'd thought of nothing but getting away from him, as he'd been doggedly following her. However, she had lost him several minutes ago, and the sounds of the crowd had grown silent.

The moon was full and the night sky clear, but not much moonlight filtered through the canopy above.

All of a sudden, thunder boomed and shook the earth under her slippered feet. Rosalind's heart raced at the strange sound until she remembered that there had been a sea battle enactment built at the end of the Grand South Walk. Some sort of cannons were to be fired.

A breath of relief whooshed past her lips. With

her gloved hand skimming along the trunk of an elm tree, she altered her direction to the sound. She would find her way out soon enough. She only hoped she wouldn't run into Lord Stokes again.

After a minute, the canopy above her head broke up as the trees were spaced further apart here. Light blue moonlight bathed the forest before her in a latticework pattern. Thank the Lord for that. Up ahead, a nest of exposed tree roots and broken limbs littered the ground. If not for the light, she would have twisted her ankle for sure. Suddenly a tall shadow separated from a tree.

She jolted in fright.

"Nicholas."

He looked menacing in the dark. By the light from the moon, she ascertained that his hair had come unbound from the queue. It fell in smooth, dark waves around his high cheekbones, and down further against his corded neck. His eyes were hard upon her, and she was suddenly overcome with the wild thought that if it had not been for his gentleman's clothes, he'd have looked like a savage.

"Lose someone?" he asked, his voice tight and angry.

Her breathing quickened once again. "Indeed,"

she said lightly, hating the way her voice shook.

"Well, you won't find him, lassie."

She swallowed. "Did . . . did *you* find him?"

"Aye."

"Is . . . is he alive?"

One side of his mouth lifted briefly. "For the love of God, woman, I am not a murderer."

Her brow darted up in disbelief.

"Why did you go off alone?" he asked brusquely.

"I didn't," she answered with a small shake of her head. "I had become separated from my aunt and then he followed me through the crowd . . ." *And you befuddled my mind by watching some strange young woman.*

He took a step toward her. "That man has been watching you since your trip to the bookshop. That man was standing outside your house the night of the ball, gazing up into your windows." He advanced toward her.

She took several quick backwards steps, but her legs quivered so much that she nearly stumbled over the roots. But he kept advancing and she kept retreating until she could draw back no more. Before long, she found herself standing on a particularly thick root at the base of a tree. They now stood eye to eye.

"I found him wandering around these woods. He claimed he lost you. He claimed he had no idea where you were."

"I did get lost. He-he wanted me to go with him to Gretna Green. I ran."

His jaw hardened and it sounded as if he growled. "I didn't know what I'd find out here. You can't even imagine—" He broke off and ran his hand through his hair with a frustrated sweep. "That man is dangerous."

Boldness bloomed at her newfound height. "Really, Kincaid?" she asked tightly. "He's been watching me? Following me? Then I see no difference between you and him."

His eyes fixed on her mouth. "Unlike him, I don't have any nefarious intentions—"

"You have *no* intentions toward me. I am aware of that," she said, unable to keep bitterness out of her tone. "But unlike him, you despise me. So tell me, who am I really safer with?"

"I don't despise you, Rosalind." His throat convulsed with a swallow. Heat radiated in the small wisp of space separating their bodies. Both of their mouths were slightly parted, their breath mingled.

"Are you . . . are you still frightened?" he asked.

She didn't answer because the truth was she *was*

frightened of him, but not in the way he meant, she realized.

She wanted to tell him that she loved him. Right now. But she wouldn't. He did not feel the same way. Would her love ever fade? When would it stop hurting? Her mother's pain never did. Perhaps hers wouldn't either.

A soft breeze sifted through the tree branches high above them, bringing with it the smell of rain. She shivered. "I am not afraid of you," she lied.

She was suddenly overcome with the need to touch him, to force herself to be brave. Seemingly of their own accord, her arms raised. Placing her hands lightly on his broad shoulders with a reverence she couldn't hide, she allowed her fingers to tighten on the hard muscle, then slide slowly down to test the strength of his upper arms.

She marveled at his size. He was so different from her. Harder, broader, hotter it seemed. Underneath coat, waistcoat, shirt were sun-kissed muscle and sinewy grace. How she wished she could feel his bare skin.

His chin dipped down to watch her movements, his slightly bristled cheek brushing hers.

Gloved fingers splayed over his chest, feeling each breath he took. He was so powerful; he could snap her in half if he wanted to, she imagined.

She must stop touching him. What must he think of her? This beautiful, stubborn man who ensnared her attention and ignited her temper like no other.

She leaned in to push against his chest. "I've got to find my aunt," she whispered. "She's undoubted worried. And we are to attend the Hazelton ball . . . but then, why am I telling you? You already know."

"Enough of this," he breathed just before he reached back to roughly cradle the back of her head.

His other hand caught her jaw, his slightly calloused fingers digging softly into her skin. And for a second, his hooded gaze feasted on her mouth like she was a succulent dish and he couldn't wait to steal a taste.

"Forgive me," came his dark whisper a second before his lips descended upon hers.

Too stunned to react, Rosalind held perfectly still at first, her arms trapped between their chests. The kiss was gentle, but deep, his lips exploring, tasting, tempting. A heady combination of hard and soft, incredibly hot and increasingly demanding.

His lips and tongue were doing the most wonderful things, and Rosalind soon melted, a muffled moan of pleasure mixing with his groan. His heat and scent surrounded her and warded off the slight chill in the breeze.

Nicholas couldn't seem to get enough of her. He had thought, well, he really hadn't thought at all, but he'd assumed he could take just one taste and be done. She was so responsive. After her initial hesitation, she blossomed beneath his kiss, her lips, so yielding, fitting perfectly with his.

She tasted so damn sweet; he thought he'd go mad if she stopped him now. She put her arms around his neck, keeping him close. He had wanted to kiss her, but he hadn't expected her response, the sounds she made—hell—they made him feel weak.

They must stop, he shouldn't have done this again. This was wrong, wrong . . . His kiss suddenly faltered as she pressed her breasts more fully against his chest. Lips still on hers, their mouths opened, both of them breathing heavily.

But after coming up for air briefly, they dove under again for another round. Hungrily, his mouth slanted over hers again and again. His hand still protecting the back of her head from the rough bark of the tree, his other hand settled heavy on her hip. He squeezed, and a burst of pleasure thrummed through her. She moaned softly.

The kiss escalated, drowning Rosalind in a flood of sensation. She gasped into his mouth and he seized the opportunity to slide his tongue into her mouth to mate with hers. Melting, she was melting with heat, with pleasure. And trembling. She felt trembling, but she couldn't tell if it was Nicholas or herself.

The hand at her hip slid roughly up her rib cage, to her back, his thumb edging under her arm. Another inch and he'd be grazing the side of her breast. She would not stop him.

And then, finally, his large hand covered her breast. Her moan sounded overly loud in the woods.

He pulled his hand away.

"No," she murmured from under his lips, sighing with pleasure once again as his hand returned to her.

He kneaded her while she pushed herself more fully into his grasp. His fingers threaded through the crisscross bodice, seeking the edge. The tips of his fingers grazed her soft flesh and he squeezed once again, swirling his palm over the tight bud of her nipple nestled under the fabric.

He trailed a fiery path down her neck with his lips and tongue. His breath feathering hotly against the downy flesh of her bosom, he hesitated, staring at her as if she was a feast. And then he descended, first gently biting the swells, and then kissing them reverently in return.

She didn't want him to stop. Seeming to sense her need, he kept up his tender torment, dipping his tongue under the edge of her bodice in teasing flicks. Her nipples seemed to ache for his touch, just out of reach.

Her breath came in panicked gasps of sensation. "Nicholas," she choked out, holding on to his shoulders.

And then with a sudden rough tug, one of her breasts popped free. Nicholas didn't hesitate. Their gazes met and held as he dragged his tongue over the pebbled peak. Again and again he encircled, teased, and flicked before latching on to suckle her.

Her knees crumbled, and she would have fallen to the ground if not for the support of the tree trunk at her back and Nicholas's very solid thigh, which he wedged high and hard between her legs. Her body was awash in sensation so intense that she almost feared it, almost pushed him away.

Instead, she held him close, one hand threaded

through his hair, the other roaming over his chest.

His hand at her hip rocked her on his thigh, the other grasped her waist, then molded up her rib cage to sculpt her other breast. She cried out as sparks of intense pleasure buffeted her entire body.

Cannon fire from the exposition boomed once again.

They broke apart. She almost lost her balance, but she steadied once his large hands clamped over her waist as he set himself apart from her. They were both panting heavily.

She looked at him and his eyes shown like shards of gray glass in the soft light. He stared at her intensely as they fought to stop the trembling and regain their breath.

"Oh, my," she breathed, her fingertips pressed to her swollen lips. "What . . . what was that?"

He shook his head and swallowed, yet unable to speak. After a moment, his hands dropped away, and he brought them to his waist. He looked adorable, arrogant, and very masculine. "I don't know. I didn't expect that . . . we must never . . . never again."

"You keep saying that. It keeps happening." Not that she was opposed to it happening over and over again.

He nodded and she adjusted her bodice.

Strangely, she understood what he meant. They came together and all logic fled. Their passion was powerful, earth shaking. And frightfully dangerous.

"Go," he said, with a nod to his left. "Return to Tristan. He's waiting at the edge of the path."

She nodded and pushed away from the tree.

"And tonight," he said darkly from behind her, "when you return to the house after the ball, make sure to lock your window tightly."

Her brow furrowed. "What is it? Do you think Lord Stokes will try something?"

He shook his head. "No, lassie. But I might."

Chapter 12

Four hours later, Rosalind stood before the window in her bedchamber, staring at the latch as if it was an impossible mathematical challenge.

Arms akimbo, she pursed her lips while soundlessly tapping her toes upon the carpet.

The demure, sophisticated, well-schooled-in-the-art-of-comporting-oneself-as-a-lady Rosalind ought to have put on her primmest nightdress and thickest wrapper, lock the latch, and climb into bed with a book of scriptures.

But the other Rosalind, the grown woman who had been in love with a particular man for the past seven years, wanted nothing more than to throw open the window, toss her wrapper to the floor, and flounce over to the chaise lounge and strike a come-hither pose as she awaited his arrival . . . and his kiss.

And what a kiss it would be.

She reached out with one finger, lifting the latch.
Unlocked.

The pair of windows parted slightly and a
soft summer breeze wafted through. The skirts
of her cream-colored night rail billowed around
her ankles. She shivered and closed her eyes, and
there, in the dark, were flashes of memory.

His head tilting to hers. His broad shoulders,
blocking out the world. His hair, free and wild.
He loomed before her, seductive and breathtak-
ingly handsome. His mouth swooping down to
devour hers. His intense gaze locking with hers
as he passed his tongue across her breast.

If it hadn't been for the cannon fire, what would
have happened? What would he have done next?
What would she have done? Would she have
surrendered herself to whatever fate he'd had in
mind? She shivered anew at the possibilities.

But then, hadn't he admitted to being enticed to
guard her with a case of whisky? That wasn't very
flattering, was it?

Lips pressed together tightly, she reached out
with one finger.
Locked.

But at the Hazelton ball, he'd been remarkably
reserved. He'd watched her from a distance, only

scowled on occasion, and had even managed to persuade her sour-faced aunt Eugenia to dance with him to the surprise and delight of the guests. She had never seen her aunt so lighthearted. By God, the woman had actually giggled.

Rosalind sighed, smiling reluctantly.

Unlocked.

Hmmph. But he hadn't danced with her.

Locked.

Quite honestly though, he wasn't supposed to be dancing with her, he was supposed to be watching out for her, which was what her brother expected him to do. And, unlike at the Devine ball, he hadn't danced with anyone save her aunt.

Unlocked.

She stared at the window for a second, thinking her mind was made up when she suddenly remembered how the fair-haired young lady in the pleasure gardens had caught his attention.

Rosalind nodded, once, and with grave conviction.

Locked.

Her mind settled, she snatched her wrapper from the chaise lounge, threw it around her shoulders, and exited her bedchamber. It was time for chocolate and a good book.

She returned to her room minutes later, a cup of chocolate in one hand and, clutched in the other, a gothic novel entitled, quite appropriately, *The Nocturnal Visit*.

Alice must have been in her room while Rosalind had been below stairs, for the fire had recently been stoked and the flames burned bright and hot.

After shutting her door, Rosalind ambled toward her bed, placed her chocolate on a small table close to her bed, shrugged out of her wrapper, and turned over the counterpane. She was just about to crawl inside when a man cleared his throat. Rosalind froze and her book dropped to the floor with a dull thud.

"Your lock is inferior."

Rosalind blinked, astonished. Inch by inch, she turned her head to face the direction of his voice.

And there, in the corner, sprawled on her chaise lounge, was Nicholas. He wore no coat, no cravat, just a loose white shirt. His breeches were black, as were his boots, and he remained in his reposed position, ankles crossed, arms folded above his head despite her notice of him.

Indeed, his pose might have been leisurely, but it was contradicted by his scowl. He was looking directly into her eyes.

He looked . . . wonderful, handsome, and so very wicked in her room.

She faced him fully. "What are you doing in here?"

He lowered his arms and swung in his legs. Sitting forward, he rested his elbows on his knees and steepled his fingers, his loose hair falling forward. His scowl only lightened a smidgen before he drawled, "Well, I tended the fire, draped your gown, that you carelessly left on a chair, over the screen, and put your slippers in the wardrobe."

"Thank you," she said lightly. "What gallant service. If ever I require a new maid, you'll be my first choice."

He grinned, all lopsided and a touch condescending. He stood and the room suddenly shrunk. There was a dangerous glint in his eyes—like he knew some dark, wicked secret.

She lifted her chin a notch and crossed her arms over her breasts in a defensive manner.

"Why are you here?"

"To issue a warning."

"What sort of *warning*?" Her eyes narrowed on the word.

"Well, I've behaved," he intoned. "I watched you tonight while keeping my distance. I didn't even

255

interfere while you danced with yet another renowned rake."

"How very commendable. Did you come here for my praise?"

"No," he murmured, smiling ruefully. "I came here because I needed to . . . disabuse you of my level of patience. I have none. Or, at least, what I had is gone. I will not play games any longer and chase you across London, nor will I sit idly by while you pick out a bonnet for half a day just to spite me." He flicked his long, loose hair over his shoulder with an impatient jerk of his chin.

Rosalind remained silent. He looked as if he wanted to tell her something . . . something that was painful.

"I want . . . I need to make something very clear," he announced, giving her a direct stare. "You are never to go anywhere without me by your side. What happened at Vauxhall—"

"I was perfectly fine, Nicholas."

"And what did he want?" He advanced slowly, his steps measured. "He wanted you to elope with him."

She wasn't expecting a line of questions—she hadn't expected to find a sigh-worthy, hostile Scot in her bedchamber, either, for that matter.

He sighed heavily. "Do you realize what could have happened?"

"It turned out fine," she stressed.

"You have no idea. He could have caught you. What then?"

"He *wouldn't* have caught me," she said simply. "I am rather quick."

He huffed with disbelief. "Right then." His eyes raked her from top to bottom and back again. "Show me."

Her brow furrowed. "Show you?"

"Show . . . me."

She held up a hand, her middle and index finger walking in the air. "You want me to run? Now?"

He nodded, impatiently. "Yes. Now. Let's put you to the test, lass." He made a shooing motion. "Go."

"Well . . ." She eyed him like she would a completely mad person. "All right. I . . . guess." And then she turned to sprint across the room lengthwise. She made it to the wall fairly quickly. Her hands touching the wallpaper, she pushed off slightly and turned.

Nicholas was right there, blocking her escape. Her back thumped lightly against the wall. She tilted her head back to meet his gaze. Large hands splayed on either side of her head. He had effectively trapped her with his body without even touching her.

"You're fast?" he asked, his gray eyes sparkling with mischief.

She nodded, her thoughts too muddled to form words because the truth was he was slightly intimidating—in the melt-your-stockings-off sort of way.

"Well, I'm faster," he intoned. "And if Stokes *really* wanted to catch you, he would have."

After a brief hesitation, she realized he'd left her space enough to get away. Swiftly, she ducked under his arm. "Ha!"

She took three measly steps before Nicholas's muscled arm anchored around her waist, abruptly halting her. She gave a grunt as her breath was momentarily trapped in her chest. But he wasn't done.

He jerked her roughly against him. She wiggled to free herself, but before she could think, she was flat on her back on the carpet with Nicholas atop her. Her chin hardened and she swatted at his arms, careful not to rake him with her nails, for she knew he posed no threat; he was only trying to prove a point.

Pinning her to the floor with some of his weight,

he grabbed her wrists. He held them tightly and high above her head with ease in one of his hands. The other drifted down to gently remove a lock of her hair that had slashed across her face, obstructing her view.

"Sadly, you are not nimble enough," he murmured, shaking his head in a maddeningly derisive manner.

Her eyes narrowed into slits. "Yes, but I'm hardly fighting you."

He raised a brow.

A challenge?

She bucked beneath him. He hadn't expected it, she knew, because the force of her movement sent him rolling onto his back, taking her with him, for her wrists were still imprisoned by his hand.

Now, straddling his waist, she froze, not entirely sure what she should do next. She twisted her hands, trying to free her wrist.

"Is that where your plan ends?" He chuckled darkly, his free hand molding to her side.

Before she could utter a retort, he bucked his own hips, keeping his free hand behind her to cushion her spine as he flipped her over to her back.

"You might as well admit it, 'tis easy to overpower you."

"Oh, but I haven't yet begun. I've two brothers. I know how to punch and kick." Her gaze flicked downward. "And where to kick."

"Do your worst," he invited darkly.

She kicked out wildly, thrashing her legs . . . and quite suddenly found Nicholas wedged heavily between her thighs. Her nightgown had rucked up to her hips, leaving the sensitive skin of her legs to rub against the warm fabric of his breeches and the granite of his thighs. Scorching heat blossomed at the center of her being.

She was utterly bare underneath her nightdress.

His face above her, Nicholas's jaw hardened, a tick pulsing in his cheek.

"Did I get you?" she asked, breathless from exertion and from the surge of sensation. Had she kicked him? He looked as if he was in pain. "I did not mean—"

"Do not talk," he said through his teeth. "Do not move." He closed his eyes.

She waited quietly, her entire body flushing with heat.

"What a mess." His nostrils flared. "I'm going to get off you now. I'll keep my eyes shut. Cover yourself as quickly as possible."

She nodded.

"If you understand, you may say something. I cannot see through my lids."

"Hmm-hmm," was all she said.

Slowly, his face relaxed and his breathing slowed.

He opened his eyes, his heated gaze settling on hers. Their mouths were so close, she imagined they shared the same breath.

He released her wrists, leaned up on his forearms, then stared down at her in this utterly submissive position. A myriad of expressions crossed his features. Gently, reverently, he brushed the back of his fingers across her cheek, his thumb then tracing the whorls of her ear, spurring a delightful shiver.

And then, with a look of wonderment, he shook his head. "You're so . . . lovely. I-I hadn't meant . . . I wanted to show you how easily . . ." He swallowed. "I was wrong." He shifted to extract himself from her.

And then Rosalind did something she'd never thought she had it in her to do.

With an instinct she had not known she possessed, she wrapped her legs around his thighs, anchoring him there, then grabbed the front of his shirt and pulled him back down atop her for a kiss.

He hesitated for mere seconds, then sunk his mouth down to meld with hers. Desire exploded. This kiss was not gentle or slow. It was carnal, primal. This was a man and woman on fire, seeking a quenching they could receive only from the other. His hair around her, he thrust his tongue deep inside her mouth with thorough, blazing sweeps.

Knowing what to expect, Rosalind matched the rhythm of his ardor and dueled right along with him. She whimpered beneath his mouth and he answered it with a deep groan of his own.

The kiss was wild and out of control. Her hands rubbed at his strong back, down his sides and at his waist, where he seemed to be moving in a restrained, undulating fashion. She suddenly wanted to feel that rhythm against her. She needed to.

She angled her hips and pressed upward. Hard met soft. Her mouth broke away from his on a moan.

Swirls of sensation thrummed at her core. Grinding his hips into her, he bit and suckled the side of her neck and her mouth opened with silent, breathless pleasure. With tongue and teeth, he worked up to her ear, licking and sucking on the lobe. She cried out and he caught it with his mouth, the thrusts of his hips now matching the sweeps of his tongue.

She pulled his shirttails free from his breeches, her hands finally making contact with skin. And he felt glorious. Warm and muscular. She ran her hands over his stomach and it jerked beneath her touch.

Reaching between them, Nicholas's hand slid possessively from her neck, down her flimsy bodice, across her stomach, and around her hip. Squeezing and rubbing her leg, his thumb pressed into her inner thigh, coaxing her to open wider for him. Yielding, he surprised her by sliding his hand upwards to replace the press of his arousal.

She gasped at the feel of his fingers, at first tickling as he sought to separate her folds and then delightfully intrusive as he slid his fingers slowly downward, back and forth, back and forth. She gulped and fluttered her eyes open, seeking his gaze. He was watching her, his eyes like gray shards.

The sweeps grew steadily deeper until one of his fingers dipped inside her slick sheath.

"You like that," he whispered, knowingly, possessively. Over and over, he repeated his movements.

She couldn't answer, she couldn't think. She

shuddered and he kissed her, deeply, coaxingly. And then his thumb flicked a particularly sensitive spot and she choked back a sob.

Looking down, she gave a low whimper at the sight of his large tan hand, cupping her between her pale thighs, his fingers disappearing and reappearing, his thumb flicking within her dark curls. Her head dropped back and she panted.

His mouth slid downward to the swell of her breasts. He bit gently, then soothed the spot with his tongue. Using teeth and that deft tongue of his, he pulled down the square bodice until one breast bobbed free.

"Nicholas," she gasped.

His warm breath feathered the ruched tip a second before he fastened his mouth over it, alternating sucking hard and flicking his tongue until she thought she'd go mad.

If Nicholas showed her indifference before, he certainly wasn't now. Rosalind arched her back, reveling in the waves of sensation, marveling in his ardent attention, pushing all doubts to the far corners of her mind.

He feasted upon her breast while his fingers relentlessly moved. Her hips seemed to move of their own accord, a frantic pace.

Rosalind moaned low and deep. Pleasure built inside her, budding a strange frustration that was equal parts maddening and wonderful. All of a sudden it burst through her, sending shocks of bliss that startled her with their intensity. Her shoulders lifted from the floor.

Nicholas muffled her startled cry of pleasure with a kiss. She clamped her thighs tightly shut, trapping his hand there, but he never stopped moving. Not until she breathed again, her shoulders lowering to the ground.

Breathless, she peeked open her eyes and found his gaze hot upon her. He brought up the finger he had sunk into her and gave it a savoring lick.

"Nicholas," she breathed, another wave of pleasure rippling through her. "What was that? Did you . . . did you feel it, too?"

"To the depths of my soul."

They looked at each other intently for another full minute before he turned away.

He pulled her nightdress down to cover her damp thighs. He was out of breath and too stunned by the beauty of her climax to feel guilty. But it would come, no doubt.

Allowing himself to stare down at her for only one more moment, he rolled away, giving her his back, his erection aching from thwarted desire.

Behind him, he heard her descent back to earth. Her breathing was returning to normal, but she was very still.

Nicholas took several deep breaths. He felt a tugging at his sleeve.

Leaning on one arm, he looked over his shoulder. She was gazing at him with wonder in her eyes.

She was relaxed and sleepy now, and her sable hair swirled around her like a goddess, her normally pale skin now a dusty pink, and her mouth slightly swollen from his kisses.

She lifted a listless hand and gently ran her fingers down his jawline. He kissed her fingertips and she smiled.

Shame wormed through his thoughts. He closed his eyes against the sight of her.

Dear God, he had ravished his best friend's sister on the carpet in her room. He was a beast. A monster. He deserved pistols at dawn.

"Nicholas," she said softly.

He shook his head, unable to look at her. Standing, he held out his hands and helped her to stand. He held her to him for a brief moment, cradling her head to his chest.

Placing a kiss in her hair, he whispered, "This changes nothing. And everything."

"I-I don't understand," she said, her tone husky and confused.

"I shouldn't have touched you," he said, surprised his brogue had thickened.

"I wanted you to," she said quietly.

He shook his head. "Here I was warning you away from the advances of men. I wanted to show you how easily a man can overtake a woman. And then I overtook you." He dropped his arms, releasing her, and took a step away.

"No. No, Nicholas," she said hurriedly. "I grabbed you. I pulled you down."

"Aye, but I didn't have to follow you." He walked away from her and headed toward the window.

"You're upset," she announced.

"Aye. I am. But not with you. I'm sorry, lass."

"I don't want you to be sorry," she exclaimed, irritation laced in her voice.

"Well, you should," he replied. At the window, he swung a leg over the sill. "It shouldn't have happened."

"But it did," she said, sounding almost shrill. "It did and now you want to pretend that it was nothing?"

He shook his head. The breeze at his back increased, blowing ominously into the room, making the flames in the hearth bend and brighten. His loose shirt, untucked by Rosalind's own hands, billowed in the storm-charged air.

"I can't pretend anymore," he said softly, his tone grim. "The truth is I want you. I think I've wanted you for a very long time."

"And now you're done," she stated with a shrug of irritation.

He flicked his hair out of his eyes, chuckling low and self-deprecatingly. "If only I were that easily appeased."

"Why couldn't we—"

"I owe much to your brother," he said forcefully. "I cannot dishonor my promise."

Her smile held no warmth. "It's a little too late for that, no?"

He gave her a solemn nod. "Aye. But it stops here. We will go no further. "

Her eyes seemed to brighten, and he hoped it was with anger, not tears. Nicholas was stricken again by the way she tugged at his heart.

But instincts told him that he must treat her coldly now. If he didn't, if he was tender, like he wanted to be, she might foolishly invite him in her bed, and then he would surely make love to her. She must think of him as the lowliest of scoundrels. After all, he felt like one.

"Rosalind, you must realize I was asked to protect you."

"Indeed." She stared at the fire in the grate, a growing resentment smoldering in her gaze. "And who will protect me from you, Nicholas?"

He swung his other leg over the sill and reached for the limb of the sprawling oak next to the house. "You will be safe from me." He gave her a nod, then ducked away into the turbulent night just like the thief he feared he was.

If he would have hesitated a moment longer, he would have heard Rosalind whisper, "Indeed, Nicholas. But you certainly won't be safe from me."

Chapter 13

Rosalind rather thought that two days spent moping around the town house was sufficient time to execute a proper sulking.

Not to mention the fact that staying indoors was, in an indirect way, making the current situation rather easy for Nicholas.

Did he think they could go back to the way things were after what had happened? Would he regain his aloof façade, expecting her to forget coming blissfully apart under his sensual command? Did he think she would simply continue matchmaking and flitting from ball to ball, all the while casting narrow-eyed glares in his direction? Did he think *she* was so easily appeased?

Stepping into the foyer, Rosalind headed for the oval mirror near the door to check her appearance. She felt an unbidden need to see him again—she adjusted the bit of lace spilling from her bodice—and for him to see her.

After she finished sulking this afternoon, she decided a small outing was in order and informed Alice of her plans. Her maid responded enthusiastically, and Rosalind ordered a small luncheon to be packed and the carriage brought around.

Satisfied that all was working out as planned, Rosalind swirled into the study to talk to Tristan before she left.

"All right, I admit it," Rosalind proclaimed as she entered.

Seated across from Briggs, a game of chess positioned on a small rosewood table between them, Tristan studied the board, rubbing his jaw in thought. "Admit what?"

"That I am not perfect."

He gave a small puff of air, indicating he thought her very arrogant. "I was not aware that you thought you were."

"In my *matchmaking* capabilities," she remarked impatiently. "I've found that I have certain limitations."

He sighed, his fingers poised over his black bishop. "What happened?" he murmured, sounding resigned. He flicked a quick glance at her, his eyes returning to the chess game for only a second

272

before swinging back to her in shock. "What in God's name are you wearing?"

"What?" she asked, looking down at her pale pink frock. The bodice was scandalously low, but she and Alice had stuffed a bit of lace into her corset in order to conceal the swells of her bosom. "Is it not suitable for the park?"

"Suitable?" he squeaked out, looking angry. "That color is parallel to the shade of your skin, Rosalind. For a second I thought you were naked."

She smiled, a breath of relief whooshing through her. "So you think he'll notice?"

"If he doesn't notice you, it's because he's dead. Dare I ask just who in particular you are trying to attract?"

Her eyes swung to Briggs, widened meaningfully, then swung back to Tristan.

"I assume you'd like our butler to give us a bit of privacy?" His lips quirked with a smile. "Or is Briggs the poor fellow you've set your cap for?"

The old man chuckled softly and stood.

"Will you excuse us, Briggs?" Rosalind asked. "I hate to interrupt your game."

"Pay no mind, my lady. Master Tristan here is thrashing me soundly, and I should like a respite."

Bowing stiffly, he backed out the door, closing it as he left.

Tristan eyed the door with a wry smile. "Blast that old man."

"Tristan!"

"Do you not recognize veiled sarcasm when you hear it, Rosie? He wants you to think he's yielding to my superior chess mastery . . ."

"Chess mastery?"

" . . . when the truth is, I've never met his match playing chess. He's cunning and ruthless. I highly suspect that on the rare occasion that I *do* manage to win a match, it's because he let me." He shook his head slowly, glaring at the chess board.

"If you cannot best him, why do I often find the two of you engaged in this game?"

Tristan just glared at her.

Rosalind's brow quirked as the distinctive sound of Briggs's mocking cackle resounded from the other side of the door.

"See? He's not to be trusted." Tristan stood and stretched. "So, who is it that caught your interest? I will not lie and say that I'm not intrigued."

"Well," she started, swallowing nervously. "I'm not prepared to disclose that information. However, I would like to ask for a bit of . . ."

"Yes?"

"Gabriel isn't here and I should like to ask him. Although I don't know if I would have enough courage to, and it really wouldn't be prudent. No." She shook her head. "He might not take me seriously. Perhaps Madelyn. Yes, I would ask Madelyn if I could. I could never ask Lucy. Lucy wouldn't leave me be after she found out."

"Rosalind, you're babbling."

She blinked. "So sorry. It's just that . . . I seem to know how to make matches for others, just not myself."

His brow scrunched together. "I think I told you something similar the other day, did I not?"

She nodded, unsmiling. "I realize you may have no advice to impart, you being one and twenty, and well, a man, but if one knows someone might be, no, *is* attracted to them but is holding themselves back for some reason, is there any way to make oneself irresistible to them?" Her smile felt more like a cringe. Her little speech didn't quite come out as she had thought it would.

"Irresistible?" Tristan's scowl looked frighteningly like Gabriel's. "Nicholas?" he asked, his voice so low she almost wasn't sure he'd said it.

She hardened her chin. "Yes."

Something akin to relief crossed his features, making him look older and wiser than his years. "Well," he said, placing his hands behind his back and rocking on his heels. "My brotherly advice would be to let him come to you. Don't chase, make no demands. He'll figure it out sooner or later."

"That's it?" She couldn't keep the pang of disappointment from her tone.

"I'm your brother." He held up his hands in a defensive gesture. "How can you expect me to tell you what to do to attract a man?" He sounded baffled and astounded.

Rosalind became amused. "Surely you can do better than 'Don't chase, don't demand,' " she said, mimicking his baritone. "Come on, then! Tell me something good! Something wicked!"

"I will do no such thing!" He was starting to look embarrassed.

"AHA! So you do know things," she accused.

He started backing toward the door. "I admit nothing. Now, don't you have to go shopping? And where's Aunt Eugenia?"

Rosalind sighed impatiently. "In the garden working on her needlepoint."

"Ahh," he said with feigned admiration. "I've

always enjoyed watching that woman work at her needlepoint."

"Oh, stop. You do not."

Tristan did a remarkable job at looking earnest. "So sorry, but I must away. Don't want to miss a single stitch, you know."

Rosalind laughed. "Wait. I seem to remember you murmuring something at the Fairfax musicale last year—something about watching Miss Marianne eat a piece of fruit? What was it? I can't recall."

She would swear Tristan blushed. "I don't know what the devil you're talking about."

"Oh, yes you do."

He jerked his chin in the direction of the window. "If you've planned an outing, you'd best hurry. Looks like rain again."

Sighing, she strode to the window. Unsurprisingly, she saw nothing but blue sky.

"You're such a sneak . . ." she said as she turned, but he was gone.

Shaking her head, Rosalind walked into the hall. Alice was standing at the open door speaking quietly to Briggs.

"Are you ready, Alice? I thought I'd do a bit of shopping, and then have luncheon in the park. A good plan, I think."

"Indeed. It's such a fine day, and my Nellie should be there with the new baby."

Rosalind smiled genuinely, descending the front steps and ducking inside the carriage. "Wonderful."

The storm that had blown through the city the night Nicholas had come to her room had been followed by two full days of bright sunshine, but the air yet held a dampness to it, as did the ground.

Finding a shady, reasonably dry patch for her picnic was difficult indeed. The air smelled fresh, for London that is, and was matched with a warm breeze and bright summer sunshine. The fine weather coaxed many to enjoy the delights of Hyde Park.

Men flaunted their horsemanship, children rode alongside their papas on their ponies, while others played lawn games or flew kites with their nursemaids. Ladies strolled the clipped lawns and graveled paths with pretty parasols shading them from the glare of the sun.

Rosalind stifled an impatient sigh, thinking of the pretty parasol she'd seen in the Wedgwood shop an hour before. She'd had her heart set on buying it, but when she'd inquired after it, they'd told her they were to wrap it up for a customer who had purchased it mere moments before she'd gotten there.

Rosalind heard the coo of a baby and turned her head. Alice sat on a bench in the shade at a distance, cradling her new grandchild in her lap, her daughter chatting next to her.

Nicholas sat on a bench in the distance, his top hat low and his head bent as he feigned reading a book. Oh, he was watching her. She could feel his gaze upon her. But he hadn't made any pretense to approach her at all, and she was starting to get a bit annoyed.

After all, she had eaten at least seventeen strawberries (they were rather small) and she was starting to feel quite ill. This was rather silly. Here they were at the park together, but separate. Dear Lord, she was tired of this game.

She was four and twenty and every season was the same. She'd come to London, dodge a plethora of hopeful suitors, dance, make merry, and, of course, pine for Nicholas secretly.

Was this all there was? Would she simply grow old waiting for Nicholas to make some sort of indication, either way, of his feelings? She knew he felt lust for her, but was that all? She refused to believe it.

He'd mentioned in the morning room the day she'd stuffed cake in her mouth that some men feared love, avoided love, thought love brought them unbearable vulnerability—as if they believed, she mused, that in opening their hearts, they opened a wound.

Could he have been talking about himself?

She looked down at her pale pink skirt, shooing a tiny beetle from her hem.

This season was different from all the others. He was here—Nicholas, not the beetle—and while perhaps he wasn't here for the reasons in her romantic daydreams, it occurred to her that she should seize this opportunity to tell him how she felt once and for all.

She was going to tell him that she loved him. She needed to.

Resolved, she collected her plate and napkin and placed them in her basket. As soon as she was all packed up, she was marching straight over to him and confess. In truth, she rather thought that he might already know.

A pair of tall, polished boots came to a stop at her side.

She looked up to find Nicholas staring down at her. He grinned.

"May I join you?"

She nodded.

He settled himself beside her, one knee bent, his other leg slightly gaping. He leaned back on his hands.

Rosalind had never felt so very feminine, just by having a man sit next to her on a blanket. Her gaze fell to his lap, where a long box rested on his taut thighs.

Looking up at him, she noticed that his gray eyes shown like shards of broken glass. Those eyes drank in every inch of her.

Her breathing sped up in response. "What is it?" she couldn't help but ask.

"That dress."

She raised a brow. "Do you like it?"

A short, low chuckle rumbled in his chest. She felt it all the way through her bones.

His smile was devastatingly handsome . . . and dangerous. "You think I don't know what you're doing, lass?"

"I don't know what you're talking about."

"Oh, yes you do. And I like the dress."

"Thank you," she responded pertly, straightening her spine.

"And the strawberries," he swallowed. "You

have such a delightful way of eating them. Sucking slightly before popping them into your mouth."

"Enjoyable for you?"

Shaking his head slowly, he chuckled, low and quiet. "I don't like to be teased."

She swallowed. "Teasing implies that I wish to arouse your hope, only with no intentions of giving you satisfaction."

"And do you?"

"You can have what you want, Nicholas."

He licked his bottom lip and dropped his gaze to her mouth briefly before speaking again. "Be careful, Rosalind. You may think you know exactly what I want, but you can only imagine."

With those words hanging in the air, he leaned toward her, handing her the box.

"What is it?"

"A gift."

She blinked in surprise. "A gift? For me? Why?"

He nodded, his brow furrowing in such an adorable fashion that she couldn't help but grin. "Is it not the eighteenth?" he asked.

She shrugged. "I suppose. But what would that have to do with—?"

"Isn't it your birthday?"

Her mouth opened on a gasp. It was her birthday, and she had completely forgotten all about it. "You knew it was my birthday?"

"I know a lot of things about you. Here." He handed her the long, narrow box, a neat band of blue ribbon looped artfully on the top.

She stared at it for a moment, not sure what to do.

"Take it," he said.

Quickly untying the ribbon, she balanced the box on her hip and lifted the lid. She gasped in delight at the contents. Tucked inside was the parasol she had seen at the Wedgwood Shop.

"How did you know?"

He grinned. "Not telling."

"It's lovely, Nicholas. Thank you," she murmured.

"You're very welcome." He stood suddenly, holding out his hand to assist her to stand. "I have something to ask you as well."

"Hmm?"

"My niece's birthday is a week after yours, but my sister is having a party for her two days hence. Would you come?"

"I'd love to."

"Your aunt is welcome, of course."

"Thank you, but she's not feeling very well."

"Good." He cleared his throat and she laughed.

"I mean, that's too bad. Certainly you could have Tristan bring you?"

She nodded, smiling.

"I'll walk you back to your maid." He looked off in that direction and cringed. "It seems she's caught your butler's cold as well."

Rosalind looked over to see that Alice was handing her grandchild back to her daughter. Once the baby was settled, Alice shook out a handkerchief and sneezed into it.

Nicholas plucked Rosalind's blanket and basket from the grass. Together they crossed the lawn. She took out her new parasol and opened it, marveling at its beauty.

"Nicholas?" she beckoned softly once they were halfway there. It was time to declare her love.

"Yes?" He stopped, turned, and looked down at her patiently.

"I want you to know. I . . . I've always . . ."

"Yes?"

"I've always . . . I've always wanted a parasol just like this one."

What a coward.

Chapter 14

"The road's washed out ahead, my lady. We'll have to turn back."

"To London?" Rosalind shouted over the sound of raindrops pummeling the carriage rooftop like the pounding of a hundred drums.

The driver shook his head, rain dripping relentlessly over the brim on his hat. "No. I'm to take you to an inn, Bleak Hill."

She smiled, her eyes widening. "My, it sounds welcoming."

"Pardon?"

"I said, it sounds lovely," she shouted, sitting up. "Is it nearby?"

He gestured behind the carriage with a nod of his head. "His lordship says it's back down the road in the village. You'll wait out the storm there."

"Did my brother say how close we are to Lord Winterbourne's sister's?"

After a brief hesitation that gave Rosalind the

impression that she had somehow confused the man, he shook his head. "No, my lady. But you'll be spending the night. Even if the rains stop, it'll take some time for the water to recede."

She nodded and settled back against the squabs.

He gave her a queer look before shutting the carriage door.

"Lud, whatever did I say to provoke such a look?" she asked no one in particular, being quite alone in the carriage.

Alice and Aunt Eugenia were back in London suffering from the atrocious head cold Briggs had undoubtedly passed to them. Rosalind couldn't have been more pleased—not that they were ill, of course, but she was delighted that she would arrive without her disagreeable aunt in tow.

Of course, she wasn't traveling *completely* alone. It had been agreed upon that Tristan would escort her to her destination. He had been riding behind the carriage for the past several miles. They'd had a late start, and evening was fast approaching.

Reaching up to unbutton the clasps of her midnight blue pelisse, she sighed, suddenly feeling overheated.

Where London could be at times cold and damp, the southeast had some of the warmest temperatures in England. Rain often brought a warm humidity and, being from the North Country, Rosalind soon deemed it positively sweltering and shrugged out of her coat completely.

She gazed out the window at a darkening gray sky. The rain had lessened to a steady drizzle, but it showed no signs of stopping. Still, the landscape was quite marvelous—fruit orchards and fields of strawberries, hop gardens, and oast houses, with their steeple-like kilns.

A blur of a shadow at the window caught her attention. Rosalind leaned forward and spied the shadow of a rider practically fly past the carriage.

"Oh, Tristan, you reckless boy," she said with a wry smile.

Before long, they rolled to a stop, the carriage jostling a bit as the driver jumped down.

"Thank the Lord," Rosalind muttered, the muscles in her back stiff from a long day of travel. Scooting to the edge of the seat, she stretched, thrusting out her chest with her arms thrown over her head.

Sloshing footsteps approached, and in the next second, the carriage door flung open. "Sweet Christ," someone shouted, then slammed the door shut.

Rosalind's eyes widened. "Nicholas?"

Slowly, she opened the door and looked left and right. Finally, she spied him, carrying her heavy trunk up the steps and into the Bleak Hill Inn.

Bemused, she sat there for a moment, staring out into the drizzle.

A second later, Nicholas reappeared and strode over to the carriage with such brisk, determined strides that she almost shrank away.

Without saying a word, he grabbed her pelisse, threw it over her head, scooped her up and out of the carriage, and started toward the entrance of the inn.

Or, at least she thought he was. She really had no idea, for she couldn't see a thing but the inside of her coat.

"Where's Tristan?" she asked, her voice muffled.

"He rode ahead about two miles ago."

"Oh, dear."

"Precisely. Where's your maid?"

"At home, ill, with my aunt and her maid."

"How bloody convenient," he muttered with disdain.

His tone had her writhing in his hold. He had no choice but to put her down, she supposed, or he might drop her. Feet on the hard surface of what could only be the front step of the inn, she flung out her arms, fighting with her coat until she managed to pull it down from her head.

She could tell that her bonnet now sat at an awkward angle on her head, but she didn't care. Fueled by her agitation, her chest rose and fell rapidly and her eyes narrowed on him. "Are you implying that the maids and my aunt are sick on purpose? Just to make things inconvenient for you?"

He didn't answer but continued to scowl down at her from under his low-brimmed hat, his hair sodden and resting on his shoulders, his broad chest blocking out the view of the narrow, cobbled lane at his back.

She poked him in the chest, her temper ignited by his suspicious gaze. "I'll tell you what's inconvenient—being saddled with a surly guardian. Oh!" She looked about her. "And let's not forget the implication that I am worth my weight in whisky! Indeed, this whole experience has been nothing but unadulterated pleasure."

He sighed, an odd sparkle in his eyes. Truly, he looked as if he would smile. Rosalind rather thought she'd stomp on his toes if he did.

"Are you finished, love?" he asked rather nicely, grinning like the handsome devil that he was.

She sniffed, shifting her stance. "I think so."

"Good. Let's go in."

Clutching her pelisse to her chest, she allowed him to guide her inside, his hand at the small of her back.

A rather tiny wrinkled man with a full white beard greeted them. His name was Mr. Peters. While Nicholas spoke quietly to the proprietor, Rosalind removed her bonnet and looked about her, noting that her heavy trunk sat near her feet.

The glorious scent of roast beef and—she inhaled deeply—batter pudding wafted over to her, making her stomach growl. Lord, she hadn't had batter pudding since she was a child. Her gaze flicked over to the room adjacent to the one they stood in. It seemed to be a small banquet room of sorts, and it was packed with hungry overnight guests.

Eager for a bit of privacy, a room to relax in, and a plate of food, she edged closer to where Nicholas spoke to the innkeeper.

He was trying to explain something to Mr. Peters, and she wished he'd hurry.

Her temper was still steaming with the notion that Nicholas thought she'd had a hand in the fact that she had no maid or chaperone. As if she was trying to orchestrate some sort of seduction. What arrogance, she thought with a roll of her eyes.

A scowling Nicholas came over to her then, bending his head low. "I'm going to have to lie, Rosalind. There is only one room left and you well know that there could be a hundred rooms and you still cannot travel alone and keep your reputation intact."

"I suppose you think I anticipated this outcome and sent word ahead, asking the good people of Kent to rush to the Bleak Hill Inn and book all the rooms so that we'd be stuck together. Hmm?"

That curious sparkle returned to his gaze. "Just hush," he drawled.

Her brow rose, as did a new facet of her temper.

Nicholas stepped away from her. "Mr. Peters. The one room will be fine. My wif—"

"Sister," Rosalind announced rather loudly. "Sister, I am his sister." If he wanted to treat her coldly and pretend there was absolutely nothing going on between them, then she certainly wasn't going to allow him to play into some sort of fantasy wherein they got to pretend to be man and wife.

If he could be aloof and cool, then she would be an Ice Queen.

Nicholas's gray gaze froze on her for a long

moment before turning back to Mr. Peters. "Aye. My sister and I will share a room."

"Splendid," Mr. Peters beamed. "Shall I send up a tray of food?"

Nicholas nodded, then tossed the man a coin.

"I regret that I have no one to carry up your trunk, I could—"

"That's all right," Rosalind assured the old man, who was now shuffling toward the narrow staircase, step by rickety step.

She looked pointedly at Nicholas, gesturing to her trunk with an open palm. "Nicholas, my trunk."

A tight smile stretched across his mouth as he passed her by without picking it up. "Come now, *sis*. You remember my leg injury? I couldn't possibly carry that up all those stairs."

Her lips hardened into a thin line. Exhaling on a huff, she grabbed her trunk with two hands and dragged it laboriously toward the steps, mumbling her displeasure along the way.

Mr. Peters had a hard time with the stairs, ascending them at a turtle's pace. Nicholas offered to assist the man, but the innkeeper politely refused.

Thankful for the slow ascent, Rosalind found it easier to pull the trunk on the carpeted stairs.

Reaching Nicholas, she pulled hard and the trunk slid up the next step rather quickly. The corner rammed into the back of Nicholas's knee.

"Ow!"

Rosalind smiled.

Mr. Peters looked over his shoulder. "Everything all right?"

"Indeed," Rosalind chirped. "It's just his bad leg." She gave a happy sigh. "Everything is perfect now."

He abandoned her.

Well, perhaps she was being a touch melodramatic.

After the "accidental" leg walloping on the stairs, Nicholas helped her carry her trunk the rest of the way to their room.

And if the Scot had the power to make a room appear smaller just by his mere presence, he made this room look positively tiny.

On the right, dominating the room, jutted the bed, a large and rustically designed four-poster, with a clean counterpane of ivory. A small dressing screen stood in the corner, closest to the door. In the opposite corner stood a small washstand and side table.

On the other side of the monstrous bed, a small hearth crouched in the center of the far wall. Before it sat a tiny scarred wooden table and the room's only chair—a rather nice armchair with salmon-colored cushions that had probably been dark pink when new.

Rosalind reposed there now, plopping the last square of cheese in her mouth.

Nicholas had been gone for two hours, at least. She didn't know precisely, as there wasn't a clock in the room.

He'd claimed he would see that the horses were being properly cared for and expressed some interest in returning to the washed-out road to ascertain a way to drain it. Then he'd locked the door behind him and left.

Would he return?

Common sense told her that he would, but she wouldn't be at all surprised if he didn't return until the morning—having deemed a muddied road infinitely more exciting than spending the rest of his evening with her.

No. She knew what he was doing. He was avoiding being alone with her in this room.

Her eyes flicked over to the bed. Where would they both sleep?

Just then, the lock on the door clicked and Nicholas swept inside the room, setting a small bundle on the side table near the door.

Sparing her the briefest of glances, he shrugged out of his carrick coat and hung it on a peg on the wall near the door. His beaver hat joined it. Next were his riding gloves, which he took a ridiculously long time to pull off. He laid them on the side table next to the bundle.

Rosalind stood, patting the wrinkles out of her dark blue frock. "Ah, good evening?"

He grunted while pouring a splash of water in the basin.

"Did it stop raining?" It was a stupid question. She could have just looked out the window for herself.

He nodded and looked about the washstand. "Do you have soap in that trunk of yours?"

"Yes," she answered. Loping over to her trunk, she flipped it open, located the small, square wedge, and handed it to him. "I hope you don't mind . . . it's slightly floral. Jas—"

"Jasmine and cream."

She blinked, astonished that he knew. "All right, then," she murmured, taking a step back from him. "Do you like it?"

"Too much."

"Ah," she remarked, not quite sure how to respond. "Would you like me to get you some for your private use? I could order it for you."

"On you. I like it on you."

"Oh."

Dear me. He was certainly a man of few words this evening.

Hands folding demurely in front of her, she watched him wash up. There was nothing else to do, nowhere else to look. She supposed she could look out the single window next to the fireplace, but it only showed the side wall of the neighboring building—not terribly exciting.

The bed. All she could think about was the bed and where they would sleep. Quite honestly, with Nicholas in the room, the bed seemed to come alive, demanding she take notice of it.

She handed him a towel once he was done. After he finished drying himself, he took off his boots, set them near his coat, and began unbuttoning his shirt.

Rosalind gulped. "What are you doing?"

"Getting ready to go to sleep." In seconds, he stood before her, bare-chested, all that glorious, sun-kissed muscle bunching as he shook out his shirt, then hung it next to his coat.

Her heart started to race at the sight of him.

"Mr. Peters loaned me an extra blanket," he said, pointing to the small bundle he had brought in the room. "And a shirt." He unfolded it and shrugged it on. Bringing his arms together in order to button it, a ripping sound rent through the room.

He looked over his shoulder and down his back.

Rosalind gasped, a hand thrown to her throat. "Oh, Nicholas. I think the shirt was too small."

Pressing his lips together, he nodded.

Unable to stop herself, she giggled. "No! No! Don't take it off."

"I can't button it."

"Yes, but it covers you mostly. And I think you'd get cold without a shirt." And she wouldn't be able to stop looking at him.

He shrugged out of it anyway.

Silence reigned for some time while she busied herself dragging his wet clothes over to the hearth, where she laid them on the table to dry by the fire.

When she was done, Rosalind supposed she ought to ready herself for bed as well. After rifling through her trunk, she located her brush, prim nightdress, and a pair of thick stockings that she liked to wear when she was away from home.

As Nicholas had nicely dumped his water in the bowl on the floor, Rosalind poured herself fresh water and began her nightly regimen. She thought perhaps she might ease the tension in the room by talking to him.

But then again, it wasn't an easy task when the other person wouldn't look at you and only responded in grunts.

"Did you eat?" she asked.

"Yes. Downstairs." He was sitting in the chair. "Did you?"

"Yes. Thanks for ordering it for me."

He grunted.

"The strawberry tarts were delicious. I ate all four."

"Good," he said with some satisfaction. "I knew you would like them."

"How?"

"Hmm?"

"The tarts?" Gently, she patted her freshly washed face with a small, clean towel. "Were you just guessing?"

"Actually," he said smoothly, "I remember an incident Gabriel had mentioned a while ago involving the last strawberry tart at a spring luncheon. Your birthday picnic, if I remember correctly."

She laughed. "Oh, yes, I remember. Tristan challenged me to an arm wrestling match. The winner got the last tart. He won the match within seconds, of course, but I snatched the thing from his grasp before he could take a bite."

"Thief."

"Indeed. I ran all the way to my room and locked the door behind me. I was just about to take a bite, and then it dropped, fruit side down, on my dirty shoe."

His lips twitched with a suppressed smile.

"I suppose you think I deserved such an outcome?"

"No. I think your brother should have let you have it. It was your birthday, after all."

"Good," she replied, folding the towel and placing it on the washstand. "We finally agree on something."

Finished, Rosalind approached the dressing screen, sudden trepidation taking hold. She hadn't fretted over the potential problem of not having a maid with her until that moment. She assumed that his sister would have a maid who could assist her in dressing and undressing. But she hadn't planned on spending the night at an inn.

She took a deep breath and nodded. *I can do this,* she told herself.

Flinging her nightgown over the screen, she removed her boots, and then her stockings, replacing them with the soft, wooly ones. With her chin hardened in determination, she reached behind her to begin unfastening the row of buttons marching down her back. Several minutes later she'd managed to get three or four done before her arms cramped from the awkward position and her elbow whacked into the screen.

"Ouch!"

A heavy, masculine sigh erupted from the other side. "What the devil are you doing, lass?"

"Trying to remove my gown."

Silence.

She tried once more, but her arm cramped again. "Oh, I surrender! I will simply wear the dratted thing to bed."

"Although I think it might kill me," came his quiet, deep baritone from across the room, "do you want me to help you?"

She thought about it for a moment. Somehow

300

sleeping in yards of damp muslin was not appealing. "Yes, I require it."

"Come here, then," he muttered in resignation.

She walked around the screen to see Nicholas sitting in the chair, long legs spread out before him, white shirt open, revealing a beautiful expanse of his chest. His dark brown hair had curled slightly at the ends from the humidity. It simply was not fair that a man should look so devastatingly handsome with no effort.

She swallowed, her heart beating a wild staccato with anticipation of his touch.

She came to his chair and peered down. His eyes were shut and he lifted a hand, motioning her closer.

"Oh, for heaven's sake, Nicholas! Just unbutton the back of my gown. And please hurry."

He grinned but didn't open his eyes.

She sat on the arm of the chair and he went to work on the buttons. Shivers danced all along her spine. "Now the corset."

He sighed, and it sounded quite like a moan of pain. Deftly untying her laces, he soon loosened the corset, and goose pimples fanned up her arms and down her chest, hardening the tips of her breasts as well.

"Done?" he asked, voice almost pleading.

"Yes, thank you," she intoned.

He nodded and she returned to the screen, where she finished undressing and donned her nightclothes. Brush in hand, she plopped down on the bed, surprised at how soft it was. She began the process of unpinning her long hair.

She watched Nicholas while she worked, waiting for him to open his eyes. When the silence stretched, and his eyes remained closed, she allowed her gaze to rake his entire body freely.

"Are you comfortable?" she asked.

"Yes."

"Don't you want your blanket?"

"I'm not cold right now."

She loved how the muscles of his abdomen twitched as he spoke. "Are you going to sleep in the chair?" she asked, brushing out her hair now.

"Yes." A short pause. "Rosalind?" Her name rumbled sleepily from his lips.

She shivered. "Yes, Nicholas."

"Go to sleep."

She froze for a moment, her thumb smoothing over the soft bristles of the brush. She couldn't possibly sleep. Not with him sprawled within reach. Did he *want* her to look at him? Was this some sort of test? Why couldn't he just cover himself up with the blanket?

She had the most scandalous urge just then. In her mind's eye, she slid off the bed, stepped between his long legs.

She cleared her throat in an effort to steer her thoughts into a different direction. "Why have you never married?" she asked. After a long silence, however, she regretted the intrusive query. "I'm sorry. I tend to pry on occasion."

He shifted more comfortably in the chair. Lifting his arms, he settled them behind his head like a makeshift pillow, which made him look even more enticing, if such a thing had been possible.

"I have never had the inclination," he finally answered.

"Oh." She suddenly felt happier for some reason. And a touch brazen. "Ah . . . should you have the inclination," she began carefully, "what sort of woman would suit you?"

He raised a brow but did not open his eyes. "What sort?"

"You know," she murmured, her tone casual, "looks, temperament, situation. I-I'm just curious, really."

"Looks. Hmm. Perhaps tall, blond."

Rosalind's mouth twisted as she looked down at her rather petite legs. She sighed audibly, then began braiding her long, black hair with a pensive tilt to her head. "Is that so?" she murmured, her voice small.

"And she needn't be a lady of some social rank, either."

"No?" Good Lord, she wanted to cry.

"In fact, a country miss might be just what I need."

She swallowed the lump in her throat, remembering his casual notice of the tall, willowy blond at Vauxhall. Apparently, Rosalind was in the mood for a bit more self-torture, for she couldn't help but ask, "And what of her temperament?"

"Now that's the most important requirement of them all."

"Is it?"

"Aye. Above all else, she must be quiet. No chatty lassies for me. Especially in the evening . . . when I'm trying to sleep."

She had been dwelling so miserably on the words "tall" and "blond" that it took a moment to realize he was only teasing her. Or, at least she hoped he was. Good Lord, she hated this dreadful cloud of uncertainty she was plagued with.

Silence reigned between them for several moments. Her hair now in one long plait, she sat back, pulling the covers up to her chin. "Nicholas?"

"Yes, Rosalind?"

"Why will you not look at me?" she asked.

"I already know what you look like."

She threw her pillow at him.

He sat there for a moment, pillow on face and chest before he pulled it away. His expression terribly serious, he murmured, "Thank you," then placed it behind his head.

Which left Rosalind without a pillow.

She inhaled sharply. "That was *my* pillow."

"Then you shouldn't have thrown it at me. It was rather childish of you."

"Childish!" She crossed her arms tightly over her chest. "I'll tell you what's childish. *You*, refusing to look at me."

"Why the pressing need for me to look at you? Have you been away from your admirers too long and are suffering from the effects of inattention?"

"Oh, I think I despise you."

"Good."

"Why is that good?"

"Because usually," he drawled, his voice low and deep, "people don't converse with individuals they don't like. And I'd like to sleep, but I can't if you don't hush."

"Now I'm positive I don't like you."

"Yes, you do. I could tell by the way you looked at me once I relieved you of your burden and carried the trunk the rest of the way."

"I was relieved that I didn't have to hurt you again."

He shrugged, the faintest smile curving his lips.

"And do you like me?" she blurted without filtering her thoughts.

After a brief hesitation, he shook his head, the corners of his mouth turning downwards. "No," he said simply.

"*NO?*" she couldn't help but shout.

"Maybe a wee bit."

"Oh, how my heart swells."

He chuckled low and quiet.

She sighed, long and drawn out. "I *can't* sleep," she complained.

"Strangely, neither can I."

"Do you want to know why I can't sleep?"

Silence.

She decided to answer anyway. "I can't sleep because you look so uncomfortable over there."

"I'm not."

"But you appear to be." She bit her lip. "Your neck will undoubtedly be sore tomorrow."

One gray eye opened a tiny bit. "Then where should I sleep, Rosalind?"

She suddenly felt like she had been prodding a sleeping bear, only to find out it was a dangerous game. She toyed with the edge of the coverlet. "Well, I mean . . . it's a fairly large bed."

"Quite."

The other eye opened and heat pooled low in her belly. He looked like he wanted to gobble her up. "An invitation?"

She nodded.

To her surprise, he unfolded himself from the chair and stretched.

Rosalind watched him, realized she just might be drooling, then turned away. She scooted over and opened the blanket.

Eyes trained on her the entire time, he replaced the pillow she threw at him, then slid in next to her. "Good night," he said, somewhat stiffly.

"Good night," she answered, matching his tone. "May you have pleasant dreams about tall, blond mutes frolicking in the countryside."

He chuckled, silently, his mirth shaking the bed. "I'm afraid I'll have nightmares instead."

"Oh?"

"Aye. I've a suspicion there will be a raven-haired pixie in my dreams." A smile was in his voice. "She'll have the sweetest smile and the most beguiling blue eyes, the color of a Scottish loch in spring. She tortures me and I ache for her something fierce. But she'll not let me rest—"

"Until you kiss her good night. I never got my birthday kiss, if you remember."

"I'm not kissing you, Rosalind. If I kiss you, I'll not stop." He nodded slowly, his eyes intent upon her. "You'll find yourself naked and spread across this bed in whatever position suits me."

She forgot to breathe. "Oh."

"Exactly." He gave her a fearsome scowl, though the silver in his gaze made it a sultry stare instead. "You trust me because your brother does, and you respect his opinion. And, aye, I've always been an honorable man, but around you I think honorable is pretty damn boring. Stop tempting me, Rosalind."

She said nothing but met his harsh stare.

He leaned toward her and kissed . . . her nose. She was too stunned by his declaration to react.

"Consider it a warning. You only get one." And then he rolled over and presented her with the broad expanse of his back.

Rosalind had about two seconds before she rolled helplessly toward him, bumping into his warm, solid back.

"Oomph! Sorry," she mumbled. She scooted back to her side of the bed, tightened her muscles in order to stay put, but ending up giving in. She rolled back into him.

"Sorry," she repeated, her face pressed between his shoulder blades. "I'm not trying to ravish you, you may depend upon it. I couldn't help it. Perhaps if you roll over . . ."

Nicholas flipped over onto his back, his laughter shaking the bed. "It doesn't matter. You're such a wee thing. This mattress is misshapen and I'm heavy—you're going to keep sliding into my side."

"Oh," she said, rather distractedly, as she was now snuggled against his bare chest. She looked down at him, knowing he saw the yearning in her gaze.

"I think," Nicholas said quietly, "I should return to my chair."

She shook her head. "Stay."

They stared at each other for several moments before he gave her the slightest nod. "Well, if you think you can keep your hands off me . . ."

Her jaw dropped. "If I didn't cherish this pillow so much, I think I'd happily wallop you with it."

"Aye, you're such a fearsome lass." He grinned and closed his eyes. "Good night, Rosalind."

Rosalind settled back onto the pillow, her body tense to keep from rolling into him.

After several minutes, she picked up her head and looked at him. Thick, dark lashes fanned against his cheekbones. His glorious chest rose and fell, deep and even.

Ever so slowly, she inched closer and closer still. Sure he was asleep, she pressed against his side and carefully rested her cheek on his upper arm.

She didn't plan on a sigh of contentment, but it came all the same. She didn't think she'd ever been so comfortable in her whole life.

To her surprise, Nicholas lifted his arm, wrapped it around her, and held her close.

And then her heart truly did swell. "See, Nicholas," she whispered. "I knew you liked me."

To her chagrin he said nothing. She hoped it was because he had fallen asleep. Too afraid of what answer he **might** give her if she pressed and repeated herself, **she** merely sighed, then pressed her cheek against his chest.

Soon, she drifted off to sleep, but eventually doubt reared its pernicious presence in her dreams. She dreamed she was back at Wolverest, traversing the long, tree-lined lane her mother had named Canopy Row. As she approached a whimsical Aphrodite statue, Rosalind smiled at the goddess's expression, her lips pursed as she blew a kiss in the wind.

And then the air around them changed. The skies darkened to an ominous shade of purple, and fat, cold drops rained down sporadically, landing on Aphrodite's stony cheeks and rolling downward, making her lighthearted expression transform with tears from the heavens.

Chapter 15

He dreamed of her.

That is, in the handful of minutes he actually managed to stay asleep.

It was impossible to dismiss her presence. Her soft, feminine sighs nearly made him groan in response, her alluring feminine scent kept his mind alert as well as another part of his anatomy, and the way her warm curves melded so perfectly to his side made his hands tremble from the restraint of not pulling her atop him and begging her to let him worship every inch of her with his hands and mouth.

He reached up and grabbed his forehead. Christ, the images weren't helping matters.

He should have insisted Tristan accompany her all the way to the manor. Or at least Nicholas should have insisted on sleeping on the chair. To hell with the chair—he should have slept in the stable with Buttercup.

Having awoken with the most uncomfortable erection he'd ever had in his life, he spared her not a single glance before sliding out of the warm, tempting bed. Quickly donning his clothes and cloak, he left to find the nearest, secluded body of water. After swimming for twenty minutes, he deemed that the cold depths had sufficiently chased the lust from his body. Only then did he trust himself to return to the inn to fetch her.

Stomping up the steps of the inn, he shook a lock of his sodden hair from his eyes. It was well past five in the morning and the lass should be awake and ready for departure. He'd ordered a plate of breakfast to be sent to her room nearly an hour ago with instructions for her to eat, dress, and pack as quickly as possible, for they would be leaving before six. They needed the clinging darkness to ensure no one recognized her with him.

What Nicholas needed was to get to Francesca's, and fast. Before he threw caution to the wind and took Rosalind in every sense of the word.

He sighed once he reached the top of the steps. Her trunk was supposed to have been waiting outside the door, as he had instructed a maid to inform her, but its absence meant either she wasn't ready or she was being stubborn again. His vote was for the latter.

He rapped a light knock upon the worn oak door, waited several seconds, and then tried again. After no response came at his second round of knocking, he shifted his stance and spoke as close as he could to the crack of the door. "Rosalind. Are you ready?"

"Just a minute more!" she called from inside the room.

Rumbling came from the other side of the door, and he assumed she was dragging her trunk toward it.

"Just leave it," he ordered. "I'll get it."

Silence.

He sighed and pressed his forehead to the door, leaning his full weight into it. "Did you hear me?"

The door sprung open and he tumbled forward, his body connecting with Rosalind's willowy form. Together they flew backward, their momentum giving them no choice but to land wherever they would.

They landed on the bed, Nicholas on top and between her thighs.

Her very breath knocked out of her for a

moment, Rosalind looked up into eyes of silvery gray. "Have you no patience," she squeaked out, all too aware of their provocative position.

"With you?" he practically panted. "No."

He went to roll away from her, but Rosalind grabbed his simply tied cravat.

Tucking in his chin to look at her hold, he raised a brow, then met her gaze. "The door, Rosalind, is open."

"Of course," she muttered. The weight of him atop her was intoxicating. She didn't want him to move.

He withdrew himself from her and took the three steps to the door. There, he hesitated, and Rosalind was quite sure he was fighting some sort of inner battle.

She sat up, leaning back on her elbows, and watched him.

Grabbing the scuffed handle, he opened the door wider and sighed, resigned.

The sound tore at her heart.

Was she such a witch, then? This man was only trying to protect her. To do his job and move on. Clearly they were attracted to each other; clearly they both recognized this. She looked down at her feet, embarrassed now for making him feel bad for agreeing to watch her, for purposefully aggravating him by shopping for hours. Why had she been so determined to make this as difficult for him as she could? What had he ever done to her to deserve this?

The answer was suddenly obvious. He'd made her fall in love with him, effortlessly, completely, and irrevocably—yet she inspired only lust in him. But then she was being such a brat, so difficult, how could he have fallen for her? Shame flooded heat to her cheeks. What had happened to her good sense, her levelheadedness?

Indeed, it was her pride. It smarted once she'd discovered that Nicholas would most likely never interact with her unless forced to by his sense of obligation to her brother.

In a sea of admirers and would-be suitors, the only man she wanted to cling to didn't want anything to do with her. She was a *responsibility*, nothing more. And she had been making this man's life miserable.

Well, it would stop now. She would . . . behave.

Chapter 16

"**A**re you a princess?"

Standing at the threshold of Nicholas's sister's house, Rosalind blinked down at the tiny, cinnamon-haired sprite who had just opened the door. She wore a bonnet three times too big for her head and stared up at Rosalind with round gray eyes.

An even younger little girl, a curly-haired blond, stood next to her, her smile overshadowed only by the chubby finger stuffed up her nose.

"Ah, . . . no. I am not a princess," Rosalind answered. Looking up, she spied someone she presumed to be the butler. The gray-haired man stood slightly behind the door, blinking as if this conversation was quite ordinary and boring, too.

The little girl in the big hat sized her up. "You look like a princess," she said in the tiniest-sounding voice Rosalind had ever heard.

"Well, thank—"

" 'cept for that dot on your forehead."

Rosalind's hand flew to her hairline, her fingers dusting across a tiny blemish she hadn't known she'd sprouted. "Oh, dear," she mumbled.

"It's all right. You are still quite pretty."

"Are *you* both princesses?" Rosalind asked.

Gray eyes sparkled, as if the imp thought the idea rather marvelous, and she nodded, giving her skirts a swish. The blond just kept picking her nose.

"Are you going to marry Uncle Nicholas?"

Lud, the girl was direct. "Well . . . I . . ."

Scrunching up her lips, the girl shook her head slowly. "I didn't think so. He said you gave him a great ache in his head."

Rosalind laughed. "He did, did he?"

"And then, there's Miss Polk."

Rosalind's mind, which had been keeping up with the child's abrupt way of speaking, suddenly came to a stumbling halt. "Miss Polk?"

"Aye," she said, sounding a bit like her uncle. "You don't know about her?"

Rosalind shook her head slowly. At the moment she wanted nothing more than to launch a list of questions about this Miss Polk.

"Who exactly is M—"

"Gracie! Isabelle!" a young woman gently admonished as she strode into the room. "Show her ladyship inside, please."

At some distance behind the woman Rosalind presumed was his sister, Nicholas sauntered into the room, watching her intently. Had he heard what his niece had said?

"I'm so sorry, my lady. I had no idea they had opened the door." She glanced briefly at the butler. "Jameson here indulges them terribly, I'm afraid."

The butler nodded, his downturned lips hinting of a suppressed smile.

Nicholas stepped forward, handsome as ever, his jacket nowhere in sight and his cravat loosened slightly. "Please come in." He guided her inside with a hand at her lower back. "Your brother was held up as well yesterday. He only just arrived before we did. He'll be in shortly. I believe he's appraising the stables."

She nodded.

"Allow me to introduce my sister?"

"Of course," Rosalind readily responded.

"Francesca, this is Lady Rosalind Devine. Lady Rosalind, my sister, Mrs. Francesca Colton."

"Colton? That name is very familiar to me."

"Is it, my lady? Perhaps you remember his

name from Wolverest? I believe His Grace's solicitor, Mr. Ashton, worked with my husband on occasion. We moved to Kent shortly after we married but spent much time in Yorkshire on business matters."

Rosalind smiled. "I do believe you're right. And please, call me Rosalind. I shall not have it any other way."

Nodding, Nicholas's sister smiled a little nervously.

Rosalind felt a tugging on her skirt and looked down to find the pretty girl in the floppy bonnet smiling up at her. "I'm Gracie. I'm five."

"Pleased to make your acquaintance, Gracie."

"Likewise."

Rosalind giggled. Her laughing eyes met Nicholas's serious ones, and instant heat pooled throughout her body.

"And that's Isabelle," Gracie pointed out. "She's only three."

"I four."

"Ah," Rosalind said, "is your party today?"

She nodded.

"Good. I brought you a present, Miss Isabelle, and your sister, too. I didn't want anyone to feel left out."

"I like her, Uncle Nicholas," Gracie said, looking up at him.

"As do I, wee one. As do I."

Three hours later, after much present opening, game playing, and conversing with numerous guests and their families, Rosalind found herself quite out of breath and in need of a respite.

She hadn't been able to get within five inches of Nicholas before her attention had been requested elsewhere. And she'd happily complied.

Her own family, though dearly loved, was small, and she was the only female other than her aunt. Of course, now they had Madelyn, but Rosalind would have to wait until their return before she could relish in the rare delight of "sisterly" companionship once again.

But here, well, one would have thought that she would have been the perfect picture of aristocratic snobbery at the informality of the entire affair. But the truth was, Rosalind hadn't had this much fun since . . . well, since never.

And every so often she would look up from whatever she was doing, be it playing with the children, assisting someone atop a pony, or soothing a wee one with a scrape, and she'd find Nicholas watching her with an exacting gaze that took her breath away.

And he was marvelous, too. A giant to the children, but with the most tender of hearts. He even agreed to partake in a "tea party" hosted by his nieces. Rosalind nearly toppled over with laughter when they talked him into eating one of their "biscuits" but failed to tell him it was made of dried mud. He spit it out, making a great show of it, and the children laughed uproariously.

She never would have guessed how much fun she would have here.

Tristan seemed to be having a nice time, as well. He was currently playing a rather lively game of cricket with a group of children across the way.

Rounding a fat oak tree, Rosalind found Nicholas sitting beneath it, his back against the trunk. His two nieces sat before him, watching his hands intently as he worked something in his hands.

Flowers. Tiny daisies, to be precise. He was chaining them together.

Quietly, Rosalind sank down next to him on the blanket, careful to arrange her pale green skirts.

"Just in time for the crowning," he intoned.

"Am I?" she responded lightly, with an easy smile.

Holding up the crown of daisies, he placed them upon his nieces' heads in turn. They giggled and sprang up, eager to show their friends what their uncle had made for them.

"Nicholas," Rosalind said softly. "Thank you for inviting me."

Those beguiling gray eyes met hers, the corners creasing slightly from the glare of the sun behind her. "It's your turn."

Her brow knitted. "My turn?"

He nodded and raised his hands, another circle of daisies laced over his fingertips. Leaning toward her, he placed them atop her head.

"Perfect," he muttered, his tone light, but his eyes held a dark promise that made her shiver.

Despite this, a bubble of laughter tumbled past her lips. "Oh, I don't know. Are you sure you didn't give me one with a bee nestled on one of the blooms?"

He chuckled softly and Rosalind was quite sure something inside of her melted.

And then, because she couldn't help but ask, for the need to know was burning her insides, she asked, "Who is Miss Polk?"

He shrugged. "A neighbor near my Yorkshire residence."

"What does she look like?" She swallowed, uncomfortable that her jealousy was apparent.

Squinting with his face turned to the sky, he murmured, "Rather tall, blond, I think."

The woman he looked at in the pleasure gardens perhaps?

Her stomach knotted. "Is she rather soft-spoken?"

He shrugged. "I suppose. Compared to you, she's a mute."

"Your perfect girl, then?" She tried to laugh, to keep the conversation light, but her execution left a lot to be desired.

"Not perfect," he murmured, his eyes connecting to hers.

She gave a tiny shrug herself, trying to affect an air of nonchalance. "Why have you made no offer for her? If she's nearly perfect, that is?"

He shrugged.

"I saw her at Vauxhall," she guessed. "You saw her, too."

"Aye. I was surprised to see her. You sound jealous, lass."

"And what if I was, Nicholas?" she asked, suddenly having had just about enough of his evasion for a lifetime. "What if I was jealous? Would that be permissible?"

"Lady?"

Rosalind turned to see Gracie standing behind her.

"We're going for a walk in the woods, would you come?"

Rosalind exhaled all her anger. "Yes, yes, of course."

Nicholas stood and reached down to help Rosalind stand.

She didn't accept his assistance, however, and sprinted off behind his enthusiastic niece.

Nicholas knew the path Gracie and a few of her friends liked to frequent. It was a party of four. Gracie, three of her slightly older friends, and Rosalind.

A twinge of worry marred his brow. His nieces seemed to have grown very attached to Rosalind in a very short time. He couldn't blame them. Rosalind was simply lovable. So, why couldn't he admit it to her?

A sudden weariness came over him, no doubt from a lack of sleep, and quite possibly years of suppressing his feelings for one particular woman.

Nicholas gave his head a shake to clear it, noticing Gracie running across the field, her skirts hitched up nearly to her waist.

She probably needed to use the privy. But she

kept charging straight toward him. As she got closer to him, he realized that tears were streaking down her cheeks and panic was evident in her huge eyes.

"The lady! Uncle Nicholas, the lady!"

Kneeling down, he caught her at the shoulders. "What is it? Where is she, Gracie? She was with you, was she not?"

Gracie's breaths came in big gulps. "The lady . . . she's in the water."

Chapter 17

⟨ᴏᴏ⟩

"**O**h, I-love-you-I-love-you-I-love-you," Rosalind chanted to the skinny limb of the plum tree she clung to.

Fortunately, because of the recent heavy downpour, the still flowering branches hung low and heavy over the pond, their lush, pink blooms holding rain, which weighed them down.

Both hands grasping the branch, Rosalind eyed the footbridge that had collapsed when she'd tried to cross it moments ago. She was relieved that it had been she that had fallen into the pond rather than the little ones.

Twisting in the water in order to eye the shore, she mustered up a smile for Gracie's friends, who were standing frozen on the grassy bank. "I'm all right," she shouted.

They stood motionless, blinking at her.

Oh, who did she think she was fooling? She

couldn't stop trembling and she figured she had to be as pale as her bed linens. Fortunately, the water was moderately warm, but the good Lord only knew how she was going to get back to the shore. She knew one thing for sure, she was never going to let go of this lovely branch.

Running footsteps approached, but Rosalind couldn't tell where they were coming from. In another moment, Nicholas came bursting through the trees, launching himself in the water.

She'd never seen that look on his face before. He looked terrified and angry at the same time.

Out of the corner of her eye, Rosalind watched as Francesca ushered the children back down the path, Gracie latched to her mother's skirts.

Nicholas swam toward her, cutting through the water with a speed Rosalind envied. "What the hell happened?" he shouted.

The combination of being submerged in water and being terrified made her teeth chatter uncontrollably. "The b-bridge," she managed, speech becoming a bit difficult. "I d-don't know how to swim."

"Christ," Nicholas muttered, glancing over at the splintered wood.

Reaching her, he wrapped a very warm, very

solid arm around her back. "Let go," he ordered, looking at the branch.

She shook her head.

"Rosalind," he said patiently. "Let go of the branch."

"I can't."

"Yes, you can. I've got you."

"And who has you?"

He let forth a mighty sigh. "I have me."

"It won't work," she chattered. "Too heavy t-together. We'll s-sink."

He cradled the side of her head in one of his hands. "Look at me, lass. I'm not going to let anything happen to you."

"You will not be able to do it."

"Yes, I will."

She shook her head again.

"All right," he said with a slow blink. "Is there anything I can give you, a promise of some sort, anything, to entice you to let go? Perhaps some chocolate cake?"

"Not f-f-funny."

"Something else, perhaps?" he prompted when she failed to answer.

She was quiet for a moment, and then nodded quickly.

"Yes? Great. What do you want, Rosalind?"

"A k-kiss."

"From me?"

"Yes, you. Y-You d-dunderhead."

"That's all?" He bent his head toward her.

She pulled away. "Not n-now."

His brow rose.

"Later," she explained, "when I c-can enjoy it."

He nodded, a wide, secret smile curving his lips.

"And it better be g-good."

"Oh, it will be, Rosalind. It will be."

Nearly ten o'clock in the evening, and Rosalind still hadn't gotten her kiss. However, she did have plenty of visitors . . . of the little moppet variety.

Upon returning to the manor, Rosalind had been settled inside a guest bedchamber for the night. Dripping wet and shivering uncontrollably, she had quickly shed her sopping wet clothes with the help of Francesca's maid and had soaked in a gloriously hot bath for nearly an hour.

After Rosalind had dried, donned a clean gown of light blue muslin borrowed from Francesca, and had her hair dressed in a loose bun atop her head, Gracie and Isabelle had snuck inside her room, plopped themselves upon her bed, and proceeded to ask her about a hundred and seventy-eight quick-fire questions.

Rosalind didn't mind, however. In fact, she found she rather liked their company.

They wanted to know everything about her. Her favorite color, her favorite dessert, what her governess was like, and if she ever rode a horse without a saddle. The stream of questions was seemingly without end.

And then they asked the inevitable: do you love our uncle Nicholas?

She was saved from exposing herself by a knock on the door.

Francesca poked her head in. "Rosalind, may I have a word with you . . ." She clucked her tongue. "Girls. I told you to allow our guest to rest." She glanced at Rosalind. "I'm terribly sorry."

Rosalind hurriedly set her at ease. "It's rather nice, actually."

Nicholas's sister smiled, but she gave her daughters a stern look. "It's time to go to sleep. Now off with you."

The girls scooted off the bed.

"Good-bye, lady," Gracie called out.

Isabelle smiled and waved, nearly walking into the doorframe.

Rosalind giggled.

Francesca cleared her throat. "I wanted to thank you for the music box and the doll you brought for Gracie. It was very kind of you."

Rosalind shook her head. "I loved shopping for their presents. Truthfully, I've never had the opportunity to purchase a child a toy. And I must say to see the look of delight upon their faces makes me want to positively spoil them."

Francesca laughed. "You might not feel that way after you've been here for several days. They can be quite the troublemakers." Sobering, she bit her bottom lip, clearly hesitating.

It was obvious she wanted to say something but hesitated. "What is it?" Rosalind urged.

Francesca gave her head a tiny shake and glided in the room. "I hope I'm not being too bold, but I wanted to ask you . . ." She took a deep breath, then exhaled slowly. "Be patient with him. I know he's rather vexing, but I fear he's hardened his heart."

Rosalind sat up straight in her armchair.

"You see, I think he fears loss. He'd never admit it, but the truth is our parents dearly loved each other. They were openly affectionate, and I daresay," she paused to chuckle, "sometimes Nicholas and I felt invisible to them, as they were both so wrapped up in each other."

"You were very fortunate to remember your parents with such fine memories."

She nodded, a sadness welling in her eyes. "Yes, but when our mother passed, our father sunk into the depths of despair. He hardly slept and barely ate. He missed her terribly and was never the same person again. Never."

"I'm so sorry," Rosalind said with genuine sorrow.

"Nicholas. I almost think he's afraid to love, as silly as it seems. He's afraid of loss." She sighed, giving her head a shake. "Anyway, I thought you might like to know."

"Thank you," Rosalind remarked. "I had my suspicions."

"Yes, he always said you were very perceptive. I believe that's why, back in Yorkshire, he pretended to ignore you."

"He did ignore me," Rosalind added dryly.

Francesca sighed with a smile. "I have my own suspicions about that, as well." She patted at a fold in her skirt. "Is there anything I can get for you?"

Can you send your brother up? "No. I think I shall retire early, actually."

Francesca smiled. "Very well. Good evening, then."

"Good evening."

Francesca quietly left.

Rosalind sighed, her mind mulling over the information Francesca had imparted. Then she stood, thinking to close the door and retire for the night, when someone knocked on the doorframe.

She turned to find Nicholas standing in the hall, two steps from entering.

"Well, I didn't think I'd see you again today."

He smiled, all lopsided and heartbreakingly handsome. His feet were braced apart, his arms neatly behind his back, which did a delightful job of showing his broad chest to the best advantage.

"I'm going to get my kiss now?"

He shook his head slowly, his eyebrow rising in a most beguiling fashion.

"Then what have you come here for?"

"I came with a message," he said quietly.

"And that is?"

"Keep your door unlocked tonight."

He had to drag her out of her room.

No, that wasn't quite the thing, Rosalind demurred.

When Nicholas came to her bedroom and she realized his intent, she balked—in fact, she held onto one of the posts of the bed with a death grip.

But her puny hold was no match for him. In the end, he pried her hands loose, slung her over his shoulder in a most savage manner, snatched up his basket—filled with only the good Lord knew what—and stomped down the hall, down the stairs, out the servant's entrance, across the lawn, and through the woods, where he then deposited her on the grassy knoll before the pond she had dropped in several hours ago.

It was then that he pulled her to him and dragged her into the pond.

Wearing nothing but a night rail, waste deep in the warm water in the middle of the pond, she glared at Nicholas in such a fashion that, if she'd been able to cause physical pain with her eyes, he'd be dead.

It had taken him nearly a quarter of an hour to get her in the water. She'd put up a good fight, but he would have none of it.

The stubborn man insisted she learn how to swim. Right now. Because apparently he could not go on living unless he knew that she could save herself.

But it was done. For tonight, that is.

It was grueling, but he was finally satisfied that she at least knew how to tread water and float on her back.

"May I go back to my room now?" she bit out. "I'm wet and I'm tired, and I don't think I like you right now."

He threw back his head and laughed, powerfully handsome. His long, dark hair was wet and smoothed back, and his bare chest glistened with droplets of water. Light from a dozen beeswax candles set in lamps on a flat patch of grass bathed the sinewy ropes of muscle in a golden-brown glow. Water lapped at his waist, teasing her to imagine that he was not wearing anything at all.

Rosalind, despite her initial irritation, found herself in awe of his male beauty. His eyes sparkled this evening, and she shivered as his laughing gaze settled on her.

And then something rather slimy brushed against her thigh.

"Oh!"

Standing three feet in front of her, Nicholas froze. "What is it?"

"I-I don't know. Something . . ." She felt it again.

With a great leap, she tossed herself in Nicholas's direction, water splashing all around them. Wrapping her arms around his shoulders, she jumped up, wrapping her legs around his waist. "Get-me-out-get-me-out!"

"For the love of Christ, calm down, woman. It's probably just a fish."

She relaxed slightly, belatedly realizing that her wet gown rendered her dreadfully exposed.

Nicholas seemed to notice at the same time. He looked down and his eyes fastened to her breasts, their hard tips straining against the fabric.

A thrumming seemed to grow between them. A sensual pull.

It occurred to her then they were stepping over an invisible line. A new territory. She should have been insisting they return to the house. She should have been worried that someone might come and discover them.

But the only thing she could focus on was the sensation of his bare chest pressed against her breasts.

"You've forgotten my kiss, Nicholas."

He shook his head while staring at her mouth like he'd love to devour her.

"You know," he said quietly, his deep baritone rumbling through her, "it could have been a snake."

Her eyes fastened to his mouth; she gasped and pressed herself fully against him.

Nicholas chuckled, sliding his hands to cup and squeeze her backside.

Rosalind couldn't stop a groan from escaping her lips. It felt so wonderful. He was so strong, so capable. She felt as light as a pebble as he started for the shore, sloshing through the water.

Halfway there, their mouths melded together at the very same time. Seeking and wet, hot and erotic.

Reaching the shore, Nicholas laid her down on a soft blanket he had spread out between the candles. He kept on kissing her, making her dizzy with immeasurable sensation—one strong hand lifting her night rail, the other sliding under her bottom to lift her up in order to get her garment completely off.

Kneeling between her legs, he gazed down at her with such reverence, such longing, that she nearly covered herself up, but she didn't. She wanted him to see her, all of her, explore her, claim her, possess her, because she was his whether he wanted her or not. She had been the day her eyes had met his, and she would always be, no matter what the future held for them.

"Sweet Christ, you're so lovely, Rosalind." His hot hands sculpted up her calves, over her knees, and up her thighs. Reaching her hips, he gripped them, then trailed his fingers over her waist and lower.

"Let me look at you," he whispered.

She panted as his fingers traced the outer folds of her sex, separating them, stroking them. She could feel how damp she was, and it embarrassed her.

Judging by the look on Nicholas's face, he liked it.

"You want me, lass. Do you feel that?" He dipped one finger inside and she could feel herself grip him from within.

She moaned. A thousand shivers raced across her skin, her knees brushing against the roughness of his breeches.

"Cold?"

She shook her head. Truthfully, she didn't feel cold at all. What she did feel was incredibly sensitive to each and every square inch on her body.

He raised a brow. "Not at all?"

"Maybe just a little."

"Then let me cover you."

His heat engulfing her, Nicholas slipped further between her knees, sinking his strong body onto hers. Clamping a hand on her waist, he pulled her tight against his hardness. Smoothing the backs of the fingers of his free hand down her cheek, his glittering gaze bore intensely into hers before he brushed his lips over hers.

"Is this what you want, Rosalind?" he asked, his breath moist against her lips.

She nodded. A shaky breath escaped her as he licked and nipped playfully at her lower lip. Her mouth opened slightly as she dared to mimic him. And then he fastened his mouth to hers, his tongue circling hers, thrusting and coaxing.

Wrapping her arms around his torso, she clung to him, yielding to the heat, wanting to match his hunger.

He threaded his fingers into her hair, shifting pins in the damp strands. His other hand snaked around her waist to clamp onto her backside, holding her tightly to his erection.

She made a sound, half moan, half whimper, and he growled, kissing her with such utter possession, such gentle domination, that she thought she might burst from pleasure.

And then he was kissing her neck, biting softly,

lapping at the drops of water on her collarbone, between her breasts. Her hands fisted in his damp hair, holding him to her, begging him to continue this erotic torture.

Cupping her breast, he slowly descended to the impossibly tight tip, flicking his tongue until she nearly screamed.

"Nicholas, please," she breathed.

And then, to her surprise, he slid his hot, exploring mouth ever downward across her stomach until his breath whispered through the soft, dark curls at the center of her being.

Her eyes flew open and she looked down her body just as he looked up at her, his sultry lips parted.

"What are you—?" she panted, reaching for his tousled locks to urge him upward. "Is this . . . pr . . . pr . . . proper?"

With half a grin, he dipped his head between her thighs and gave her a quick flick of his tongue. "I think it is."

She gasped, no longer able to hold a thought. He kissed her there like he had kissed her mouth. Her entire body succumbed to him, to his slow, thorough lips and the maddening swirls and dips of his tongue.

Her thighs quivering, her fingers tangled in his hair, Rosalind suddenly cried out as wave upon wave of pleasure crashed over her.

And all the while Nicholas never ceased his movements, causing streak after streak of fire to ripple through her.

"I've never tasted anything so sweet," he murmured, finally kissing his way back up to her mouth.

Rosalind felt truly wild. She wanted something, something more.

He tugged at her nipples and she arched her back like a bow, unknowingly settling him deeper into the cradle of her thighs.

"Rosalind," Nicholas panted. "I can't wait any more."

"Don't wait," she breathed, running her hands down his arms and back.

He angled his hips to position himself. Grabbing her hip, he entered her, swallowing her gasp with his kiss. He gave her time to adjust, then pressed his forehead to hers. Their gazes met and held. Blue fire and verdant gray.

With one fluid thrust, he joined with her completely, breaching her maidenhead. Her eyes squeezed shut, her facial muscles tight with pain.

"I'm sorry. I'm so sorry," Nicholas murmured, raining kisses down her cheeks. "It's just this time, I swear. This first time."

It took her nearly half a minute to remember to breathe. "That hurt, Nicholas."

"I know."

"I think I like the other way better," she said.

Breathing hard, Nicholas chuckled. "You'll like this, too." He reached down, sliding his fingers between to tease the highly sensitive nub of flesh between her folds.

He teased her, nearly shuddering with his own need. She felt like liquid fire around him, like folds of the silkiest satin. Soon she began rocking her hips, little whimpers of pleasure spilling from her lips.

Slowly at first, he started to slide out and in, back and forth, each thrust a little faster, a little stronger, until she began to move with him, her head thrashing back and forth, her heels pressing into his buttocks.

The rhythm increased, her moans and his grunts mingling together, carrying each other to new heights.

Glorious tension budded to life within her and she found herself urging him onward, until she was nearly frantic with the need to grab hold of it again. Suddenly it was there, bursting over her, and she cried out.

Muscles straining, Nicholas drove into her one last time, pouring his seed with a guttural moan. He collapsed atop her, shifting most of his weight to his elbows, which were planted on either side of her shoulders.

It seemed to take them both forever to regain their breath. Long moments later, Nicholas was the first to stir. Shifting to the side, he faced her, drawing lazy swirls on her stomach.

"Nicholas," she whispered. "That was so beautiful."

"Aye, it was."

"And you are one wicked man."

He lifted a brow and gazed at her. "Why is that?" he asked softly.

She suddenly felt horribly shy. "You said I'd be safe here," she replied with a teasing grin. "You said you wouldn't touch me under your sister's roof."

He grinned. "We are under the stars, Rosalind. I kept my word."

At that moment the light in his eyes darkened and he turned pensive, his mood sobering.

Rosalind sighed shakily, fearing regret was creeping its way into Nicholas's heart.

Reaching for his breeches, he stood and slid them on. "We should go in."

When she stood, he bent to retrieve a blanket from the grass and wrapped it around her shoulders.

"What is it, Nicholas? Why does it seem that every time I get close to you, you pull away?"

"After what we just did? I hardly think I pushed you away."

"That's not what I meant and you know this. What is it? Is it because of your obligation to my brother? Do you dislike me? Is it because of your parents?"

His head snapped up, his gaze watchful. "What do you know of my parents?"

"Just that they loved each other very much. You have happy memories, I have—"

"Happy memories? You think I have happy memories? Watching a man beg for death? Sitting at her grave for hours on end. Sleeping there. For God's sake, I had to stop him from digging in the dirt with his hands. I never found out if he was trying to dig her out or bury himself with her."

"I didn't know."

"And this went on, Rosalind. For years. It was like part of his soul was ripped from him and he forever mourned his other half." He ran a hand through his slicked-back locks. "And you . . . you are my . . ."

"I am your what, Nicholas?" She spoke slowly, carefully.

He swallowed heavily, his eyes oddly glistening. Taking a deep breath, he turned his back to her. "You are my responsibility. At least until the season is over. Let us return to the house."

He couldn't have hurt her more if he'd have slapped her.

Four hours later, unable to sleep, Rosalind stood on a flagstone, gazing up at the moon, a thick cream shawl wrapped around her shoulders.

At home she'd often pace the balcony during a sleepless night, but her room here didn't have one, so she'd come down into the garden for fresh air instead.

She lifted her foot slightly, rubbing her bare sole gently across the sandstone step.

Upon their return from the pond, Nicholas had walked her back to her room and kissed her good-night with such tenderness that she'd nearly cried.

Did he feel guilt over what they had done?

They had become overcome by their attraction, helpless but to slate their desires. It wasn't right for him to blame himself or think of himself as weak. She was just as guilty.

Was he watching her even now? And when did he even sleep?

She swallowed down a lump in her throat, remembering the sound of his voice as he'd told her of his father's grief. The sound tore at her heart.

A little bird chirped in the distance, telling her that day was about to break. Tristan would be waking soon, and they would head back to Devine Mansion. Nicholas back to his guarding. He might not have it in his heart to ever love her, or maybe he was just too afraid to ever let himself, but she wasn't, and she needed to tell him.

What they'd shared was wonderful, beautiful. And she would cherish the memory forever.

Scuffling came from behind her. In reaction, she looked over her shoulder to see who was there.

And then everything went black.

Chapter 18

Throwing a coarse sack over someone and knocking them in the head wasn't a terribly creative way to abduct a person. But it worked.

With an ache throbbing fiercely in her skull, Rosalind felt herself being tossed down, only to realize it was not *down*, but *in*.

And only after the ground lurched under her did she realize she was in a carriage, her hands tied behind her back, the dark sack still covering her.

The blow to her head must have caused her to lose consciousness at some point, for she did not remember getting her hands tied. The carriage rumbled on, the sound of the hoof beats revealing that they moved over a meadow or lawn and not a road.

She twisted, trying to sit up so that her head would quit bouncing on the floor, but as soon as she managed to sit up, the carriage would shudder and lean, causing her to fall back over.

Using her feet, she felt around the carriage, seeking to discover if she was alone. After a brief inspection she deemed herself unaccompanied and sent silent thanks to the heavens above.

Whoever her abductor was, and she could hazard a guess, he wasn't doing a terribly good job. She wriggled her wrists, realizing that she would have them untied in no time. Of course, then there was the problem of deciding what to do next. She could just jump to her freedom and run for her life, but she had no idea where she was or how long they had been traveling.

A loud ruckus surrounded the carriage and it jostled to a sudden stop. Outside, voices rose in anger. Good Lord, was there more than one abductor? She knew the wager in London was ridiculous, but she'd never thought those men would stoop this low.

Footsteps surrounded the carriage and there was a great scuffle. Rosalind waited, hands secretly untied.

The carriage door was snatched open and cool air blew around her ankles. Jolting in surprise, her abductor grabbed her by her shoulders, yanked her out, then stood her on the ground. Rosalind's hand balled into a fist—just the way her brothers had taught her—as she waited for the hood to be removed.

With a swish the coarse sack was whisked away. Screwing her lips, she let her fist fly, connecting to her attacker's nose.

It was unfortunate, then, that by the time she realized it was Nicholas standing before her, she had too much momentum built up to stop the blow.

"Oh, dear. Nicholas! I didn't mean to hit you."

He covered his nose with his hand, his face red from pain. "Who the hell taught you to punch like that?"

"Gabriel."

"Och," he muttered, sounding nasal. "I don't know whether to thank him or cuff him myself once he returns." He gave his head a shake, blinking. "Are you all right, Rosalind?"

Motion behind Nicholas caught her attention. "What happened?"

He took a step aside so she could see.

Lord Stokes lay in a disjointed-looking heap at Tristan's feet.

"Apparently, your erstwhile suitor thought to force you to marry him."

She gasped, narrowing her gaze on Stokes.

"He's quite unconscious," Tristan remarked nudging the man with a toe of his boot.

"How did you know what was happening?" she asked Tristan.

"I just happened to be on the way to the stables for an early morning ride."

"After hitting you over the head," Nicholas said "Stokes carried you over to where he left his carriage on the road. By the time I got to you, he had already started tearing down the lane. Your brother rode up and took one look at me and started after him. I had saddled up Buttercup and joined him Together we stopped him, but I take the full credit for knocking him into oblivion."

Rosalind nodded, trying to absorb everything he'd said. "Buttercup? Your giant horse's name is *Buttercup*?"

Nicholas's look of triumph changed to impatience. "Gracie and Belle named him."

Tristan laughed from behind them.

"Oh, Nicholas, that is rather sweet," she said smiling.

Nicholas frowned and pulled her close. "Are you hurt?" he asked, his lips in her hair.

She hadn't expected him to hold her, but it felt simply delightful. "I don't believe so. I did get wal loped in the head, but I think there's only a small bump."

His hand gently searched her skull, stopping at a sensitive spot on the side of her head.

"Here?"

She nodded.

"I'll send for a doctor to come to the house."

"It's not necessary, really."

"I insist."

Behind them, Stokes groaned.

"If you'll excuse me," Nicholas said, striding away. He began tying up Stokes with the rope that had been used to tie up Rosalind.

One of Francesca's footmen ran up just then and offered his help. Once the men had Stokes secured, Nicholas dragged him atop Buttercup's saddle.

Waving a hand, he motioned for Tristan to walk over to him.

Rosalind watched as the men spoke in low tones. She crept closer, hoping to overhear some of their conversation, but they both looked up at her at the same time and stopped.

She sighed, suddenly feeling a bit shaky. The gravity of what had just happened, what could have happened, finally hit her, and she started to tremble.

Nicholas strode over and threw his arm around her shoulders. "Come, I'll ride back with you in the cretin's carriage and get you some tea. Charles here," he nodded to the footman, "will drive the team."

She nodded, letting Nicholas pull her inside the carriage with him.

"What about Tristan and Stokes?" she asked.

"He'll bring both horses back and we'll send for the magistrate." Nicholas settled her tight and snug to his side, pressing his nose and mouth into her hair.

Rosalind sighed, closed her eyes, and pretended that he loved her.

"What are you doing?"

Holding a finger to her lips, Rosalind pleaded with her eyes for little Gracie to be quiet.

The girl nodded in jerks, apparently wanting Rosalind to know very clearly that she understood.

Smiling with gratitude, Rosalind angled her head closer to the closed oak door, listening intently. She had to brace her slippered feet very close to the baseboard in order to keep the floor from creaking under her, which was a difficult position to hold for so long. But she was determined to find out what they were talking about.

Nicholas and Tristan had been on the other side of the door for at least an hour now.

The rumble of male voices reached her, which either meant that they were speaking louder or moving closer to the door.

She pressed her ear to the cool wood.

"Are you certain this is what needs to be done?" That was Tristan.

Rumbling.

"I am aware of this. He did inform me before they left." Still Tristan.

More rumbling.

"And you are sure?"

"I will do whatever it takes in order to keep her safe." Nicholas.

What could he mean by that statement?

The odd sound of hands clapping on backs reached her ears. She looked at Gracie with a "what in the world was that?" expression.

Gracie giggled.

A clinking sound came then, reminding Rosalind of the dinging of glass when one pulls the stopper from a decanter of spirits.

She looked to Gracie again and the little one shrugged.

Letting out a pent-up breath, Rosalind straightened.

The door swung open, startling them both.

Nicholas stepped out, scowling darkly. Silently he walked between them. With a hop, Gracie caught up to him and grabbed his hand to walk with him. The moppet looked over her shoulder, and Rosalind grinned.

Rosalind held her smile for Gracie and tried to ignore the tiny jab of pain at Nicholas's coolness.

Tristan leaned in the doorframe, looking serious and older.

"We're going home," he stated quietly.

"Home? Devine Mansion?"

Tristan shook his head. "Wolverest."

"Wolverest!" Her brow furrowed. "Why?"

"Nicholas has decided that the city is no longer safe for you."

"But Stokes was caught."

He shrugged. "There could be others."

"And they could follow me from London just like Lord Stokes followed me here."

"We are a day's ride from London here. And there's too many people in the city. Too many places to hide. Yorkshire is safer." He pushed off the frame and ran a hand over his jaw. "We'll stop by the manor first to prepare for travel. But it's done, Rosalind. You will simply retire to the country before everyone else." He proceeded to walk down the hall.

"And what of Nicholas?"

He halted at her words but didn't turn around.

"Will he be coming with us?"

"I don't know."

Chapter 19

"You have a caller, my lady."

Rosalind looked up from the open portmanteau that sat upon her bed.

Her entire wardrobe was strewn across her bedchamber as maids folded and pressed her garments, packing them for the return trip to Yorkshire.

Closing her eyes briefly, Rosalind tried to quell the unstable feeling of being adrift. He was sending her away and she didn't know if he was coming with her, and, if he was, what their relationship was going to be like once they settled into their old country routines.

She wasn't going to do the silly thing, stomp her feet and refuse to leave the city—she'd almost been abducted, for goodness' sake. She wanted to leave until the interest in the wager faded away. Although she supposed it never would—unless she married.

And if all of this was still going on when Gabriel and Madelyn returned, Rosalind was sure he'd insist she marry posthaste—for her own protection.

She wanted to talk to Nicholas. She needed to hear his voice, needed to feel his arms around her. She wanted to look into his eyes and see the warm and loving heart he hid there. She wanted him to let her crawl inside and stay there forever.

After they'd made love by the pond, she could have sworn that he'd been about to reveal *something* of the inner workings of his mind. And then the way he had held her in the carriage back to his sister's house had further buoyed her hopes. But then he'd been so cool after talking to Tristan that she didn't know what to think.

"My lady?" a maid insisted gently. "You have a caller."

Rosalind gave her head a shake and looked up at the maid standing at her open door.

"Miss Meriwether asks to speak with you. Are you receiving callers?"

Rosalind nodded. "Could you send her upstairs?"

The maid bobbed a quick curtsy and left.

Rosalind stood, brushing at her pale green

skirts. Moments later, Lucy bolted inside her room, her skirts rustling.

"I have your solution!" she exclaimed, grasping Rosalind's hands in her own.

"To what?"

"To . . ." She looked pointedly at the pair of maids working on packing Rosalind's wardrobe. "Where are you going?"

Rosalind quietly dismissed the maids. She waited until they left the room, closing the door behind them before answering Lucy. "Back to Yorkshire."

"Why?"

"Lord Winterbourne's orders."

"And just like that, you go?"

Pressing her lips together, Rosalind nodded. She'd explain the entire story to Lucy one day, but not now.

Lucy's shoulders fell. "Hmmph. That makes what I was about to say moot."

"What were you about to say?"

Lucy sighed dramatically. "Only that I found a solution to your guardian problem."

"What solution?"

"Not what, but *who*, rather. A Miss Polk. Lady

Beecham hosted yet another garden tea and she was there. We happened to talk, and in doing so I discover that she is in love with none other than Lord Winterbourne! Don't you see? I've found his distraction! It seems her family lives near his farm in Yorkshire and she's been pining for him and followed him down to London. She overheard him talking to her uncle a month ago about digging a new well, and Winterbourne said he couldn't help because he had some 'vexing business' to take care of in London."

"I'm his vexing business," Rosalind repeated, her voice sounding small.

"Yes!" Lucy declared, excited, and clearly unaware of the turmoil such a statement was causing Rosalind. "So it was a good idea, correct?"

"What idea?" Rosalind felt sick.

"That you should match Polk with Winterbourne?"

Rosalind shook her head slowly, staring off into the corner of the room. "I-I don't want be a matchmaker anymore."

Silence filled the air.

"Are you all right?" Lucy touched her shoulder.

Rosalind shook her head. "No. I don't feel very well. If you don't mind—"

Lucy held up a hand. "I understand. I want to see you before you go. Make sure of it?"

Rosalind nodded, tried to smile and failed. Lucy tilted her head sadly and quietly left the room.

All at once Rosalind felt as if the fog in her mind had cleared. She'd thought he was hiding something, possibly his feelings for her, but now it was entirely possible that the reason Nicholas was acting cool toward her was that his heart resided with someone else.

And that meant that as special and wonderful as she had thought last night had been, he had used her. He'd wanted her and he'd wrestled with his conscience because she was his best friend's little sister, she was his responsibility, she was his vexing business.

Her heart started to race and her breaths came faster. Dear Lord, she had made a dreadful miscalculation of his regard.

Someone knocked softly on her door.

"Come in," she called out, her voice crackling on the words.

The door creaked open and Nicholas walked through with slow, measured steps.

Her gaze already on the floor, she gradually raised her eyes from his polished boots, snug black breeches, flat waistcoat, broad chest, cravat, to his beautiful face.

His gray eyes narrowed slightly when their gazes finally met. "I needed to speak with Tristan," he said, explaining his presence. "I have. Just." He cleared his throat. "But now I need to speak with you."

Breath whooshed out of him and he started to pace the floor, his hands clasped behind his back.

He was so nervous. She'd never seen him behave in such a manner.

"I-I have a confession to make," he intoned. "I don't know if you realize how difficult this is for me to say. I didn't want it to be like this."

Her eyes followed his path, back and forth.

"I have kept some things from you."

Her heart skittered inside her chest. Here it was. Here was his confession—that he wanted to be with someone else.

"Don't say it," she exclaimed, a bit too forcefully.

He stopped in his tracks, his straight brows drawing together.

She advanced toward him, tears welling in her eyes. "Don't say anything."

Kiss him now. Kiss him one last time. For when he says he doesn't love you, you can't pretend any longer.

Reaching up, she framed his jaw in her hands, pulled him close, and kissed him like she had never done before. Her mouth moved over his perfect sculpted lips like *she* was the dominant one. Walking him backwards, she kissed him like she was conquering him.

Hands at her elbows, he stopped walking when the backs of his thighs met with her bed. Her tongue delved into his hot, slightly chocolate tasting mouth, mating with his.

And then his momentary shock dissolved and the roles reversed. He pulled her roughly to him, spun around, and sat her on the high bed. Just as he started leaning further into her, forcing her to recline, she pushed at him. For several moments he didn't budge. And then, as if coming out of a daze, he eased himself away from her.

As soon as she was free, Rosalind ran out of the room.

Rosalind rounded the corner that would lead her to the rear entrance and nearly crashed into Tristan.

"Whooh! Slow down there." One hand holding a copy of the *Times*, the other holding a sloshing cup of tea, he took a look down the front of himself. "Missed." He raised a brow. "Got a spot on my boot though."

She averted her gaze and made to move around him. She didn't want him to look into her eyes and see that she was upset.

She needn't worry. He was too concerned about his boot.

As she walked past him, he mumbled, "Despite the state of my boot, there is a bit of good news. Did you know, Nicholas just informed me that he has a pair of Welsh cobs? Excellent horses. I've always wanted one. I must say I'm going to like having Nicholas as my brother-in-law."

She froze. "What did you say?" She turned, bit by bit, to face him.

"My new broth— Didn't he?" His eyes grew large and guilty looking. "He said he was going to . . ."

"Oh no. Oh-no-oh-no-oh-no." She dashed past Tristan, heading for the stairs. She prayed Nicholas hadn't left.

What a little fool she was! Here he had come to propose, confess his feelings, and she'd stopped him. It was obvious speaking about his feelings was difficult for him—and then she'd stopped him.

Please let him still be here.

Dashing down the hall, she skirted past a tall figure, grabbed the newel post to launch herself up the stairs . . . and froze.

Looking over her shoulder, she glanced to where Nicholas stood next to the stairs.

"Good afternoon," she said, drawing out the words. A tremulous smile played on her lips.

Nicholas grinned like a fool.

Without taking her eyes off him, she lifted her chin toward the stairs. "Come with me?"

"As you wish." He grabbed her hand and together they trudged up the stairs and into her room.

"Quietly," she warned, pointing to her aunt's closed door.

He nodded.

Inside her room, she gently shut the door behind them, grabbed his arm, and steered him over to the stool before her writing desk.

Taking a deep breath, she patted down her skirts and then clasped her hands in front of her demurely.

"Now, you were saying?"

He laughed, suddenly feeling such contentedness that it should have frightened him. But it only made him happy.

He pulled her onto his lap and kissed her fore-head. And then, quietly, he said, "I have a confession to make."

"Indeed? Go, on."

"A few, in fact."

"You have my rapt attention."

"Some might make you angry."

This caused her to raise one delicate brow "Truly? Out with it, then."

"I can waltz."

"I suspected." She sighed. "But I shall forgive you based on your performance on the sofa afterwards."

"Should you like a repeat performance, tha could easily be arranged."

"We'll see. You have more confessions to make after all."

"Ah. Well, my next confession is that I accepted no whisky. Gabriel didn't offer me any compensation, and I wouldn't have accepted it even if he did."

"Why?" she whispered, looking unsure.

"I told myself that I was doing a favor for a friend that you're an obligation. Hell, I even told Tristar that earlier today. But I'm tired of fighting it."

He squeezed her and looked directly into he eyes. "Because I love you, Rosalind. I think I'v

loved you for a very long time. Years. I think, because of my fears, I kept fighting the feeling. I kept
telling myself that I was only attracted to you, that
it would fade, that you would marry someone else
someday."

She opened her mouth to speak and he quieted
her as he brushed the pad of his thumb across her
bottom lip.

"I tried to spend the least amount of time in
your presence as possible. Because every moment
I am near you, the pull to be with you grows stronger, my resolve to resist you weakens."

"Nicholas. I love you. And I have loved you for
a very long time, as well. But unlike you, I didn't
fear it. But I did fear your indifference."

He chuckled low. "If you only knew. I'm sorry
for misleading you. For being such a coward.
Would spending the rest of my life showing you
just how entranced by you I am suffice?"

She nodded, smiling.

"Marry me, Rosalind. Be my wife."

"Of course I will."

He kissed her tenderly, openly, holding nothing
back.

When they finally pulled apart, she gave him a
skeptical look.

"What's wrong?"

"It's just that . . . twice you told me that you like quiet, tall blonds . . . and Miss Polk is tall and blond. And she followed you all the way here . . ."

He shook his head, inwardly kicking himself for teasing her. "Rosalind. Listen. If I wanted to marry Miss Polk, I would have done so long ago. If I wanted to have any relations with Miss Polk, I would have done so long ago. My nieces are aware of her interest in me because the woman is about as subtle as a cannonball blast."

Rosalind laughed. "All right."

"However," he said, curling his arms around her to hold her tighter to him, "I should confess that I am completely obsessed with short, raven-haired, blue-eyed lassies named Rosalind."

"Indeed?"

His mouth descended to her. "Oh, am I ever."

At Avon Books, we know your passion for romance—once you finish one of our novels, you find yourself wanting more.

May we tempt you with . . .

- **Excerpts** from our upcoming releases.
- Entertaining **extras**, including authors' personal photo albums and book lists.
- Behind-the-scenes **scoop** on your favorite characters and series.
- **Sweepstakes** for the chance to win free books, romantic getaways, and other fun prizes.
- Writing **tips** from our authors and editors.
- **Blog** with our authors and find out why they love to write romance.
- **Exclusive content** that's not contained within the pages of our novels.

Join us at
www.avonbooks.com

AVON

An Imprint of HarperCollins*Publishers*
www.avonromance.com

Lakota Legacy

With the courage to bridge cultures and brave wilds,
three couples find shelter in the past—and in their love.

Three brand-new stories by *USA TODAY* bestselling authors

MADELINE BAKER
KATHLEEN EAGLE

and reader favorite

RUTH WIND

Available October 2003

Where love comes alive™

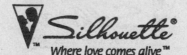